THE N... ...ACK

"Carmack once again delves into the Elizabethan Age, in all its drama, treachery, and religious mania, with this richly textured second outing for court musician Kate Haywood. . . . In Carmack's hands, this period whodunit is deliciously detailed but never heavy-handed." —*Publishers Weekly*

"Carmack takes readers from the glittery wealth and luxury of the coronation of Elizabeth I to the tawdry life in the pleasure quarters, each described vividly and accurately. Young Kate is again loyal, clever, and a shrewd detective. The setting and personalities of the time come alive as Carmack weaves a breathtaking mystery with nonstop action and emotional growth for Kate." —*RT Book Reviews* (top pick, 4½ stars)

"A very intriguing and suspenseful historical mystery that you will not want to miss!" —*Fresh Fiction*

"Kept me turning pages. A great combination of tension and intrigue. The climax was another nail-biting intox-icating ride, and the wrap-up drops a bombshell . . . that had me wanting the next book immediately. Another stellar book in this series that is exceeding expectations. Buy two copies: one for you and one for a friend." —*Mysteries and My Musings*

"This is my favorite type of mystery! An intelligent fe-male amateur sleuth solving crimes in the richly detailed setting of Tudor ... ... a puz-zle with a natura... ... heav-ily from historic... ... this book earns a we... ...elf! . . . A real treat for a... ..."

...views

continued . . .

Murder at Hatfield House

"Meticulously researched and expertly told, *Murder at Hatfield House* paints a vivid picture of Tudor England and a young Princess Elizabeth. Amanda Carmack's talent for creating a richly drawn setting, populating it with fully realized characters, and giving them a tight and engaging narrative is unparalleled. An evocative and intelligent read."
—*New York Times* bestselling author Tasha Alexander

"Amanda Carmack writes beautifully. . . . I enjoyed *Murder at Hatfield House* and recommend it; it is a cozy excursion into Tudor times with a lively heroine."
—Historical Novel Society

"An excellent start to a new historical mystery series."
—*RT Book Reviews* (top pick, 4½ stars)

"Historical suspense with a solid murder mystery and very enjoyable heroine. Near perfect."
—Mysteries and My Musings

"We see the action unfold through Kate the musician's eyes, but the most exciting revelation is not the unveiling of the mystery, but the unveiling of Elizabeth."
—Heroes and Heartbreakers

"I enjoyed this novel, with the rich descriptions and the lively and interesting cast of personable characters. I think that this is going to be a great series to follow and I highly recommend it to those who enjoy a bit of history to their mystery!"
—Sharon's Garden of Book Reviews

ALSO BY AMANDA CARMACK

The Elizabethan Mystery Series
Murder at Westminster Abbey
Murder at Hatfield House

MURDER
IN THE
QUEEN'S GARDEN

AN ELIZABETHAN MYSTERY

AMANDA CARMACK

AN OBSIDIAN MYSTERY

OBSIDIAN
Published by the Penguin Group
Penguin Group (USA) LLC, 375 Hudson Street,
New York, New York 10014

USA | Canada | UK | Ireland | Australia | New Zealand | India | South Africa | China
penguin.com
A Penguin Random House Company

First published by Obsidian, an imprint of New American Library,
a division of Penguin Group (USA) LLC

First Printing, February 2015

ISBN 978-0-451-41513-4

Printed in the United States of America
10 9 8 7 6 5 4 3 2 1

PROLOGUE

Nonsuch Palace, 1541

Amelia was right. He would very much regret doing this.

As Dr. Timothy Macey, astrologer to King Henry's royal court, hurried through the night-dark gardens of the king's pleasure palace at Nonsuch, his mistress's words rang in his head.

'Tis not fitting for people like us to be amid the schemes of people like that, Amelia had cried when she learned what his new business was. *It's not safe, and it won't end well—mark my words. Look what happened to poor Queen Anne!*

Then she had sobbed, snatched their bewildered little son up in her arms, and dashed into the cottage, slamming the door behind her.

He had cursed her folly, shouted at her that she knew not what she spoke of and that she could rot in there all alone.

She had never had a problem spending the extra coin he earned now; that was for certain.

But he worried now there was some truth to her fearful words. The doings of kings, especially *this* king, with the blood of so many on his bejeweled hands, should be none of his business. He had seen what happened to those who displeased King Henry Tudor, had seen their heads on pikes. Yet his vast knowledge, hardwon from so many forbidden books, so many long nights over a scrying stone, had made him arrogant. He had thought he was different.

Only when he read what was written in the stars had he truly seen how far he had come along a dark road.

He paused at the entrance to the garden maze and peered back at the palace, sleeping with a deceptive air of peace in the darkness. It was King Henry's pride, his great pleasure palace, meant to outshine any French château or Italian villa with its magnificence. Indeed it was surprisingly beautiful, with its carved towers and pale sculptured friezes, yet it was not finished. Despite the fact that Henry had begun to build it years ago, to celebrate the birth of his precious son, Prince Edward, whole wings around the courtyards were still left hollow, decorations half-painted.

Yet Henry had insisted on showing the house's magnificence, bringing his court here with his new queen, the young Catherine Howard—half his age, golden haired, merry, laughing, dancing. Always dancing. The king's "rose without a thorn."

Dr. Macey cursed now to think of her. She had seemed to make his fortunes only a few days ago, when King Henry commissioned him to draw up the queen's horoscope. No doubt the fat, sickly, stinking Henry was sure the stars would foretell the handsome sons she would give him, the love for him she had in her youthful heart.

But that was not what was in the future at all. Macey's hands still trembled on the scroll he clutched, the terrible chart that told the truth of Queen Catherine and her young heart. The blood that would soon taint her white skin and stain the souls of so many around her.

Nay, he could never tell the king the truth, or anyone else! He was a mere messenger, but the royal rage, so swift and lethal, would surely fall directly on *him*. Not to mention what would happen if the queen's lover knew the truth. It had to be concealed, and now, before Macey was caught.

He looked down at the parchment crumpled in his hands, and the pale moonlight caught on his rings. His night stone, whose power he had treasured ever since his old teacher had gifted it to him so many years ago, and the fine emerald set in wrought gold, a gift from King Henry that had once seemed such a treasure, both glinted in the light.

Now the emerald was a chain, dragging him down to the waiting demons of hell.

He heard Amelia's sobs again, saw her fear-filled eyes. He had scoffed at her, but she was right in the end. His powers should never have been put to the service of a madman like King Henry and a strumpet like Queen Catherine.

Worse, he had given in to the basest temptation and taken coin from the queen's lover—a man who was young and hot-tempered and who had killed before without thought or care—and played him off the king. That was what haunted him now, what chased him in the night.

They would find out what he had done in those papers, for the stars never lied, if they had not already, and they would take their revenge.

Macey spun around and hurried into the dark safety of the maze. The thick, thorny hedge walls rose around him, blotting out the sight of that cursed house, and only moonlight guided his steps.

He knew Queen Catherine used the center of the maze for her secret trysts. Where better to hide her secrets, and his own?

He had sent a copy of the chart to his best student, young John Dee, at Cambridge, instructing him not to read it unless it became necessary. John had the wisdom and discretion of men three times his age. He would know what to do with this knowledge, if need be. This copy, Macey would destroy now, before the king or the others could find him. He would have to draw up a false horoscope for Queen Catherine.

Suddenly, there was a shout behind him, from beyond the entrance to the maze. Booted footsteps pounded on the ground, and he heard someone call his name.

He knew that voice. It was Thomas Culpeper, the queen's young ruffian of a lover. He and his friends Lord Marchand, who had hated Macey since their own days at Cambridge, and Master Dereham, the queen's secretary, had already paid Macey for his secret knowledge of alchemy. And now he knew he truly was betrayed. They would try to destroy the horoscope and silence him.

But they still did not know the secrets the stars had told him. If he survived this night, he would make certain they never did.

He ran faster through the twists and turns of the maze, as the racing footsteps of his pursuers grew louder behind him. If he could only reach the safety of the next turn.

Yet it was too far away. He couldn't breathe; his chest felt tight; his legs burned. He tumbled into the maze's center just as a rough fist snatched a handful of his robe and shoved him to his knees. Pain jolted up his legs as he landed in the mud. The emerald fell from his finger and the paper was snatched away from his hand.

"Bastard!" Thomas Culpeper cursed. "You will get us all killed. Where is the horoscope? I know you have it; the maidservant who saw you told me."

"May God forgive me," Macey whispered. He had not considered the servants. He thought of Amelia, of their little Timothy's face. And he feared it was much too late for anything at all.

CHAPTER ONE

August 1559

"Make way, you varlets! Make way for the queen!" The guards in Queen Elizabeth's green-and-white livery galloped along the dusty, rutted lane, pushing back the eager crowds who gathered to watch the queen ride by. They had left the nearest village behind, with its rows of cottages and shops, its stone gaol, but the crowds were still thick.

Along the road, the royal procession seemed to stretch for miles. Hundreds of people rode with Queen Elizabeth on her summer progress, an endless stream of horses, wagons, and coaches. Baggage carts were piled high with chests and furniture, maidservants and pages clinging to them precariously as they bounced along. The courtiers on their fine horses were a many-faceted jewel of bright velvets and feathers, a brilliant burst of color emerging from the brown dust of the hard, rutted summer pathways.

None were more glorious than the queen herself. She rode in her finest coach, a gift from one of her suitors, the Prince of Sweden. It was an elaborate conveyance painted deep crimson and trimmed with gilt paint, lined with green satin cushions. Six white horses drew it along, green ribbons braided in their manes and tails fluttering in the wind. Queen Elizabeth, resplendent in white-and-silver brocade, her red-gold hair piled atop her head and twined with pearls, waved her gloved hand at the crowds who clamored to see her.

"God save our queen!" they shouted, falling over one another, tears shining on their faces. Parents held their children up on their shoulders to glimpse a real queen.

"And God bless all of you, my good people!" Elizabeth called back.

Sir Robert Dudley rode beside her on his grand, prancing black horse, almost like a part of the powerful beast himself in his black-and-gold doublet. A plumed black hat trimmed with pearls and rubies sat on his curling dark hair. He laughed as he caught some of the bouquets tossed to the queen, and he leaned into the carriage to drop them in her lap. Elizabeth smiled up at him radiantly, the very image of a summer queen, full of heat and light and pure, giddy happiness.

Kate Haywood could barely glimpse the queen's coach from her own wagon farther down the lane, but even she could see the sunburst of the queen's smile. It had been thus all summer, from Greenwich to Eltham, a procession of dances, banquets, and fireworks over gardens in full, fragrant bloom. After so many years of danger and fear, it seemed summer had truly returned to England at last, and everyone was determined to enjoy it to the hilt. Especially the queen.

Kate looked down at her lute, carefully packed into its case and propped at her feet. She let the stewards load her clothes chest, filled with her new fine gowns and ruffs, into the baggage carts, but never this, her most prized possession. It had once belonged to her mother, who died at her birth, and she had grown up learning to play her music on it. It was her most trusted companion, and now that she was a full member of the queen's musical consort, it earned her own bread as well. It had seen much activity in the last few weeks, playing deep into the night as Queen Elizabeth danced on and on—mostly with Robert Dudley.

Kate flexed her fingers in her new kid gloves. They, too, had seen much work lately, and she couldn't afford for them to grow stiff. Once they reached Nonsuch Palace, there would be much dancing again. It was said that Lord Arundel, the palace's owner, was much set on wooing the queen and had planned many elaborate pageants to advance his suit.

For a moment, Kate thought of her father, content in retirement at his new cottage near Windsor. She received letters from him on this progress, full of his news as he finally had time to work on the grand Christmas service cycle he had longed to finish. He also had words to say about a kindly widow who lived nearby and who brought him fresh milk and new-baked bread. He seemed happy, but Kate often missed him a great deal. They had been each other's only family for so long.

And yet—he had kept her mother's secret from Kate all her life. And she hadn't yet been able to bring herself to confront him about that. She didn't know if she ever could. It made her feel so very lonely.

Kate leaned farther out of the wagon into the choking clouds of dust to study the coach in front of her. Catherine Carey—Lady Knollys—the daughter of the queen's aunt Mary Boleyn, rode there with her beautiful daughter, Lettice, the fine new conveyance a sign of their high favor with the queen. Beside them, talking to the ladies through the open window, was Lady Knollys's brother, Lord Hunsdon.

He threw back his head and laughed, his red beard glinting in the sunlight, and his sister peeked out the window to laugh with him. She caught her plumed hat just before the wind would have snatched it from her dark hair.

Whenever Kate saw Lady Knollys, she wondered if her own mother had looked something like her, with her delicate face and shining black hair—Boleyn hair, they called it. Kate's own mother, Eleanor, was the illegitimate half sister of Anne and Mary Boleyn, a fact Kate had discovered in a most shocking way only a few months before.

Not that the Careys, or anyone else, ever spoke of that fact or acknowledged it. Though sometimes Kate thought she saw Lord Hunsdon looking at her. . . .

The convoy suddenly lurched to a halt, startling Kate from her brooding thoughts. She clutched at the wooden side of the wagon to keep from tumbling to the floor.

"Are we stopping *again*?" cried Lady Anne Godwin, who sat across from Kate. "We shall never get to Nonsuch at this pace! I vow we could walk faster."

Mistress Violet Roland, from her perch on the bench next to Kate, smiled and said, "Of course Queen Elizabeth will wish to stop and talk to the people whenever she can. Most of them will never see such a sight again."

Kate smiled at her. She had come to like Violet very much on their travels, for they often found themselves in the same conveyances and sharing lodgings in the palaces and manors of the summer progress. She was one of the queen's newest maids of honor, small and pretty, with blond curls and a quick smile. She enjoyed music and could help while away dull hours on the road talking of the newest songs from Italy and Spain. She was also a fine source of gossip about the court, conveyed in quick whispers and giggles. Who was in love with whom, who was seen speaking to whom.

Information that seemed most frivolous but could prove deadly useful—as Kate often discovered lately.

Violet seemed especially excited today, for her brother served as a secretary to Lord Arundel, and she would get to see him at Nonsuch.

"And it is such a lovely, warm day," Violet said. "Who can grumble about being out in the sunshine?"

"I can," Lady Anne muttered, readjusting her silk skirts around her. Unlike Violet, she was not often very merry. "My backside is aching from this infernal, jolting wagon. And your nose will grumble, too, Violet, when you get hideous freckles."

Violet just laughed and leaned out to see what was happening. Kate peeked over her shoulder to see that the queen had halted her carriage to call forth a man with a little girl in his arms. The child shyly held out a bouquet to Queen Elizabeth, who accepted it under Dudley's protective watch.

Kate felt a pang of strange wistfulness as she watched the tenderness Sir Robert always showed the queen, the affection that was always so obvious between them. It had been many weeks since she had seen her friend Anthony Elias, who worked to become an attorney in London. Yet she thought far too often of his smile, his beautiful green eyes. The safety she had found in his arms when she nearly died on the frozen Thames. If he ever looked at *her* as Sir Robert looked at the queen . . .

But Anthony would not. And she had her own work to do. She had to cease to think about him.

She sat back on the narrow wooden bench and made sure her lute was safe still. Music was all she ever knew for certain.

Violet turned and gave her another smile. "Have you had your horoscope done by Dr. Dee yet, Kate?"

Kate shook her head. "I have not yet had the time," she said. She had seen Dr. John Dee's bearded, black-robed figure hurrying around the court, his apprentice, the pasty young Master Constable, dashing after him with his arms full of mysterious scrolls and books. Having one's horoscope cast was considered essential by many people at court in recent days. Dr. Dee had forecast the queen's coronation date, as well as where she should visit on this progress. Queen Elizabeth relied on his wisdom entirely.

But Kate was sure the hour of her own birth, which had been the hour of her mother's death, could not augur well for the future. She had to learn how to make her future for herself. It seemed best not to know her destiny.

"Oh, but you must!" Violet cried. "Everyone is doing it. Dr. Dee had no time to cast mine, so Master Constable did it. He said I was born under Saturn, and am thus of melancholic disposition. I should marry within the year, but never to someone born under Mars, or great misfortune will ensue. I must make sure all the humors are in balance." She glanced toward a group of men on horseback nearby, and a small frown fluttered across her lips. One of the men was her persistent suitor, a certain young Master Longville, and Violet showed no signs of returning his favor. But she was soon laughing again.

Kate shook her head. She thought of Violet's frequent laughter, her love of dance and song. It seemed Master Constable wasn't learning much from his apprenticeship.

"I am surprised the learned Dr. Dee would even wish to return to Nonsuch," Lady Anne said with a smirk. "Surely that would be a most bad omen for him."

"What do you mean?" Violet cried.

"Have you not heard the old tale?" Lady Anne said. Her eyes were shining with the pleasure of gossip. "I know not much about it, but my uncle was there when it happened. It was in old King Henry's time, when he was married to poor Queen Catherine Howard."

Catherine Howard—who had lost her head in the Tower when she was barely more than a girl. Kate remembered all too well the chilly feeling of dread that surrounded the Tower. She thought of that dark, cold night when she knelt on the stone floor of St. Peter ad Vincula in the Tower with Queen Elizabeth, sure that unseen eyes watched their every movement.

"Oh, do tell us!" Violet urged. Kate said nothing, but she was intrigued.

Lady Anne smiled. "'Twas on a summer progress just like this one. Nonsuch was the king's then, and not yet finished, but he was determined to bring his new queen there. When Dr. Dee was very young and first at Cambridge, he was an apprentice to a man called Dr. Macey, and King Henry wanted Macey's advice that summer and summoned him to Nonsuch."

Kate glanced ahead to where the queen greeted more of her subjects, smiling and holding out her hand to them. The radiance of the scene seemed so far away from when the old, mad king had come this way with his frivolous, flirtatious young queen. Had King Henry require some dark magic from Dr. Macey that year? There had been such frightening tales, of alchemy and spirits. . . .

"What happened?" Violet whispered. Her eyes were wide, as if she, too, feared to know of ungodly arts.

"A courtier named Lord Marchand accused Dr. Macey of—of *treason*!" Lady Anne hissed the last word. "He declared Dr. Macey predicted the king's death and the queen's black fate, which is a burning offense."

"Was he executed, then?" Kate said, appalled.

Lady Anne shook her head. "That is the strange twist of the tale, Mistress Haywood. This Lord Marchand took it all back. No such horoscope predicting the king's death or the queen's downfall could ever be found, but poor Dr. Macey quite vanished. He was never seen again. Dr. Dee went abroad after he finished his studies at Cambridge, and they say he never speaks of Dr. Macey. Lord Marchand died soon after; they say he went mad or something of the sort. And it all happened at Nonsuch. What can Dr. Dee be thinking to go back there now?"

"How terribly sad," Violet sighed. "And Dr. Macey never reappeared at all?"

"Never," Lady Anne said with obvious relish. "My uncle said some people declared a demon spirited him away at his own conjuring."

"A demon!" Violet shrieked.

"Don't be silly," Kate said. "How would a demon appear in the midst of a crowded court? Surely there would at least have been the smell of brimstone."

She laughed, but she couldn't help shivering. The warmth of the summer sun couldn't quite banish the old, dark memories of the past.

The procession jolted forward again, and Lady Anne and Violet talked of happier matters—the latest style of ruff from France, the new Spanish ambassador, Bishop de Quadra, who was betrothed to whom, and whose heart was broken. Horoscopes and mysterious vanishings seemed forgotten, especially when they rolled over the crest of a hill and Nonsuch Palace came into view at last.

Even Kate was stunned by the sight of it, despite the paintings and etchings she had seen. She had heard many tales of Nonsuch, of course—King Henry had begun building it the year his precious son, Prince Edward, was born and intended it to surpass in luxury and grandeur any châteaus of the French king. He had demolished a whole village, old Cuddington, to make way for it. It was to be the most lavish palace in Christendom. But he never finished it, and Queen Mary sold it to Lord Arundel. They said the last time Henry visited was when he brought his new queen Catherine Howard to show it to her.

It was dazzling, all golden stone and rosy brick in the sunlight. It rose above the lush green parks and gardens like a palace in a troubadour's tale. Gilded cupolas crowned octagonal towers at every corner, and crenelated walkways joined the two inner courtyards. The walls were decorated with enormous colorful stucco reliefs of classical gods and goddesses. Above it all rose a marble statue of King Henry himself, looking out on all he had dreamed of and not quite accomplished.

It was beautiful, elegant, joyful. Hardly a place where treason and dark magic could ever triumph.

Hardly a place where anything as evil as murder could ever happen at all.

CHAPTER TWO

Kate leaned out of the open window casement, caught by the song that floated up to her from the garden on a warm, rose-scented breeze. She was meant to be on an errand for the queen, fetching a book from the royal bedchamber, but the sound was like a siren song she had to follow. She was always captured by snatches of music.

The scene below her window was so wonderfully idyllic it could have been a painting or a tapestry. Queen Elizabeth sat on a marble bench beneath an arch twined with climbing roses in Tudor red and white. They perfectly framed her green satin gown and the pearl-twisted loops of her red-gold hair. Some of her ladies sat around her on cushions scattered over the ground, like flowers themselves amid petals of white and silver and sky blue silks. They passed around apples, sweetmeats, and goblets of wine, giggling and blushing over the romantic song.

Or perhaps they blushed over the *singer*, who strolled among them as he strummed on his lute, and Kate could not really blame them. It was young Master Green, a secretary to the queen's—and now Kate's—cousin Lord Hunsdon. Master Green came from some obscure family in the North, and his fortune seemed merely adequate, yet the favor and employment of a royal kinsman could take him far. Lord Hunsdon often declared he could not do without Master Green's services, his sharp wits and unflagging energy, and such a high patron was not an asset a young lady could discount.

Nor could she discount his personal assets, for Master Green was a bonny lad indeed. Kate nearly laughed behind her own hand as she watched him sing, and giggling was not something she often did. She was far too busy for ogling young courtiers, but any lady would have to be blind not to look twice at Master Green. He was tall and elegantly slim in his fashionable dark red doublet and striped hose. He wore no cap today, and the dappled sunlight of the rosy arbor gleamed on his glossy curls.

" 'Come, oh come, my life's delight! Let me not in languor pine, love loves no delay, thy sight the more enjoyed the more divine. . . .' "

Yet, for all his charms, Kate felt rather as if she admired a fine painting when she looked at him. She marveled that a real person could be so lovely. He certainly rarely took notice of her, and when he did she never felt that sudden fluttering in her stomach, the flight of all words from her mind, that happened when she looked at someone else.

Someone she hadn't seen in months.

Kate frowned at the sudden shadow on the bright day. It seemed as if a grayish cloud suddenly blotted the golden scene as she was reminded of Anthony Elias and his green eyes, his all-too-rare dimpled smiles. The way it felt when his fingers, ink stained from writing out so many legal documents, folded around hers. Or the warm, perfect safety when he caught her in his arms after she feared she would die on the icy river.

Yet she hadn't seen him in so long. Not that she expected to. He had his work in London. Soon his apprenticeship with the attorney Master Hardy would end, and he would have to build his own career. Her place was here at court with Queen Elizabeth, as it always would be, and the queen's summer progress had taken them all across the countryside. With her music, the banquets and masques, her compositions, and the secret tasks she had lately undertaken, she had no time to think of anything else.

Except when she paused for a moment between duties, between banquets and hunts, and remembered. Then memories, both good and ill, caught up with her and tugged at her skirts again.

Kate leaned farther out the window and took a deep breath of the flower-tinged summer air, so clean and green. Memories surely had no place in such a moment, at such a place. Not memories of feelings she wanted to forget, to push away. Certainly not memories of the fear and panic of that freezing night in January, when she had nearly died in the river at the hands of a madman. That was gone now, all of it. The summer was for merriment and frivolity, for rejoicing anew that Elizabeth was queen and had been for many months now.

Not that everyone rejoiced at that fact. Mary, Queen of Scots, the new Queen of France, waited across the water for her chance, as did her mother, Marie of Guise, just over the border in Scotland, massing her armies. Spain lurked, waiting its chance, as did Tudor relatives much closer to home. Elizabeth refused to worry about such things, choosing to ride and dance and laugh as she had never been able to do before, but her chief secretary, William Cecil, looked more gray and worried every day.

Kate studied the gardens, which rolled away in a perfect series of riotously colored flower beds, sweet-scented herbal knot gardens, white-graveled walkways, and emerald green meadows, peppered with the tents so many courtiers had to lodge in. On hilltops and in groves waited Grecian follies, just perfect for trysts and secret meetings. An ornamental lake, dotted with boats, shimmered blue and green in the distance.

Nonsuch was beautiful indeed, built and lavishly appointed to be a place for summer joy. A place to forget the perils of the outside world, forget illness and war, and just—dance. Old King Henry had intended it thus, a pleasure palace to rival those of the French kings, when he showed it to his young and beautiful— and supremely frivolous—queen Catherine Howard, and Lord Arundel had made it even lovelier since he bought it from Queen Mary. It was said he thought to use its pleasures to lure Queen Elizabeth into marrying him, elderly and Catholic though he was.

Yet there was little in its rare beauty that could truly protect a vulnerable queen, her throne still tottering beneath her. No high walls, no moats. Dreams could do so much, but they couldn't keep enemies at bay forever.

Kate swallowed hard as she remembered how very many enemies there were out there. Her own body bore the scars of some of them, and William Cecil's lessons in reading codes and breaking locks showed her how very vast the web of wickedness was. So many enemies, both bold and hidden, did not want Elizabeth as queen, and they all had to be vigilant to keep England from sliding back into the chaos and fear it had known with Queen Mary.

She studied the scene below her window anew, and this time saw more than the beauty of it. The silken petals of the roses concealed poisonous thorns.

Standing behind the queen was her now-constant companion, Sir Robert Dudley. He leaned lazily against a pillar of the trellis, dressed in glorious counterpoint to Elizabeth in a pearl-embroidered green satin doublet. His arms were loosely crossed over his chest, and his foot, encased in a glossy black leather boot, tapped in time to the song. He smiled lazily, the very image of an indolent courtier at his leisure, but Kate knew now how deceptive that image was.

Sir Robert's dark gypsy eyes were constantly on the watch, past the queen and her laughing ladies, past the music and the wine, to see all that lurked in the shadows. His sword was strapped at his lean hip, and even here at fairy-tale Nonsuch, his hand would be swift to grasp its honed steel hilt.

Everyone thought him a creature of burning ambition, grasping to raise his formerly disgraced family by the jeweled hems of the queen's skirts. A man of impulsive action, of battle and rash daring, who sought only to wed the queen and become king—despite his ill wife locked away in the countryside.

And surely he was all of that. The court was filled with people of just such hungry ambition, such eagerness to play for the very highest stakes, despite the dangers of royal favor. They were always with the queen: the Howards, the Greys, the Carews, her Boleyn cousins, the Douglases. Rumors that one or the other was rising or falling were always floating in the perfumed air of court. Robert Dudley had learned in the hardest of schools to be more adept than most.

Yet Kate had seen a different side to him last winter, when he'd helped her chase the evil villain who would have turned Elizabeth's triumphant coronation into a bloodbath. Behind Sir Robert's laughter, his piratical dark looks, he was solemnly watchful. Courteous, aware, and even admiring of the intelligence of others, willing to die for Elizabeth—both the queen and the woman. Kate couldn't help but admire him, despite his blatant courtship of a woman he could not have, not while his own wife lived.

Which was a feeling not many shared. The Duke of Norfolk, the highest nobleman in the land, despised Dudley and his brand of brash "new men." Cecil distrusted him. The new Spanish ambassador, the Bishop de Quadra, spread rumors of Dudley and the queen throughout the courts of Europe. Dudley would have to protect himself and his family along with the queen.

Sir Robert noticed her at the window and gave her a small nod. Kate nodded in reply, suddenly remembering why she was standing there at all. She was meant to fetch the queen's book, not loll about in windows thinking up fanciful notions of danger and romance. The queen was surrounded at all times, by Sir Robert and his men, her ladies, by Secretary Cecil and his retainers, by all her suitors and their ambassadors. She couldn't be reached by her enemies, even at Nonsuch.

Not if Kate had anything to say about it.

She glanced once more at Elizabeth, sitting in her rosy arbor. Master Green had finished his song and knelt on one knee as the queen and her ladies applauded. Elizabeth teasingly tossed him a sweetmeat, and he caught it in his mouth. She laughed even more and clapped her hands in delight. The sound of her laughter was a joy, her merriment like a balm for the whole country after the perils of the coronation.

All her ladies giggled too, falling against one another in a wave of frivolous mirth. All but one of them. Lady Catherine Grey, who sat at the edge of the group with her best friend, Lady Jane Seymour, glanced back over her shoulder at the gardens beyond, a frown on her pretty, heart-shaped face. She tucked one of her golden curls back into her cap and sighed, plucking at her silver-and-white skirt.

Lady Catherine surely should have been rejoicing. After Mary Queen of Scots became Queen of France and brazenly declared herself the rightful Queen of England as well, Elizabeth had drawn Catherine Grey closer as her other Protestant heir. She restored Catherine to the post of Lady of the Bedchamber she had enjoyed under Queen Mary and kept her nearby at every banquet and hunt.

"One must keep one's rivals closer than one's friends, Kate," the queen had told her one morning, frowning as she watched Lady Catherine dance with her friends. "Always remember that."

Yet Lady Catherine only seemed to grow sadder and paler as the summer days passed, smiling only with Lady Jane, and, more worryingly, with the new Spanish ambassador. Was it because the handsome Edward Seymour, Lord Hertford, was not yet at court, and in her boredom she played with political schemes? Kate was sure of it, and so was Elizabeth.

Kate turned and made her way along the empty corridor. Nonsuch was small for a palace, pretty but compact around its courtyards and gardens, forcing much of the court to lodge in those picturesque tents on the grounds. This tower was set aside for the queen's state apartments during her visit, and thus was quiet, with all her ladies outside attending her and the servants snatching rest. Only a few people loitered in the privy chamber, whispering near the open windows.

Yet Kate could hear the echo of noise from other parts of the house, the laughter from belowstairs, the bellow of Lord Arundel as he found something not quite perfect for the sight of the queen. She knew Elizabeth would grow restless sitting in the rose arbor idyll and would soon be leaping up to dash through the gardens or come inside to demand that everyone dance or play cards. She would forget then that she even wanted the book she'd sent Kate to fetch. But if she did remember and Kate had failed to return . . .

Kate laughed ruefully to think of the storm that

would ensue. The queen had thrown a shoe at Lady Clinton just that morning. But such flashes of temper passed as quickly as they came.

Her steps quickened, and she was near racing when she reached the end of the corridor and swung around a doorway. She was so distracted by her errand, she almost tripped over a man standing there. His black robes blended into the shadows of the tapestry-draped walls.

Kate's heart beat a little faster with the startlement, and she knew she had not yet recovered from what had happened on the frozen river. The man reached out to steady her, and his hand was freezing cold even through her silk sleeve. She stumbled back a step and looked up to see that it was Master Constable, Dr. Dee's apprentice, who lurked there.

She barely knew Master Constable, but she had seen him trailing after Dr. Dee around the court, his arms filled with scrolls and books. He was said to be a naturally gifted astrologer and mathematician in his own right, and some allowed him to cast their horoscopes when Dr. Dee was occupied with the queen's business.

But Kate remembered how he had declared Violet Roland of "melancholic" disposition, when Violet was one of the most lighthearted people she had ever met. So Kate had her doubts about his skills.

Especially now, as she peered up at him in the dim light. His round, pale face, still marred with youthful pimples, looked even more ghostly with his sparse fair hair tucked into a black cap. She had heard tell he had left Cambridge to study with Dr. Dee at the completion of his studies, which would put him in his early twenties, but he seemed younger. His eyes looked wide and startled as he squinted down at her, and she wondered what he was doing there. Surely he could not be on the queen's business himself?

"Master Constable," she said. "I am sorry, but I did not see you there. I thought everyone was outside enjoying the fine day."

He swallowed audibly. "Mistress Haywood. The fault is entirely mine. I was sent on an errand by my master."

"Dr. Dee?" Kate peered past him, as if she could find a clue to his task there, but she saw only the empty room. The queen's throne sat on its dais, draped in a scarlet cloth of estate. Two guards in the royal livery of green and white stood at the doorway to her bedchamber, their halberds at the ready, so he could not have slipped in there. Yet it seemed strange that he was lurking about at all. Kate did not like the glint in his eyes, the way he kept shifting on his feet and would not quite look at her.

People who lived and made their way at a royal court were usually most adept at hiding their true feelings and motives behind merry smiles and flattering words. A few, like Catherine Grey, never seemed to gain the ability for playacting all the time, but most had learned that keeping their heads attached meant never revealing what was inside them. And most would sometimes let their masks drop when only a lowly female musician was nearby.

She thought of Lady Anne's tale of murder and disappearance, here at this very palace, involving Dr. Dee so many years ago, and it made her feel suddenly cold. She wanted to back away from Master Constable, but something told her he was hiding something.

He seemed to be more of the Catherine Grey sort of courtier, unable to completely hide his feelings. But that seemed most odd for someone who was meant to be studying the deepest secrets of the universe.

"Aye, I must return to him immediately," Master

Constable said all in a rush, sidling around her. "If you will pardon me . . ."

He scurried away in a rustle of stiff black robes, a whiff of some strange chemical from no doubt fathomless experiments. Kate looked after him, puzzled.

"Ned," she said to one of the guards at the bedchamber door, a young man who enjoyed music and was always ready for an idle chat, despite his stern face. Guards, much like musicians, could become invisible when needed and heard many interesting things. "Was that man here very long?"

Ned gave a snort and shifted his halberd to his other hand so she could slip past. "Not long. I think you frightened him. He was tiptoeing around the dais, as if we couldn't even see him, but he didn't touch anything."

"Most odd," Kate murmured. She studied the dais, which was grand and gilded, draped in swaths of brocade and cloth of gold, but it held no concealed secrets that she could see. "If he perchance comes back, would you let me know?"

Ned's eyes narrowed. Like everyone else at court, he did enjoy an intrigue. "In trouble, is he?"

"Not that I am aware of. But one never knows." Kate gave him a quick smile and hurried into the royal bedchamber to find the queen's book. She, like Master Constable, had an errand to perform, and she had already been too long at it.

The bedchamber, like the privy chamber outside, was grand and beautiful, but also small and intimate, perfectly designed to appeal to Elizabeth. The four-poster bed, with its massive carved headboard, had been carried from palace to palace and was draped in purple velvet and gold tassels, piled high with lace-edged pillows. These matched the cushions scattered across the floor for her ladies. Tapestry frames with half-finished work were propped up along the walls, among clothes chests and locked boxes of state documents waiting for the queen's changeable attention. Lapdogs snored among the pillows, and the scent of flowery perfumes and the smoke of beeswax candles hung in the air.

Queen Elizabeth's desk was placed near the open window, and the soft breeze from outside rustled the documents held down with a carved crystal weight. The books were stacked beside them, and Kate hurried over to find the one she sought, a slim volume of poems lately arrived from Milan. No sermons or philosophy to be read today, not here at golden Nonsuch.

As Kate took up the leather-bound volume, her glance fell on the papers waiting for the queen's fleeting attention before she was distracted by a dance or a song. The one on top appeared to be written in some code, a mix of strange letters and numbers, but the tiny seal at the top showed it came from the queen's embassy in Paris. Curious, she took it up and read it. Master Cecil had given her a few lessons of late, but her skills were still very elementary. All she could make out was Queen Mary Stuart's name.

A sudden loud noise from below the open window snatched her attention from the document. A burst of trumpets, like a royal fanfare. She quickly slid the paper back into place and leaned over the casement to peer outside.

The view below the bedchamber faced away from the rose garden, toward the long, winding drive that led from the road, past the elaborate confection of the gatehouse to Nonsuch. The gilded gates were thrown open, and a crowd of curious onlookers gathered along the graveled lane. Satin-and-velvet-clad courtiers jostled together like children at a market fair. Even the most jaded among them needed some excitement now and then.

Kate shielded her eyes from the glitter of the sun and saw a most intriguing sight indeed. A caravan of brilliantly painted carts, drawn by black horses caparisoned in gold, wheeled by musicians who walked alongside, clad in more black and gold, with their drums, tambours, and trumpets. Bright flags flew from every corner of every vehicle. Banners snapped in the breeze. It was like a market fair on the move.

"Kate! Kate, are you here?" someone cried, and Kate turned to see Violet Roland rushing through the door. Her pale blue skirts swirled and shimmered, and her pretty face was flushed pink with excitement.

"I'm here, just fetching the queen's book," Kate said, holding up the volume of poetry. The music grew louder outside the window, an alluring, winding tune that was strangely—familiar.

Kate suddenly realized it was one of *her* songs, a merry tune she had written for the queen's favorite dance, an Italian volta. She started to spin back to the window, but Violet grabbed her hand.

"Her Majesty says you must come at once," Violet said breathlessly. "There is ever such a marvelous sight to be seen!"

"A company of players?" Kate gestured to the window behind her. 'Twas true that *she* was not so jaded as to fail to be excited at the prospect of a new play. Long years of quiet exile in the countryside were not so far behind her that she didn't long for every bit of color, of music, of loveliness.

But the months since the queen's coronation had been filled with pageants, banquets, and masques. What made this one different? Why did the queen need her there now?

And why were they playing *her* song?

Before she could peer out the window again, Violet tightened her grip on Kate's hand and pulled her along for a mad dash along the corridors and down the stairs. Kate held tight to the book with her other hand, laughing. Violet's sense of fun always reached out and grabbed everyone else around her.

They tumbled out into the garden, where Violet's brother, Thomas Roland, secretary to Lord Arundel, waited with his friend the lovely Master Green. Master Roland was as handsome and golden as his sister, and the three of them looked like an image out of a poem as they linked arms, laughing together.

The music was louder there, the notes she'd written winding and twisting to a glorious crescendo. She had never heard it played thus, and it was quite thrilling.

Violet drew her right up to where the queen waited, on the marble steps leading to the open doors of the palace. Elizabeth looked like a goddess in a beam of sunlight, with her bright hair and green gown, the gleam of her pearls and emeralds. She was framed by the marble statues flanking the doors, of Athena and Hera and Aphrodite, and by her ladies in their flower-like gowns.

"Ah, Kate. Good, there you are," Elizabeth said. "I need you to help us welcome an old friend to Non-such."

Elizabeth held out her hand to beckon Kate closer, the ruby-and-pearl ring that had once belonged to Anne Boleyn sparkling beside the large coronation ring. Some of the courtiers closest to the queen edged back and threw Kate puzzled glances as she hurried past them, as if they wondered at this mark of favor. But Catherine Carey, Lady Knollys, Elizabeth's Boleyn cousin, who stood just behind the queen, gave Kate a nod and a small smile.

Kate stopped on the marble step below the queen and curtsied. "A friend, Your Majesty?"

"Aye, someone who has come to amuse us in these long summer days." Elizabeth leaned closer and whispered with a teasing smile, "Or mayhap especially to amuse *you*."

Kate turned to see that the bright, noisy procession had wound its way to a halt on the graveled drive. The horses tossed their ribbon-braided manes, and the trumpets gave one last fanfare. And, at the procession's head, mounted on a pure white horse clad in green and gold, was a figure surely designed to make all the ladies sigh. Tall, strongly muscled under close-fitting green-and-white silk, sparkling with gem-scattered sleeves.

He swept off his plumed cap, and the sunlight shimmered on pale golden hair. He looked up, laughing, and gracefully leaped from the saddle to fall to one knee before the queen. It was Rob Cartman.

Kate pressed her hand to her lips to hold back a startled gasp. When last she had seen him, he had been thin and drawn tight with fury, gray faced from days in Clink Gaol and burning for revenge for the murderer of his mistress. That was right after the queen's coronation, when a murderer was loose in the queen's court. Now . . .

Now he looked like a golden god, a phoenix rising from the cold ashes of last winter's tragedy to new heights of beauty.

"Rob," she whispered.

He tossed back a shining wave of hair and grinned up at her, and she saw he was indeed the Rob he had been when they first met at Hatfield House and his troupe appeared to lighten their dull days of exile. Young and eager, shining with ambition.

The queen held out her hand for him to kiss. "Master Cartman, we are happy to welcome you back to our court at last. You and your company amused us much at Hatfield last year. We trust you have a new play for us now?"

Rob bowed over her hand in an elaborate salute that made her laugh. "We have a farce to make Your Majesty laugh—or a romantical tragedy to make her weep, whichever she may prefer. Our talents are always at your complete disposal."

"Most excellent. A comedy, I think. Nothing to make us cry in these warm days. You must consult our musician, then. Mistress Haywood will help you anon." With one last smile, Elizabeth took Robert Dudley's arm and swept into the house in a flurry of grass-green skirts. Everyone scurried to follow, Lord Arundel practically tumbling over himself to try to wrest her from Dudley and claim his rights as host.

Kate was left with Rob Cartman. His company still moved around the drive, led by the queen's footmen, and some of them waved at her and called greetings. Harry, the company's tall, gangly apprentice, whom Kate had forced to lead her through Southwark to find Rob last winter, gave her a low bow and a wincing expression that made her laugh.

It was hard to tear her gaze from Rob, though. His golden glow was almost blinding.

"Greetings, fair Kate," he said. "You are looking very well indeed." He took her hand from where it rested against her pink silk skirt and kissed her fingers, callused from her lute strings. It was different from the salute he had made to the queen, simple and lingering, no theatrical flourishes. His touch was warm through his gloves.

"And you, Rob," she managed to answer. She was much too flustered by his touch, remembering a long-ago kiss by the frozen river. Did he remember it, too? "You are looking—very well indeed."

CHAPTER THREE

"What has brought you to Nonsuch, then, Rob?" Kate asked as they strolled around the decorative lake near the palace. Swans glided serenely on the placid blue waters, the white marble follies reflected in their paths. Across the water, set off by itself like a jewel, was a small, round classical temple with a domed roof and covered walkway. The towers of the house rose above the trees planted in shady groves along the banks, and purple and white flowers tumbled underfoot in a fragrant carpet. Like everything else there, it was designed to enchant and beguile.

Just like Rob himself, Kate feared.

"Would you believe me if I said *you* brought me here, Kate?" he answered.

She turned to look up at him, startled. His expression in that one unguarded instant was solemn, his pale blue eyes shadowed. Then he laughed and gave her one of his theatrical bows.

"Nay, not a bit," Kate said, making herself laugh, too. She knew all too well the dangers of taking a man like Rob at all seriously. He was much too handsome and charming, and he knew how to use those assets to get his own way. She saw it with the men of the court every day. "I would not believe it."

Rob shook his head and pressed his hand over his

heart. A gold ring on his smallest finger gleamed next to the fine silk and the silver embroidery. Whatever he had been up to of late, it seemed profitable.

"Your doubts wound me, fair Kate," he said with a deep sigh. "It has been much too long since we met, and I have thought of you often."

"But it was not me who summoned you to Non-such."

"Nay. 'Twas Master Benger, the queen's Master of the Revels, who wrote and asked if we would present a masque for Her Majesty's summer progress. It seems the queen expressed a wish to see us perform again herself."

"And how did this letter find you?"

"Surely the queen has eyes everywhere. A troupe of players cannot make themselves obscure." His gaze shifted away, over the lake, and Kate studied him carefully.

It was true Rob was a fine actor, a practiced player since his childhood, and he was adept at donning a merry mask whenever needed. But Kate was a player, too, a musician making her way through the thorny thicket of the nobility, and she had learned a thing or two since she and Rob had last met. She had learned much from *him* as well. The dangers of a fiery temper. The pain of losing what one loved. The importance of always moving forward.

And she could see in his eyes that he was hiding something.

"What have you been doing since the coronation?" she asked. She sat down on one of the carved stone benches overlooking the water and carefully arranged her pink-and-white silk skirts. She pretended to be not much interested in his answer, one way or another. Another thing she had learned of late at court.

Rob propped his foot on the edge of the bench beside her and leaned his elbow on his knee. She saw that his boots, too, were very fine, of soft, polished Spanish leather. "Much the same as you, I would suspect. Singing for my crust of bread."

Kate snorted. "I am no fine singer, I fear, no matter how I practice."

"But you do well enough by your lute, I see."

"My music is all I have," she said softly, all too aware of how true those words were. Music was the only thing that was constant, the only thing that was always the truth.

"I am sure that won't be true much longer."

"How so? Do you think I shall take to the roads and the public stage like you?"

Rob suddenly reached out and gently touched the garnet earring she wore. His fingertip tangled in a dark curl of her hair, and she drew back from the heat of it. "The queen does make a pet of you."

In a flash of anger, Kate jerked her head away from his touch. "These earrings were my father's gift at Christmas. But certainly the queen does not neglect those who serve her. She enjoys my music, and I work hard for her. I will not starve here."

"Then surely she will find you a prosperous marriage soon."

A marriage? Kate almost laughed, remembering all the times Elizabeth had railed against marriage. "Her Majesty does not wish her servants to leave her so soon."

"And mayhap she has more reason to keep you close than your way with a lively dance tune?"

Kate peered up at him suspiciously. His expression was too bland, his tone too tense. What did he know? What was he trying to discover—and why? "You speak in riddles today, Rob Cartman, and I have no time for such nonsense. I do indeed have to earn my bread and must play for the dancing tonight."

She started up from the bench, but Rob stopped her with a touch on her sleeve. "Pax, Kate. I don't want to quarrel with you. I have few enough friends as it is. I don't want to lose one."

Kate slowly sat back down. Lose her? He had never had her, not really. They sometimes seemed friends, but then he vanished again. And when he came back, it was to insult her with his strange words. Yet she had seen his kindness, too, the caring heart he tried to hide. "I hope you know I am truly your friend, Rob."

"So you have proven time and again, fair Kate. I would have been hanged, or at least left to rot in gaol, if not for you." He sat down beside her with a heavy sigh, and for an instant the golden mask dropped and he looked older and harder. Tired. What was amiss with him?

"The troupe has had some good fortune since the winter," he said, "playing at noble houses around the countryside. There is a fine lord who speaks of becoming our permanent sponsor, since Lord Ambrose's downfall. Perhaps he would even provide a real theater for us."

"But that is wonderful, Rob!" Kate cried. Surely this piece of fortune was not what had him so down-hearted? But he looked doubtful even as he said the words. She wondered who this "fine lord" could be. "Your plays deserve to be seen by so many people. Surely once this patron hears you have been commanded to perform for the queen herself, he will agree to sponsor you in an instant." A sudden dark suspicion struck her. "Unless you have been dallying with his wife . . ."

"Not I, Kate! Your low opinion of my morals wounds me." He flashed her a sudden brilliant grin, banishing the dark cloud of an incipient quarrel she didn't even understand. "His wife is fifty at least."

"His daughter, then?"

"Nor her. I have learned my lesson since the terrible events of January last. I must see to my troupe, and the only way to do that is to pay attention to the business before me. I cannot become greedy and lustful, as my uncle did. He came to Nonsuch once himself, when he was young, to play for King Henry. I hope to play for royalty, as my uncle did, but hopefully avoid his fate."

Kate nodded, remembering the terrible end of Rob's uncle at Hatfield, the events that had left him in charge of the then Lord Ambrose's Men. His uncle had been murdered because he meddled in affairs of state that were beyond his understanding. She shivered to think of Rob ending thus, slaughtered in the woods. "I hope that may be so, Rob, truly."

"I have your example before me, do I not? Your fine dedication to your work, your loyalty to Queen Elizabeth. I must emulate you now, I think."

Kate frowned up at him, but there was only sincerity in his face now. A rueful certainty. "If you are teasing me again . . ."

He held up his hands. "I vow I am entirely serious. I have missed you, Kate. I did not know quite how much until this moment."

She had no idea how to answer that. Flustered, she turned her gaze back to the lake. Across the sparkling expanse of water, a group of courtiers played at boules on the grass. Their jeweled doublets and gowns made them look like a veritable field of flowers, yellow and purple and apple green. Behind them, the fancifully carved red-and-white towers of the palace gleamed in the light, a fairy-tale realm. Beyond the lawn stretched the rows of tents, their embroidered pennants snapping in the breeze.

It looked like a storybook scene indeed, something

from a tale of Arthur and his knights. All perfectly golden, suffused with light and warmth and laughter, ripe for romance.

Yet look what had happened to King Arthur and his realm—all the blithe, romantic perfection torn apart by the darkness of lowest human greed and jealousy. And look also at what had happened to Queen Catherine Howard only a few decades before, beheaded after her king brought her here to this lovely place.

Kate remembered Lady Anne Godwin's story of the long-ago disappearance of Dr. Dee's own teacher, right here at Nonsuch. It seemed the most beautiful of palaces could hide the greatest darkness of all.

Kate trembled at the thought, the perfection of the scene before her suddenly sinister.

"Are you chilled, Kate?" Rob asked. "Perhaps we should go inside."

"Nay, I think . . ." Whatever she was going to say was cut off by the rustle of the grove of old oak trees behind their bench. This interruption to her brooding thoughts made her jump to her feet, and she whirled around to find the queen's cousin, Lord Hunsdon, emerging onto the winding lake path. His wife, the tiny, merry-faced Anne, held on to his arm, and a party of friends clustered behind them, including the handsome Master Green, who had sung to the queen in her rose arbor.

Kate felt a wave of confusion, as she always did when she found herself facing Lord Hunsdon or his sister, Lady Knollys. She had learned how to behave with almost everyone at court, how to use words and smiles to flatter, deflect, conceal. But with the Boleyns, she could not quite forget the tale old Lady Gertrude Howard had told her in London, the truth of her long-dead mother's parentage.

Lord Hunsdon had never said anything to her of the matter. She wasn't really sure if he knew the tale or not, though surely he missed little about his family. His smile was warm as she curtsied to him, and she was struck by how much he resembled the queen. His fair white skin, his pointed chin and long nose, his dark Boleyn eyes—eyes much like the ones Kate saw looking back at her from her own glass. His hair and beard were reddish brown, darker than Elizabeth's, and his gray velvet doublet was finely cut yet simple, no jewels or embroidery.

She was suddenly very aware of Rob's tall presence at her back, his close, watchful attention on the royal party before them. Hunsdon gave them an elegant bow.

"Mistress Haywood," he said. "And Master Cartman. Enjoying the fine weather, I see."

"Nonsuch is very beautiful, my lord," Kate managed to answer.

"The perfect setting for your music, I would say," Lord Hunsdon said. "I can see why the queen would wish to bring in players to amuse her here. We shall be most merry."

"And Arundel has certainly spared no expense on this visit! I am put in mind of the knights of olden years," his wife said cheerfully, echoing Kate's own earlier thoughts of Arthur and his knights. "Shall you play for the dancing tonight, Mistress Haywood?"

"Aye, and I should return to the house to make sure all is in readiness," Kate said. She glanced up at Rob, who gave her a small nod. She couldn't read his expression at all.

"I will go with you, Kate," Violet Roland said happily. Kate saw her friend had been standing behind Lady Hunsdon, next to Master Green, her cheeks much too pink against her windblown blond curls. She took Kate's arm, and together they hurried back through the trees toward the palace.

At the turning of the pathway, Kate glanced back

over her shoulder. Lord Hunsdon and his group had continued on their way around the lake, but Rob still stood by the stone bench, staring out over the water. He looked deep in his own, unfathomable thoughts, where Kate knew she could not follow.

"Kate, you sly girl," Violet whispered teasingly. "Everyone is full of speculation about that handsome actor, and here you are talking to him all alone. So scandalous of you!"

Kate smiled at her friend and hoped any gossip would spread no further. Her usefulness to the queen depended much on her obscurity. "I knew him in London."

Violet's eyes sparkled. "Did you? Oh, you must tell me all!"

"There is not much to tell. You would find it dull fare indeed."

"You are surely no pallid Puritan, Kate, like my suitor Master Longville," Violet said with a teasing pout. "We are allowed a tiny flirtation now and then, aren't we?"

Kate laughed. Nay, she was certainly no Puritan, despite the lack of "flirtation" in her days. She was finding she loved pretty gowns and soft slippers far too much to eschew them for plain gray wool, not to mention the lack of elaborate music at chapel and no dancing. And she found she did not quite mind a flash of admiration from handsome eyes, either.

Eyes like Rob Cartman's?

She pushed away such thoughts. Surely she knew better than *that*. She knew him too well.

And anyway—how had Lord Hunsdon known Rob's name?

"I would wager any romantic tale I could tell would be nothing to yours," Kate said. "Young Master Green seems to admire you . . ."

Violet shook her head and looked away, but her blush deepened. Kate thought she must care for Master Green more than she would want to admit. "He admires all the ladies. He only talks to me because he is friends with my brother. I hope I am not such a fool as to pay attention to his pretty words. But this does feel like a magical place, does it not? As if anything could happen here."

Violet suddenly twirled around, her arms outflung, as she hummed a dance tune. Kate laughed and impulsively joined her as they spun and leaped in the air, kicking out at their skirt hems before they took off on a mad dash across the lawn. In just that one moment, she forgot all the darkening clouds that hung over beautiful Nonsuch, forgot her father and the Boleyns and the changeable Rob Cartman, and just laughed.

Violet snatched up Kate's hand and drew her up the steps into the palace. The marble-floored entrance hall was dim and cool after the brilliant day, and Kate paused for an instant to let her eyes adjust. Her fashionably tight stays were too constricting after running, and she drew in a shallow breath.

Violet seemed to need no such respite. She dashed up the winding staircase, fancifully carved with grinning goblin faces and twisting leaves and vines, past servants laden with basins and freshly sponged gowns, past frowning courtiers bent on their own vital errands.

"Race you to our chamber, Kate!" she called.

Kate laughed ruefully, sure she should not be "racing" anyone. She needed her energy for that night's banquet, for surely the queen would want to dance into the small hours again. And a royal musician should not be seen to be undignified, especially if she did not want to bring any attention onto herself. She followed Violet at a slower pace.

The small chamber she shared with Violet and Lady

Anne Godwin was tucked away at the very top of the house, at the end of a narrow corridor overlooking a kitchen courtyard. Many of the queen's young maids of honor were quartered near there, watched over by the stern eye of Lady Eglionby, Mistress of the Maids. From behind their closed doors, Kate could hear the bursts of giggles and the rustles of fine silks and taffetas. The air smelled of perfumes, rose and jasmine and lavender.

At the end of the corridor, near her own chamber, it was quieter. The door was already closed, so Violet must have won the race and gone inside. Kate reached for the handle, but she was stayed by a sudden rush of whispers behind her, in a small window alcove half concealed by the drape of a tapestry.

"... have broken your word!" a woman sobbed brokenly. "I have believed you too many times. I can do it no more."

Kate's curiosity clashed with her instinct to leave the romances of others completely alone. They brought nothing but trouble in the airless world of the royal court. But she knew now that her curiosity was more than that—anything that happened in the queen's palaces could be a threat to her royal safety. Secrets had no place in her court now, not with birds of prey like Mary, Queen of Scots and Philip of Spain circling every day. Robert Dudley and William Cecil might hate each other, but they both believed ardently in Queen Elizabeth, and they had impressed on Kate the vital importance of the mission of keeping the queen safe.

Pressing her hand to her own silk skirts to quiet their rustle, she carefully peeked over her shoulder.

The tapestry, a scene of a sunlit picnic, half concealed the couple, and the shadows were thick in their hiding place. The tall man had his back to the corridor, and his garments were dark, but Kate caught a glimpse of the woman's blond hair twisted up in elaborate curls under a lace cap, and a bright flash of silver-and-white skirts.

Catherine Grey. And surely she would have no new lover yet. Edward Seymour must have arrived at court and wasted no time in seeking her out.

"You know my feelings for you, sweeting," he said in a soft, cajoling tone. "But we must be most careful if we are to gain our deepest desire. We will never achieve it if we are tossed into the Tower."

Kate winced. This was the second reminder in just a day of the darkness of that night in the Tower before Elizabeth's coronation, the unseen eyes that seemed to watch her every movement. She would not wish such a fate on anyone. But surely these two could not be *that* foolish, to toy with the queen's goodwill already?

"No one would dare do such to *us*!" Lady Catherine hissed. "Not even *her*."

"Of course she would dare. She is queen now. My father thought he was above monarchs, too, but he learned differently."

"I do not care a fig for all that! We have waited much too long. I grow older every day. I had my horoscope drawn up by Master Constable, and my planets are aligned now for a prosperous marriage. I cannot wait any longer, biding my time, smiling as if I haven't a care in the world. If we really want this . . ."

"You know I desire it as much as you. My beautiful girl . . ."

"Then we must fight for it. As my own grandparents fought for their love against King Henry. Even he could not gainsay them," Catherine said haughtily, and in that instant she did sound every bit the offspring of Princess Mary Tudor, Dowager Queen of France, and Charles Brandon. Kate would not have thought she had it in her, but people were ever surprising. "Your mother will have you married off to that horse-faced Talbot harpy."

"My mother will do no such thing if I gainsay her," he said in a hard voice.

Lady Catherine laughed. "When have you ever said her nay? You will jump to do as she bids, and I shall be left a lonely spinster again. You have no manly will."

She spun away in a flurry of pale skirts, and he grabbed her arm and drew her back. He pulled her roughly into his arms and up on her toes, making her squeal.

"No manly will, you say?" he growled. "What say you of *this*?"

His lips came down on hers and she moaned. Kate squirmed uncomfortably, half wishing she had ducked into her chamber when she had had the chance.

"My sweet Ned," Lady Catherine sighed as she wrapped her arms around his shoulders.

So it really was Edward Seymour, come back to court, and his rumored love—or mayhap not so rumored after all. They grew bold to embrace in the middle of the queen's own palace. What did they know that gave them such nerve now?

Mayhap it was the knowledge that a "prosperous marriage" was now written in the stars for Lady Catherine, at least according to the dubious Master Constable. Kate couldn't help but wonder if that had something to do with why the man was lurking around the queen's apartments.

She carefully pushed open her own door and slipped inside before they could see her lurking there and know they were caught. She had much to think about.

"There you are, Kate," Violet said, completely oblivious to the dramatic little scene outside their chamber. "What think you? The gold sleeves, or the blue?"

*   *   *

Rob Cartman watched Kate glide away from him, swept up by the glittering, chattering crowd, over the gardens until she was beyond his sight. Her dark hair, glossy in the sunlight; her brown eyes, touched with a hazel glow brought out by her fine silk gown; the sudden radiance of her smile. Had she always been so lovely?

The memory of her as she had looked when they last met always seemed to be with him. The thought of Kate's laugh had flashed through his mind when he meant to be writing a scene. The way she would frown, ever so faintly disapproving, when she saw some of his naughtier proclivities. The way she would suddenly laugh at a jest.

Aye, all of that was with him every day. And when he had finally seen her today, after all this time . . .

God's teeth. It was more than all his imaginings. She was even prettier now than before, wiser, deeper, her eyes so knowing. Yet she thought he had forgotten about her, about all that had happened between them last winter.

As if he could ever forget.

Rob reached into the small leather pouch tied at his belt and took out a small object wrapped in a scrap of silk. He unfolded it and stared down at the object, which glittered in the sun.

He'd had a goldsmith create it for him and had even persuaded the man to take his payment in installments. It had meant scribbling out even more penny sonnets for the printer, but at last it was done. A tiny lute, made of colored enamels and set in gold. It was set with the smallest, most intricate set of diamonds, meant to mimic the inlaid pattern of Kate's own instrument. Rob had sketched it out from memory, and he hoped it was right.

Rob closed his fist around the delicate bauble. He

wouldn't give it to Kate until his secret aim here at Nonsuch was achieved. He hadn't even spoken to his troupe about it, not in full. They knew only that they sought "a patron" from among the nobility.

They didn't know he had one particular patron in mind. Lord Hunsdon, the queen's own cousin.

Lord Hunsdon loved the theater and was said to be eager to find his own troupe to serve him and his family in their newly elevated place at court. He had seen Rob play at a tavern courtyard in the springtime and had asked about his work. If Lord Hunsdon became their patron . . .

Then Rob's wandering days could be done. His troupe could think about their own theater, and he could afford a home, in London or in some village nearby. Mayhap even a wife, a family. Things he had never considered before.

He looked across the lake at the fanciful palace, where Kate had disappeared. It shimmered in the bright day, like a fairy realm with its carved towers. Kate had seemed to know Lord Hunsdon and his family, yet another reason to hide from her his true purpose here, at least for now. He never wanted her to think he used her only for her connections, her place at court. He wanted her to know he had changed, that he could take care of her.

Soon, God willing, that would be the truth, and he could tell her everything. Everything he had kept locked up in his heart for months.

Rob put the precious lute pendant away once more and hoped that soon enough he would see it shining against Kate's white skin.

CHAPTER FOUR

" . . . And the hellish phantom carriage rolled silently to a halt, and the damned Lord Blickling saw by the glow of lightning that the coachman was—headless! And the devil himself stepped out in a cloud of brimstone to claim his soul forever."

Lady Anne Godwin ended with a great flourish, raising her arms in their pure white chemise sleeves and leaping up onto the edge of the mattress. The dark blue bed curtains swayed wildly, casting fluttering shadows on the whitewashed walls and making the candles gutter in their sconces.

Violet shrieked and dived beneath her blanket. Kate laughed, but she had to admit her heart, too, was beating a bit faster at Anne's ghostly tale.

Outside their window, the fine, clear night had turned to a chill and windy one, and the cold breeze beat at the casement and whined down their chimney. The polished wood floor creaked and groaned, almost as if ghosts truly did fly about in the enchanted night.

Kate drew her knitted shawl closer over her linen chemise. She was not quite sure she really believed in ghosts, not outside a masquerade, but tonight it felt almost as if secrets buried too long beneath the slumberous beauties of Nonsuch struggled to escape.

Lady Anne flopped down onto a cushioned stool

next to their small fireplace and reached for a plate of sweet fruit suckets they had stolen from the remains of the banquet. "Every word is completely true. I vow it."

Violet peeked out from beneath her blanket. "It cannot be. I don't believe you."

"It certainly is! I heard it from Lady Bess Martin, who heard it from Beatriz Gómez, who was once servant to Queen Mary's own astrologer, Senor Fernández, who came from Spain with King Philip."

"I thought Dr. Dee once served Queen Mary thus, as he does Queen Elizabeth," Kate said. She tried to remember all she had learned of the famous doctor, the tangled threads of old gossip that had tossed everyone about in the turbulent years between King Edward, Queen Mary, and Queen Elizabeth. The twists and turns of religion and complicated loyalties.

Lady Anne shook her head, smugly happy she had the whole tale to relate. "Surely you remember the story of when Dr. Dee was once arrested under Queen Mary. He was accused of drawing up the horoscopes of the queen and King Philip in secret and was even questioned by the Star Chamber, though they let him go. He went abroad after that, and it's said he spied for Queen Elizabeth in Europe, though I believe it not. And years before that, there is the tale of his own teacher from Cambridge vanishing here at Nonsuch. It was years ago when Dee was accused of spying. I was just a girl, but my father was at court then, and he was sure Dr. Dee was quite doomed, and that it must have something to do with all that old business."

Kate frowned as she reached for a sweetmeat. The candied cherry melted on her tongue, and she nodded as the details came back to her. She, too, had been collecting stories of late, though not of the ghostly variety. "Was Dr. Dee not quickly released back then?"

Lady Anne gave a knowing little smile. "Aye, but

why was he released? No one knows for sure. Yet Queen Elizabeth trusts him now, enough to have him cast her horoscope for her own coronation date. And he is here at Nonsuch."

"Master Green says—," Violet declared, only to break off on a blush.

"Oho, Master Green, is it!" Lady Anne answered, so teasingly that Violet's cheeks turned even more violently red. "You have been spending a great deal of time with that young man. You are quite the envy of all the ladies, I declare. Master Longville is quite downcast now."

"He is a friend of my brother; that is all," Violet muttered. She tossed a cushion at Anne's head.

Kate laughed as her friends teased and quarreled with each other, but the old tale of Dr. Dee, of his long-ago arrest and of the strange disappearance of his old teacher here at Nonsuch, lingered at the back of her mind. When Anne and Violet at last fell asleep, she slipped out of her own bed and tiptoed over to peer out the window.

They were fortunate to have a room for only three of them, even though it faced the back courtyard and kitchen gardens and not the grand front drive. They had privacy compared to the packs of maids of honor in their rows of pallets, and they were nowhere near the smell of the jakes.

The moon peeked from behind a lacy bank of clouds, casting a silver glow over the low stone walls and rolling fields. The wind trembled in the treetops, and the leaves sounded almost like a chorus of wordless whispers.

Kate shivered and pulled her warm shawl even closer. She *could* believe in spirits on a night like this. Could almost imagine King Henry and beautiful Queen Catherine Howard riding over the lanes again, chased by spectral hounds and courtiers long since dead. If magic such as Dr. Dee spoke of was real, what could not be conjured on such a night?

She stared up at the moon, so beautiful and pale, so far away, and she thought of her mother. She had never known Eleanor Haywood, who had died a few hours after her birth, but her mother seemed close to her of late. Seemed to be reaching out to her. If only Eleanor could help her, advise her . . .

The memory of Rob Cartman by the lake flashed in Kate's mind, the solemnity in his eyes, the roughness of his manner. Nonsuch was meant to be a place for joy and romance, yet instead it seemed to set everyone quite on edge. What was amiss with him, with everyone? She wished she could decipher it all.

Suddenly, something shimmered below her in the garden, a flash of light that broke the perfect solitude of the night. Kate gasped, half-afraid maybe it really was King Henry returned to his pleasure palace to wreak some ghostly vengeance.

"Don't be such a goose," she whispered sternly to herself. Ghosts were not real, surely. Were they not?

Yet it was most strange that anyone would be outside on such a night, after the long hours of feasting and music. Once the queen retired to her bedchamber, none dared stay out after her.

Kate went up on tiptoe, peering past the thick, wavy glass of the window to the endless night outside. There was indeed someone there, and surely not a ghost. Ghosts did not carry lanterns. And this figure was too solid, clad in a plain dark cloak that jerked and swayed in the fitful wind. A spirit would glide, unaffected by the weather, and would certainly not have to push open a gate to move through a wall.

Much like when she glimpsed Catherine Grey earlier, Kate was not entirely sure what she should do.

Wake a guard? But what if this person was set on some secret mission, and the villain interrupted them before they could discover what it was?

She glanced over at Violet and Anne. Both of them now slept peacefully under their bedclothes. Kate knew she couldn't wake them, couldn't let them know what she was doing, if indeed there really was anything to discover. It could very possibly be just another romantic assignation. Anne would gossip about it, and Violet would shriek with fright to go out in the night. But if something was really happening, and the queen knew naught about it . . .

Kate was scared to venture out after so much talk of ghosts, but she knew she had to. It would surely be nothing, and she could be back in her warm bed before none were any wiser.

She quickly pulled on a plain dark wool skirt and a bodice that laced up the front, as well as her sturdiest leather boots. No velvet-heeled shoes tonight. She strapped one of her new daggers—she'd soon learned she needed them in the queen's court—beneath the loose sleeve of her chemise, where she could quickly grasp the reassuringly solid steel hilt if needed, and wrapped her shawl over her head and shoulders before she slipped out of the chamber door.

The tapestry-hung alcove where Lady Catherine Grey had so unwisely embraced Edward Seymour was now empty. The whole corridor was silent, no laughter or whispers echoing from the maids' rooms, no fall of furtive footsteps. The palace seemed to slumber under an enchanted spell, yet something hovered deep in Kate's senses, telling her the night was not quite so empty as it seemed.

She hurried lightly down the back stairs and through the kitchens to an unguarded side door. The vast stone space was just as quiet as the warren of royal rooms above, but the banked fires made it seem warmer, not as eerie, sending out the reassuring scents of wood-smoke and freshly baked bread. A cat sat on the ledge of one of the high windows, blinking at her sleepily as she rushed past.

Out in the garden, cast in the shadows again as the clouds slid over the moon, she found the gate where the cloaked figure had disappeared. It was still ajar, and when she pushed it open she found herself in an open pathway, exactly the sort of place where a ghostly King Henry would lead his hunt. Beyond it, past a low stone wall, was a narrow lane that she knew would eventually lead to the nearest village.

She glanced up at the sky, half-afraid it would start to rain again, half-afraid of what lurked in the darkness. She pushed the fear away and plunged ahead.

In the distance, at the crest of a low, softly rolling grassy hill, she caught a glimpse of the cloaked figure's lantern bobbing in the night. The flutter of a cloak. Then it was gone. She ran after him, glad of her sturdy boots on the damp, soft ground. She followed her quarry at a distance, until the smoke from the chimneys of another house nearby blended with the wispy, rushing clouds.

Suddenly, the cloaked figure stopped at the gate of a small cottage set back from the lane beyond a shallow ditch and a low wall. Kate ducked behind a tree and watched carefully as the person knocked at the door and slipped inside. He glanced back for only an instant, but she clearly saw his face, his wispy pale hair escaping from a dark cap, in the glow of candlelight behind him.

It was Master Constable, Dr. Dee's apprentice, who had been lurking around the queen's privy chamber only that afternoon. Master Constable, who had been drawing up Catherine Grey's horoscope, among others. What was he doing here now, creeping about away from the palace?

Kate was quite sure this could not be another romantic assignation.

She carefully studied the cottage. It looked most ordinary, with whitewashed walls and a steep thatched roof behind a small overgrown garden. But all the windows were concealed with thick wooden shutters, so securely latched that only tiny chinks of light escaped, like pinpoints in the night.

Smoke curled from the chimney, and when Kate drew in a deep breath she realized it did not smell like ordinary woodsmoke. It had a strange metallic tinge she could not quite decipher, something like biting down on a coin and feeling it catch at the back of the throat.

She listened closely, yet it seemed there was naught behind those walls at all. Even the cries of night birds were silent here. All she knew for sure was the rough bark of the tree under her hands, the cold wind through her skirts.

As she watched, waiting for something to happen that would tell her more about this strange little place, guarded by Master Constable of all people, she felt the faint tremor of the ground beneath her feet that warned of a horse galloping by swiftly. She tucked herself further behind the tree and glanced back along the lane.

It was a fine black horse, almost one with the night with such a dark, glossy coat. A groom on a smaller mount followed close behind. The rider drew up at the gate and swung down from the saddle, tossing the reins to the servant. As he strode up to the door, the groom led the horse away, and Kate gasped. She recognized that tall figure, that confident stride. Robert Dudley.

The door swung open once more, and it was not Master Constable this time. It was Dr. John Dee, his spare figure draped in fur-trimmed black robes, his bearded face smiling in welcome. The two men clasped hands in greeting, and Sir Robert vanished inside.

If Robert Dudley was here, surely the queen already knew of it? Yet what if she did not? Confused, Kate spun around and ran back the way she'd come. She couldn't help but feel that the night was chasing her, full of things she could not hope to understand. Something strange was happening in that place, something she feared she could not yet begin to fathom.

But she would find out what it was, very soon indeed.

CHAPTER FIVE

"Your thoughts seem far away today, Kate. Do we not have enough to divert you here at Nonsuch?" Queen Elizabeth asked. She stood on a low stool as her ladies dressed her for the banquet, fluttering around her as they tied on the sleeves of her black-and-gold gown, fastened her necklace, held out caps for her approval.

The queen's words snapped Kate out of her brooding thoughts. She sat in the window seat of the royal bedchamber, playing a madrigal on her lute that was meant to entertain Elizabeth as she went through the tedium of being dressed, but in truth Kate's mind was far away from her task. She was wandering down a dark, moonlit lane to a strange cottage, in fact, and cursing the way she had run away in such a cowardly fashion before she could discover what was really happening there.

Had she struck a sour note in the song? She sat up straight, her fingers falling from the strings. As one of the queen's few female musicians, she was the only one allowed to play in the royal bedchamber. She could not ruin that privilege.

"I'm sorry, Your Majesty," she said hastily. "Is the song not to your liking?"

"Nay, the song is fine. But you are my own musician,

and yet you look as if our festivities are not diverting you." Elizabeth held out her hand to let one of the ladies slide rings onto her fingers, and shook her head at the third cap offered.

"I was merely thinking of the night ahead, Your Majesty," Kate said.

"You have no duties tonight, Kate. You must enjoy yourself for once. Nonsuch is meant for pleasure, is it not?" Elizabeth glanced down at a goblet Lady Catherine Grey held out, and she impatiently pushed it away. A drop of dark crimson wine splashed on the shoulder of Lady Catherine's white gown. "Not the port wine, cousin! You know I do not care for it. What could you be thinking?"

For an instant, Kate saw raw fury flash across Lady Catherine's face, distorting her delicate features. But she quickly composed herself and stepped back with her head dipped in a show of deference.

Kate remembered the angry words Lady Catherine had thrown at Lord Hertford when they were hidden behind the tapestry, the Tudor temper that lurked beneath her beauty.

"Forgive me, Your Majesty," Lady Catherine said, her voice as sweet as the sugar wafers Elizabeth loved. "I will fetch whatever you like right away."

"Let me find some sack wine, Your Majesty," Kate said, suddenly eager to escape that overly warm chamber filled with too many mingled perfumes, too many barking lapdogs. She had barely been able to sit still all afternoon; even music hadn't carried her completely out of herself, as it usually did. Now she seized on the chance to perform some errand, any errand.

Elizabeth nodded, distracted by Mary Sidney fastening a collar of pearls around her neck. Kate carefully set aside her lute and hurried from the bedchamber.

The privy chamber outside was scarcely less crowded,

with courtiers lingering around the door in hopes of catching the queen's attention as she left. They played cards, gathered around a lady playing at the virginals, and stood by the windows to catch a stray breeze, always talking in low voices, always watching. It made her feel closed in. But the farther she went from the royal apartments, the quieter it became, and she was finally able to breathe.

She found a footman to take the wine to the queen, but she didn't want to return just yet, so she slowed her steps down the corridor. The light that flooded through the windows was a beautiful golden pink, bright and warm, yet she seemed caught in the night, watching that strange cottage. Nonsuch had been built for pleasure, aye, but she could sense little of that in its air. Something strange had her spellbound, it seemed, and she had to brush it away if she was to be of use to the queen.

She turned through an arched doorway, still lost in her own thoughts, and almost collided with the solid bulk of a man rushing in the other direction.

"Forgive me! I was not paying attention," she gasped, falling back a step. She had been doing that far too much of late and knew she needed to be far more cautious. To watch every ripple of what happened around her.

The man took her arm to steady her, and she looked up to see it was Lord Arundel himself who stood before her. He was magnificently dressed as always, in a gold satin doublet that blended into his graying auburn hair, but his face was deeply creased.

"My lord," she said, quickly dropping a curtsy.

He shook his head, as if to clear his bad thoughts away, and squinted at her closely. "You are Mistress Haywood, are you not? The queen's musician?"

Kate was startled he would know her name at all.

There were hundreds of courtiers crowding his estate, and he was one of the wealthiest lords in the kingdom. "I am indeed Mistress Haywood, my lord."

"I wonder if I could ask your assistance in a most important matter, then."

Her assistance? Kate was baffled—and most curious. "I would be happy to help you, if I am able."

"They say the queen enjoys your music, that it often soothes her when nothing else can, and you are always with her court."

"I hope that is sometimes true, my lord. I do my best to serve her, as we all do."

"I fear—" Lord Arundel suddenly broke off, his face creasing even further, so he looked older than his fifty-some years. Kate remembered that it was said he thought to woo the queen, and now she wondered if that was indeed true. The poor man. "I fear she is not enjoying her visit as much as I would wish."

"Nonsuch is beyond compare, my lord, and I am sure the queen thinks so as well."

A smile flickered. "I wish to have a grand masquerade performed here in my banquet hall, an entertainment of Juno and Diana, and the marriage of Palamon to Emilia, a most well-known scene on the Continent," he said quickly, almost eagerly. "I have my own Master of Revels, but I am now convinced that none could organize such a performance more guaranteed to please Her Majesty than you. Would you do such?"

The marriage of Palamon, servant of Juno, wife of Zeus, to Emilia, votress of the virgin huntress-goddess Diana—the triumph of marriage over chastity. Mayhap a dangerous theme for the queen, who so far chose not to marry. But perhaps that was just the distraction Kate needed. Music, entertainment—surely that would erase thoughts of magic and danger. Ghosts. "I confess I would enjoy nothing more, my lord. But in such little time . . ."

"My stewards would be entirely at your disposal," Lord Arundel said quickly. "I would be happy to reward you most handsomely, Mistress Haywood."

Kate nodded, already thinking of music and costumes, the effects that would create the illusion of a goddess and her court. Perhaps Rob Cartman could help? But no, that would mean more time with him, the confounding man. "I shall do my best, my lord."

He nodded, his face already looking clearer. "I shall send my Master of Revels to you tomorrow, then. And the queen must know naught of it yet."

Bemused, Kate nodded and made her way back toward the royal bedchamber to make sure the wine had been delivered. The privy chamber was already much less crowded; it seemed everyone had left to prepare themselves for the banquet. But Sir Robert Dudley was there, no doubt waiting to escort the queen.

He paced the length of the polished floor, his boots ringing in the quiet evening. His black-and-gold doublet, a match to the queen's gown, gleamed. He frowned, as if deep in thought, but then he glimpsed Kate standing there and gave her a smile and quick bow. "Mistress Haywood."

"Sir Robert." Kate curtsied and hurried past him into the bedchamber. She wondered what *he* thought of Lord Arundel's efforts to woo the queen, of all the suitors who flocked around her. Mayhap that was why he visited Dr. Dee in the darkest hour of night, to ask the spirits to help his chances with Elizabeth.

And perhaps that was what made Kate feel so much disquiet. She hated what she could not understand, and the forces of magic were quite beyond her.

"Ah, Kate, you are back at last," Queen Elizabeth

cried. She stood in the middle of the bedchamber, fully dressed and bejeweled, so gloriously beautiful that surely any man would use any magic or masquerade he could to win her. "I vow I am terribly parched, and the wine the servant brought has gone sour . . ."

"Make way for the queen!"

Queen Elizabeth's heralds marched at the head of her procession, banners raised and trumpets ringing out as she made her way down the covered gallery leading from the palace to the temporary banqueting house at the top of a hill. The gallery walls were open to the night, revealing torches and bonfires flaring in the twilight. The carpet under their feet was just as deep a blue as the sky overhead, embroidered with moons and stars.

Sir Robert Dudley escorted Queen Elizabeth, matching her so well with the splendor of his velvet and gold, his plumed cap fastened with a ruby the size of an egg. His black gold-lined cloak was tossed back carelessly over his shoulder as he leaned close to whisper in her ear. Elizabeth laughed, her beringed hand pressed to her lips, and on her other side Lord Arundel looked as if he might weep—or strike Sir Robert a fatal blow. Kat Ashley and Mary Sidney followed behind.

Kate, from her place a few rows back with Violet and Lady Anne, studied Lord Arundel's quiet fury and wondered again that a man so wealthy, who had been at court through so many monarchs, could be so hard-pressed to hide his thoughts. But then, if everyone was so easy to read, the queen would have no need of William Cecil's spies. Kate would stage Lord Arundel's masquerade and be glad of the merry distraction, little good though it would surely do him.

She had little time to ponder Lord Arundel's matrimonial follies, though. The procession moved ever forward, and she had to keep up. Lady Anne gave her an impatient glance, and Kate hurried to follow the snaking, glittering line along the narrow gallery.

It opened suddenly into the vast banqueting house, and for a moment its grandeur dazzled Kate. She had seen so much in the last months with the royal court—the splendors of the coronation, palaces from Richmond to Eltham, banquet halls and gilded closets. But this was like something in an epic poem of enchanted realms and fairy spells. She remembered her earlier thoughts of King Arthur and his questing knights and realized that this would be the perfect setting for them and their fair ladies.

She knew the banqueting house was a mere flimsy wooden structure, built hastily for this visit, but it didn't look like that at all. The walls and the floor beneath the sea of satin shoes were painted to look like pale marble topped with carved gilded moldings. The low timber-laced ceiling was covered with red buckram and embroidered with Tudor roses and the crowned falcon that had once been Anne Boleyn's badge and was now her daughter's. Tiered buffet cabinets lined the walls, displaying what seemed to be all of Arundel's vast collection of gold and silver plates. Banners fluttered from the rafters, sewn with the coats of arms from all the great families.

The queen's court only added to the splendor, all their finest French fabrics and sparkling jewels on display, vying with one another in peacock colors. Kate was astonished at the beauty of it all. If she was to arrange a masquerade for the queen's amusement, she had to learn from this. Surpass it.

Lord Arundel led Elizabeth to the raised dais at the far end of the hall, set beneath a large mural painting depicting the queen herself with Nonsuch in the background, taller than the round towers.

Pages in Arundel's red-and-white livery led everyone to their seats at the rows of long tables spread with fine white damask cloths, their benches lined with soft gold velvet cushions. Every place, even that of the lowest maid, was set with a loaf of fine white manchet bread wrapped in a linen cover embroidered with more roses and falcons. A silver goblet filled to the brim with a rich red wine also sat at each place setting.

To her surprise, Kate found herself not at the lowest tables with the maids of honor and pages, but just above the saltcellar with Anne and Violet. Across from them sat the handsome Master Green and Violet's brother, Thomas Roland.

"Such a fortunate evening for us, to have such loveliness to gaze upon," Master Green said as he bowed over Violet's hand, making her laugh and blush.

Kate glimpsed Master Longville, Violet's lovelorn suitor, watching her from the next table with wide eyes. Surely he was one of the *unfortunate* ones tonight. She couldn't help but feel sorry for him; he always watched Violet with such longing.

"You are Mistress Haywood, are you not?" Master Roland said as they took their seats. Like his sister, he was delicate looking, fair colored, almost pretty, but where Violet was small he was broad shouldered and tall in his purple doublet. His smile was sweet and open.

Kate had to laugh, remembering how Lord Arundel had said much the same thing when they met earlier. She had to be careful to be more unobtrusive. "I am. And I know you are Violet's brother. She has been so excited to be able to see you again."

"And I her." His smile grew as he glanced at his sister. "We were such companions when we were children, but our duties have kept us too much apart of late."

Kate wondered what it would be like to have such a sibling—or any sibling at all. "Surely a position as secretary to Lord Arundel gives you much satisfaction, and your family as well."

"So it does, Mistress Haywood. I have been learning a great deal from the household here at Nonsuch. But I do miss my family at times."

"As we miss you, Thomas," Violet cried, tearing herself away from staring across the sparkling silver plate at Master Green. "Mama and Papa talk of you constantly when I am at home."

"I must say I am glad Violet has found such friends at court as you, Mistress Haywood," Master Roland said, laughing at his sister's enthusiasm. "My lord speaks highly of your great musical skills, which I hope we will hear more of before the court departs."

Kate was rather puzzled. There were many musicians. How could he, and his lord, have heard of *her*? "I am certainly happy my music pleases," she said. "But I had no idea anyone such as Lord Arundel would know of it."

"He heard your praises from my own master, Mistress Haywood," Master Green said. She glanced at him and could see why Violet was so dazzled. His golden beauty was astounding in the candlelight. "Surely you know Her Majesty's cousin Lord Hunsdon? He says his sister, Lady Knollys, will play no songs but yours at her virginals."

Kate was shocked. Before she could answer, a lively chorus of tambours, lutes, and pipes struck up from a curtained gallery over their heads, and it was impossible to converse. Servants appeared with great golden platters bearing a feast of venison, capons in lemon sauce, partridge, tiny larks, eels in cinnamon, game pie dressed with rare Spanish oranges, and baked lampreys, as well as summer vegetable salads.

At the end of the procession came a peacock, redressed in its own feathers and with gilt wrapped around its claws, and it was presented to the queen amid much applause.

The queen stood with a bright smile. "Much thanks to Lord Arundel for such excellent amusement this night. The summer is the time for much merriment, methinks, so let us be to it, my friends. Play on, musicians!" Then she sat down to laugh again with Sir Robert, who sat beside her on the dais. She popped a candied orange into his mouth and smiled.

The laughter flowed around Kate as she nibbled on a piece of gingerbread painted with gold leaf, listening with half an ear as Violet giggled with Master Green and Anne gossiped with the ladies on her other side about the new fashion in Venetian slippers.

Kate sipped at her wine and studied the gathering. Master Longville watched Violet with the same hopeless eyes Lord Arundel used to look at the queen, and Kate couldn't help but think of some pastoral play where the shepherd chased after his lass and was spurned at every corner. In a play it was funny. In life, it strangely made her feel like crying, especially in the midst of so much desperate summer merriment.

Her gaze turned, and she glimpsed Lord Hunsdon and his wife, Lady Anne, talking and smiling quietly together. They didn't seem sad at all, having come through so many years of travails and exile under Queen Mary to find favored places at the court of his niece Elizabeth.

Kate glanced away, just as an acrobat performed a breathtaking series of backward flips down the aisle between the tables. He was clad in tight garments of bright red-and-green stripes, which outlined an impressively muscled, lean physique. A troupe of noisy, gamboling actors in bell-sewn motley, dwarves in miniature satin doublets and tinseled gowns, and trained dogs in frilled ruffs followed him. The ladies in the crowd gasped and waved, giggling, but whether at the dogs' antics or the man's masculine legs, Kate could not tell.

It made her want to laugh herself, and she reached again for her wine. As she took a long drink, the acrobat showed off with a series of somersaults and graceful leaps, and when he finally turned his face in her direction, she almost gasped as she felt a little flutter in her lower belly. The man was Rob Cartman. She looked quickly away, not wanting to think about him tonight. He was a puzzle box of a man, and not something she needed to complicate her life.

Kate noticed Violet's brother watching her, and she saw his eyes narrow. He smiled when she caught his eye, and reached out to pour more wine into her goblet. He was all charm, yet she had the feeling he was like her—always watching. "Enjoying the evening, Mistress Haywood?"

"Very much, Master Roland," she answered.

Before Master Roland could say anything else, Master Green clapped his hand onto his shoulder, laughing loudly from all the free-flowing wine, and the conversation turned. Indeed, the whole room seemed to be growing louder and louder, the air warmer, almost lightning bright around them. Only the dour new Spanish ambassador, Bishop de Quadra, and his entourage in their corner seemed immune to it all, as they always were.

It was like a song meant to be danced to in a volta, faster and faster, almost out of control, as if the lute strings slipped between her fingers. She had a hard time breathing in her tight stays, and her cheeks felt warm from the wine. She looked to the queen's dais, but Elizabeth seemed just as frantically merry as everyone else, laughing at Rob's tricks, clapping her hands. Kat Ashley, who stood behind her, leaned close as if to whisper a motherly word, but Elizabeth waved her away.

Almost unseen in the blur of color, Dr. Dee slipped into the room in his black robes and dark beard, Master Constable his constant shadow behind him. Much to her surprise, Dr. Dee went to the dais to speak to Sir Robert Dudley, whose own laughter suddenly dimmed at whatever the magus said.

Startled by the strange scene, Kate set her goblet down on the table too suddenly. A drop of the red wine splashed over the silver rim and spots like new blood bloomed on the white damask cloth. Images flashed in her mind. Catherine Grey and the wine on her white gown when the queen pushed her away. Robert Dudley at that hidden cottage. Master Constable creeping close to the queen's bedchamber.

"Are you quite well, Mistress Haywood?" Master Roland asked solicitously. She looked at him, half-startled to find herself still in the midst of the banquet.

"I—I am very well, Master Roland," she said. She wondered if she was ale-shot, though she had been careful not to drink too quickly of the heady wine. She felt dizzy. She gestured toward the dais, where Dr. Dee and Sir Robert were still in close conversation. Sir Robert's always-ready grin vanished; the queen remained oblivious. "I was just surprised to see Dr. Dee here. I have heard he is always very busy with his studies and has no time for frivolities such as banquets."

Master Roland looked to the dais with narrowed eyes. Kate wondered if he'd had his horoscope told, as Violet had, and if so, what it said.

"More wine here, I do think," Lady Anne said firmly, and gestured to one of the servants to refill their goblets. "I think we have quite exhausted the topic of Dr.

Dee and his tiresome assistant. I am quite aching to know more about your work with Lord Hunsdon, Master Green. Do tell me this one thing . . ."

Kate was quite grateful for Lady Anne's chatter, her cool social confidence. She neatly distracted Roland and Green, especially as the latter seemed a rather belligerent drunk. Kate took a sip from her own refreshed goblet and glanced around to see what Dr. Dee and the strange, lurking Master Constable were doing now. They were nowhere to be seen, but Rob Cartman caught her eye, and he seemed to see too much of what she would rather conceal. She turned sharply away.

Robert Dudley had returned to the queen's side, and they were laughing at the dwarves' gamboling, applauding, and tossing tidbits of venison to the trained dogs. Their lightheartedness seemed to release something in everyone else, and as the wine flowed ever more freely, the waves of laughter grew higher and higher, more and more shrill. Aye, matters were swiftly spiraling out of control.

A subtlety in sugar paste molded into the shape of Nonsuch was carried in as the finale to the banquet. It was perfectly rendered, with walls of red and white inlaid with blue gossamer windows and tiny curls of almond paste smoke from the chimneys. There was even a queenly figure in the doorway, all green and gold and bright red hair.

Elizabeth clapped her hands in delight at the presentation, which made Lord Arundel beam anew. "It is too perfect to eat, I declare. Surely this is indeed the loveliest house in the world, just as my father intended."

Kate examined the candy castle, which was indeed exquisite. And unlike the real castle, surely it could not conceal old disappearances, old heartaches and betrayals, as once it did with King Henry? Illusions were fine things indeed.

Robert Dudley leaned back carelessly in his seat, his hand resting lazily on the edge of the queen's chair. His smile seemed hardened around his handsome dark eyes.

More servants followed with dishes of almond cakes and fruit suckets, sugar wafers stamped with the queen's initials, and even more wine. The queen cooed over them, for she loved sweets above all else, some days eating nothing else. Yet Sir Robert still looked on with that sharp-edged smile.

At Kate's own table, Roland and Green were talking together in low, harsh voices, too quiet for any words to be made out. Violet looked as if she was about to cry, and Anne chattered on with renewed determination. The sweets did not seem to be working their magic for any of them.

Yet the queen was above it all on her gilded dais, happy and seemingly secure. "We must have dancing now!" she cried. "A galliard. I insist."

She gestured to the musicians in the gallery, and Lord Arundel leaped up to instruct his servants to push back the tables and make room for the queen's desires. If Elizabeth wanted dancing, dancing she would have, immediately. She moved lightly around the room on Sir Robert's arm, urging everyone to dance, even a reluctant-looking Catherine Grey.

Kate felt a touch on her hand, and she looked around to find Rob Cartman looking down at her, his beautiful face expressionless. He had changed from his sunset-bright tights into a more somber purple doublet sewn with a lattice pattern of brass buttons. His blond hair was brushed back from the sharp, elegant angles of his face, revealing a new pearl earring. Despite his new elegance, he was still the same Rob—complicated and unreadable.

"May I be your partner, Kate?" he asked, his tone wary.

Kate remembered their half quarrel by the lake, her nagging suspicions that he had not told her the whole tale of why he was at Nonsuch. But she could not deny him, and she did not even know why.

She nodded, and he took her hand to lead her into the forming pattern of the dance. The queen led them off, partnered as always by Robert Dudley. The two of them still laughed together, while Lord Arundel glared and the Spanish whispered. Violet stood in front of Kate in the line of dancers, partnered by her brother, while Lord Hertford danced not with Lady Catherine but with Anne Godwin.

The musicians launched into the queen's galliard, a lively tune written in her father's time, perhaps when Nonsuch was first built. Rob took Kate's hand and drew her into the opening skipping step as they circled each other, then spun back around, her feet automatically moving in time to the familiar music. It was a quick dance, an intricate pattern around the other dancers, then back like a loop of lace, and she could think of nothing else but the movement, the notes that got into her blood every time.

She couldn't help but laugh with delight as Rob caught her around the waist and spun her in a wide circle, her skirts flying out like a bell. She did so love to dance, but so seldom had the chance, as she always played for the queen's banquets, for the other dancers. And Rob was a fine partner, quick and light, easily covering her little stumbles.

They twirled faster and faster, until the room was only a buttery blur around her, and she threw back her head to laugh, forgetting everything for one blessed moment.

But it could not last for long. The music ended amid a rush of laughter, but the gust of merriment was suddenly cut off by an angry shout. The sound of it was like an ugly splash of mud on a shimmering tapestry, and Kate heard Violet gasp as they all spun toward the noise.

"You are a lying whoreson!"

It was the handsome Master Green shouting out from near the abandoned dais, and Kate strained up on tiptoe to glimpse his face. Rage, and probably too much wine—a dangerous combination in the banked fireworks of the royal court—distorted his features. He lunged forward as the ladies nearby shrieked, and his fist shot out to catch another man's jaw with a horrible, audible crack.

Kate's eyes shifted to the man who reeled from Master Green's blow. Master Constable, Dr. Dee's pastypale ghostly student. Surely the two men could barely know each other, let alone hate with such fire that they brawled at the queen's own banquet! Yet Green leaped on Constable and his hands circled the astrologer's throat with a feral intent.

"Pig! Varlet! You lie!"

"Enough of that, you hedgepigs!" Elizabeth shouted, her merriment vanished. "Enough, I say! I will have none of this guttersnipe behavior at my court. We are not a Shoreditch bear pit."

Lord Arundel started toward them, but his secretary, Violet's brother, Master Roland, reached them first. He seized his friend by the back of his doublet and dragged him off the shrieking Constable.

Master Green swung around as if he would hit Master Roland, too, and Violet cried out in horror. But Green restrained himself at the last instant and backed away with a look of stark fear on his face, as if he had only just realized what he had done. What he had been about to do.

Dr. Dee walked toward the men like a great black bird in his swirling robes and helped his student to his feet. Blood and tears mixed together and dripped from Constable's face in a terrible mess.

Kate felt like she was caught in a bad dream, as did everyone else around her, judging from their gleefully horrified expressions.

Amid the stunned silence of the hall, Queen Elizabeth whirled around and snatched up a goblet from one of the tables. At first, Kate was sure from the dark look on her face that she would throw it at someone's head.

But Elizabeth merely swallowed the wine in one quick draft and thrust the empty vessel at Lord Arundel. He looked as stunned as everyone else and took the goblet without a word. Surely the groveling apologies would come anon.

"Too much of your fine wine has flowed tonight, I fear, Lord Arundel," Elizabeth said tightly. "Master Roland, take your friend away and dunk his hot head in cold water." She turned her glare on Master Constable. "I will speak with both of you young men tomorrow, but for now I am most weary of you all."

Elizabeth whirled around and stalked from the hall, leaving her ladies to scramble after her. Kate looked around for Violet, but she was already being led away by Lady Anne. Violet's pretty face looked startled at the sudden violent scene involving both her brother and her favorite suitor, and she went with Anne with no protest. At the doors, Master Longville stepped forward hopefully, but Anne waved him away.

Only then did Kate realize that Rob Cartman had vanished into the chaos of the hall. She stood in the middle of the banqueting hall alone as servants scurried to clean away the mess. Whispered speculation flowed all around her. The queen's courtiers loved nothing more than disgrace when it was not their own.

Lady Catherine Knollys appeared beside her and gently touched her arm. Startled, Kate turned to look at her and found her dark Boleyn eyes flash with sympathy. Her hand, as white and elegant as the queen's, rested on her softly rounded belly. She expected yet another child, but everyone knew the queen would not let her leave her side until it was almost time for the babe to be born.

"Shall we walk together back to the queen's rooms, Mistress Haywood?" she said. "I fear my brother and my daughter, Lettice, have both quite disappeared, and I don't wish to walk alone in the night."

"Of course, my lady," Kate said. They walked together in silence along the gallery back toward the palace, Lady Knollys smiling at her friends. It was a subtle difference, but Kate noticed how everyone made room for the queen's cousin, their whispers quieter, their smiles quicker. Oh, how the Boleyn fortune had changed.

"You are a fine dancer, Mistress Haywood, as well as an accomplished musician," Lady Knollys said with one of her serene smiles. She seemed so friendly, so kind to everyone, yet she was as adept at hiding her thoughts as everyone else.

"Thank you, my lady," Kate answered, not knowing what else to say.

"I saw you were partnered with Master Cartman, the actor."

"You know him?" Kate was so surprised, she blurted out the words, then ducked her head as she felt her cheeks turn warm.

Lady Knollys laughed. "My brother invited him here, with Her Majesty's approval. Lord Hunsdon is much interested in the theater, you know, and has heard much of the talents of Master Cartman and his troupe. We would be interested in hearing *your* opinion of him later. I do think my brother seeks to start his own theater."

"I—I know him but little, my lady," Kate said, half truthfully. She and Rob had certainly seen much together, murder and loss, yet she really barely knew him. He was too good at his trade, and she was learning to be. It was interesting he had come here to meet with Lord Hunsdon, which would be an ambitious move indeed.

Why had he not told her of that? Was Hunsdon the wealthy lord who might seek to be the actor's patron?

They had reached the queen's privy chamber, which was once again crowded with those who could not quite seek their own rooms until the queen retired. Laughter could be heard from behind the door of the royal bedchamber, loud with wine and the remembered drama of the banquet.

"I am having some friends in my chamber for a small supper tomorrow evening, Mistress Haywood," Lady Knollys said. "Perhaps you would care to join us? I fear I cannot promise such interest as we had tonight, though."

Once again, she had surprised Kate. She often wondered what they knew about her mother—and what she should say, or not say. This was a kindness indeed. "Thank you. I would be honored."

Lady Knollys gave her one more smile before gliding toward the bedchamber. Her daughter, Lady Lettice, joined her, the two of them whispering together, and Kate hurried toward her own lodgings, her thoughts whirling. Only a few days at Nonsuch, and so much had happened.

Anne and Violet were already in their small chamber when Kate opened the door. Violet huddled on the edge of her bed, her shoulders shaking as she cried into a handkerchief, while Anne tried to soothe her with an offered cordial.

"'Tis nothing to get so dramatic about, I vow, Violet," Anne said, making a *tsk*ing noise. "Men get ale-shot and fight all the time. The queen will forget it all by tomorrow, and your Master Green will be entirely forgiven. He is too handsome for it to be otherwise. And some other scandal will quickly take its place."

"'Tis very true," Kate said. She hurried to sit on Violet's other side, patting her friend's hand. There were so many scandalous romances just waiting to erupt—including Catherine Grey's. Surely a small quarrel between two young men was nothing.

"But why would he fight with that Master Constable, of all people?" Violet wailed. "How can they even have dealings with each other? Is it because Constable told my horoscope?"

And did it very ill indeed, Kate thought, remembering how Violet had said Constable declared her of a "melancholic disposition." "I am sure that cannot be so. Master Constable did not behave improperly toward you, did he?"

Violet sniffled. "N-nay."

"And that was ages ago," Anne said. "I am sure Master Green just did not like something about Master Constable's look tonight, and who could blame him? The man looks like a two-day-old fish left in the sun."

Violet reluctantly giggled, and they went on to speak of other things, but Kate's thoughts were still in a whirl. She thought of the sudden burst of anger tonight, the cottage to which Master Constable had tiptoed in the middle of the night. Robert Dudley and Dr. Dee, and the long-missing Dr. Macey. All so strange.

And also a supper in the rooms of Lady Knollys. Tomorrow already promised to hold surprises.

CHAPTER SIX

"I will have no such foul behavior in my court! Is that rightly understood?" Queen Elizabeth's shout was so loud that the very rafters of the privy chamber seemed to ring with it. Even Kate, standing far from the throne dais, instinctively stepped back from the fearful sound of it, bumping into the man behind her.

Master Green, standing with Lord Arundel at the queen's feet along with Master Constable and Dr. Dee, went scarlet. All the men bowed their heads before the queen's wrath, their faces hidden.

"My palaces are not a tavern for brawling," she went on, slapping her palm hard on the carved and gilded armrest of her chair. "And you, Master Green—to shame your friend's master thus, when he has gone to such lengths for our visit . . ."

Lord Arundel cuffed Master Green on the back of his head. His florid, jowled face did indeed look thunderous. He had planned every instant of this lavish visit to Nonsuch, carefully choreographed every moment to advance his suit with the queen. But he hadn't accounted for a fistfight.

Would masquerades erase the brawl?

Kate thought she saw a flash of raw fury contort Master Green's famously handsome features, but it was gone so swiftly she wondered if she had imagined it. A young man in his position could not afford such anger.

But then, nor could he afford to start fights at a royal banquet. Especially not with a man said to be learning magical arts. Master Constable's black cap hid his face, but Kate could see the greasy curtain of his hair.

"It will not happen again, Your Majesty, I do hasten to assure you," Lord Arundel said. "If we should send young Green back to his father, I shall speak to Lord Hunsdon . . ."

Elizabeth gave a weary sigh and glanced away from the penitential scene before her. Kate recognized the sure signs of the queen's boredom, so quick to come upon her in those summer days. Her dark eyes constantly changed, flashing from laughter to fury and back in an instant. "There will be no need for that. Tempers do flare at times in this hot weather, and Master Green here is young. I am sure he will learn to restrain himself in the future." Her smile suddenly gleamed. "Besides, he does sing so prettily. My ladies would be desolate without his songs to lighten the days. Begone now. We shall speak no more of this."

Lord Arundel bowed so low Kate was sure his head would scrape the edge of the brocade-draped dais. Then he turned and stalked through the staring, gaping crowd, hauling Master Green with him.

Violet, who stood next to Kate, tense with fear, tried to say something to him as he passed, but he wouldn't look at her. Violet looked as if she would burst into tears again.

"Come, Mistress Roland. These are not fit proceedings for your sweet ears," her oft-rejected suitor Master Longville said, close to Violet's "sweet" ear. "Let us walk in the garden for a time."

Violet looked as if she would refuse, but then something in her teary-soft eyes hardened. She nodded and took Longville's arm to leave the room. Kate hoped her friend would not let her disappointment with one man lead her to folly with another.

Nor could she ever afford such folly herself. She glanced across the room to where Rob Cartman stood with some of his actors, his arms crossed over his chest. He looked uncharacteristically solemn as he watched the gathering. She turned away from the sight.

"Dr. Dee, stay a moment, if you will," Queen Elizabeth said. "There is a small matter I would consult with you about. The rest of you may all go about your business. Today's lesson is ended."

A great rustle like a cresting wave rolled over the chamber as everyone quickly bowed and curtsied and then dispersed. Kate saw a number of emotions written on their faces: relief, boredom, curiosity. Any ripple of change on a summer progress amid a small court was welcome. Dr. Dee approached the dais, slow and dignified, his black robes swirling around him.

Kate looked again toward where she had glimpsed Rob. If she had a free hour, she knew she should consult with him about the masquerade Lord Arundel had requested. It was an elaborate undertaking with time so short, and she could not avoid him forever if she was to impress Arundel and thus the queen. But Rob had vanished, and she was reprieved for the moment.

"Mistress Haywood," the queen suddenly called. "To me for a moment."

Kate shook away thoughts of Rob and hurried to the dais. "Your Majesty?"

"I did forget that an important guest is arriving soon," Elizabeth said, clearly distracted by whatever she was talking about with Dr. Dee and eager to get back to it. "Can you take Mistress Ashley and perhaps Mary Sidney and await her arrival for us?"

"Her, Your Majesty?" Kate said, confused.

"'Tis Anne, the Dowager Duchess of Somerset," Elizabeth said with an impatient wave of her hand. A frown flickered over her face, and Kate recalled why the queen might be reluctant to talk with the duchess. Anne Seymour, the widow of Edward Seymour, Duke of Somerset and once Protector of Edward VI, was now the wife of the lowly Francis Newdigate, and though she kept her fine title, had long been renowned at court for her pride and difficult nature. Her complicated family history made her place at court difficult. Luckily she usually stayed at her own estate, but her children attended on the queen.

And caused their own troubles.

Kate nodded carefully. "It has been long since Her Grace was at court."

"Aye, her health does not permit her to leave her estate at Hanworth often. But someone must take charge of Lord Hertford once and for all, and who better than his mother? He has been meddling in things not his business of late, or so I hear. If only all such surly boys were so easily dealt with. Eh, Dr. Dee?"

Dr. Dee's solemn expression did not alter as he bowed. "I fear I would not know, Your Majesty. I have no children of my own as yet."

"Just misbehaving apprentices, hm?" Elizabeth said with a laugh. "Go, go, Kate, see the duchess to her rooms for me."

Kate curtsied and went to find Mistress Ashley, the Mistress of the Robes, and Mary Sidney to tell them of this errand. In the corridor, she found her steps suddenly joined by those of Robert Dudley. He was as handsomely dressed as ever, in blue and green satin, but his smile was nowhere in evidence.

"Sir Robert," Kate said, surprised to find him there instead of keeping near to the queen or seeing to his duties as Master of the Horse. His coterie, young men who were always tumbling after him, were also nowhere to be seen. But she had not spoken to him directly since their adventures at the queen's coronation. "How do you fare today?"

"'Tis long days here at Nonsuch, is it not, Mistress Haywood?" he answered. His smile at last appeared, but small, almost bitter. "Much like at Westminster, eh?"

Kate had to laugh wryly. "I hope it will not prove *that* strange, my lord."

"Those of us who care for the queen must be ever vigilant for her safety. I fear that will always be true, as enemies will always lurk in the shadows waiting to pounce. Even on the brightest of days." He nodded toward Bishop de Quadra, who stood in a doorway with his Spanish cohorts.

"The fight at the banquet last night—do you think it was more than hotheaded young men arguing?"

"I know not what that business was about—yet." Sir Robert's jaw, covered in a short, dark beard, tightened, and Kate was sure that he knew more than he said. He always did. But what did he want from her? "Master Green has a temper on him, aye, but does Master Constable strike you as any sort of a hothead, Mistress Haywood?"

Kate thought of Master Constable, so pale, so quiet. And of how he was lurking around the queen's chamber. "Nay, he seems a man who keeps to his own business. But his master . . ."

That jaw flexed again. "Dr. Dee?"

Kate hesitated, remembering how she had been told Dr. Dee had once tutored Sir Robert in his youth. "I have been hearing old gossip, of things that happened during Queen Mary's time. And here, when Henry was king."

"I fear we all had to make hard choices during the

dark days of Queen Mary, to ensure our survival in hopes of better days to come. And now those days are here." His tone was quiet, expressionless. "Dr. Dee is a man with a rare gift. He did nothing sinister, I assure you, Mistress Haywood. He has always been loyal to the Tudors, and a faithful Protestant, no matter what one hears of his more . . . obscure studies. Perhaps you have heard he was my tutor for a time, when I was a boy."

Kate nodded. She had heard such, yet Sir Robert always seemed so robustly part of the wild outdoor world that she had a difficult time envisioning his studies with such a man as Dr. Dee, so preoccupied with the world of the mind and the spirits.

But then, Sir Robert had been at that strange cottage. She couldn't help teasing him just a bit. "I would wager you were not his most assiduous pupil?"

He gave a startled-sounding laugh, and for an instant his face was so unearthly handsome, like a rakish pirate or a fallen dark angel, that Kate saw why Elizabeth was so eager to keep him near. "My brothers, Ambrose and Guildford, found it hard to pay attention, I confess. We all liked our horses and our arrows above books. But for me, Dr. Dee's lessons were—different. Astonishing, that the secrets of the world could be found in numbers. His work could do great things for England, now that Elizabeth is queen."

Was that what was happening in that secret cottage? Great work for England? "And Master Constable? Is he a worthy assistant for such work?"

Sir Robert frowned thoughtfully. "I am sure Master Constable, like so many of us, has hidden depths, Mistress Haywood. He does bear watching, I think. Perhaps, Mistress Haywood, you could keep a watch on him? You are an observant lady, and I have many duties here, too many to keep an eye on everyone. I would have the queen kept safe from everyone around her."

Kate nearly told him of how she had found Constable lurking about the queen's deserted bedchamber, but his sister Mary Sidney called out to him at that moment and rushed over to take his arm. Kate knew it was fortuitous; she needed to be cautious with everyone, even a man such as Dudley.

And there was no time to say much, anyway. She could only give him a quick nod of agreement as Mary Sidney, one of the queen's favorite ladies, a woman quick with a laugh and a song, with her brother's dark eyes, hurried to his side. "Robert, dearest, there you are! Have you heard? The Duchess of Somerset is come to court. What suppose you this means for the Seymours?" Her voice lowered to a whisper, and Kate discreetly walked ahead so the siblings could talk. Seymours, Dudleys, Boleyns, Howards—old enemies, old allies. Where did they stand now? And what was Constable up to? She agreed with Dudley that the man bore watching.

It was raining again, as it had during the long night Kate had followed Constable to the cottage. A steady, cold, gray dampness swathed the beautiful gardens in a smoky haze and held everyone captive indoors. A canopy stretched over the doorway to give some shelter to those coming or departing, and Mistress Ashley already waited under its shelter, tapping her foot impatiently. Her duties as Mistress of the Robes, and a confidante to the queen since Elizabeth was a child, kept her always busy. She had no time for fussy duchesses.

They did not have long to wait. The gates were dragged open, and a fine coach jolted through, slowed by the mud that mixed with the gravel and made the ground slide away. Painted on its door was the swan, the crest of the Seymour family. It was followed by a string of carts piled with luggage, and another, smaller carriage. Even a short visit was a large undertaking for a duchess, it seemed.

The fine coach had barely lurched to a halt when the front doors opened and two more people slipped outside into the damp day. Lord Hertford and his sister, Lady Jane, Lady Catherine Grey's best friend, quickly took their places to greet their mother, fidgeting and whispering. Their faces, matching in delicate beauty, looked doubtful, but they quickly masked their frowns with welcoming smiles.

"It does not matter why she is here, sister," came Lord Hertford's audible whisper through a gritted-teeth smile. "Only that she departs soon, so behave."

"Behave, yourself! 'Tis you she comes to inspect," Jane hissed.

A footman in the Seymour red and gold colors leaped down to open the carriage door, and the duchess climbed down slowly in a flurry of dark skirts and veils. A lady-in-waiting followed to quickly hand her a walking stick. She leaned on it carefully, and it seemed rumors of her ill health were not false, as her heavily lined face was chalk white. She had been through much in her life, the grandest highs and the lowest of disgraceful lows, and it seemed it was not over yet.

She also did not look overjoyed to see her children.

"Well, Ned, Jane," she said hoarsely, holding out her gloved hand for her son to kiss. "I hope I shall not have a wasted journey, tearing across the muddy countryside in such an ill fashion. I have had no good reports of your life here at court."

"Mother, I . . . ," Lord Hertford began, but she waved his words away. She leaned heavily on his arm as he led her inside, Lady Jane fluttering after them. Kat Ashley caught Kate's eye and raised her brows. Kate laughed, quickly smothering the sound. It did indeed seem they were a wasted greeting party, hovering in the rain for no good purpose. She started to turn away, to follow Mistress Ashley into the palace, when the door to the second coach opened and a familiar figure carefully climbed down.

"Master Hardy! What are you doing at Nonsuch today?" Kate cried, astonished to see the attorney here and not in London, where he now worked at his prosperous practice. Like the duchess, he looked rather pale after the journey, his white hair in disarray under his cap, but he smiled to see her. She hurried toward him to give him aid on the slippery drive, but he waved her back with a pained smile.

"Ah, my dear Mistress Haywood, we did hope to see you here," he said cheerfully. "You have certainly made even such a long, hasty journey worthwhile."

We? A tiny reluctant hope took hold inside of her, a hope she dared not even acknowledge, as she turned toward the carriage. That hope was rewarded when Anthony Elias jumped down from behind Master Hardy and gave her a brilliant smile.

They had last met when snow was still on the ground in London, and so many new feelings and hopes had stirred. Yet it seemed only a moment had passed now as she looked into his bright green eyes.

"Kate," he said. "How well you are looking."

"And you," she answered. It was certainly the truth. London life and work seemed to agree with him, making him seem brighter, more vital. "I am surprised to see you here at Nonsuch."

His smile widened. "Not unpleasantly surprised, I do hope."

"It is only ever pleasant to see you, Anthony." "Pleasant" sounded such a small, dimly lit word compared to how it actually felt to look up at him now. He made all the strangeness of the last few days seem distant.

They followed Master Hardy and the duchess's army of servants into the palace, so close they almost touched. So close she could smell the clean scent of him, and it made her smile even more. She felt rather foolish, like Violet and her blushes when Master Green was near. At least he could not see if she *did* blush, for the hall was dimly lit after the gray glare of the day.

"Master Hardy has been much occupied of late looking after the duchess's business affairs," Anthony said as they made their way down the crowded corridor. "He was in need of a clerk on this journey, so I volunteered my services."

In hopes of seeing her there? Kate dared not even think that. "I am glad to hear Master Hardy's business prospers."

"He has more than he can handle of late. Mistress Hardy complains she never sees him. But 'tis much preferable to the way things once were."

Kate nodded, thinking of those dark days near the end of Queen Mary's reign, when Master Hardy had been sent to gaol. "And how are you keeping yourself, Anthony? Finishing your studies must consume a great deal of time."

"So it does. Master Hardy thinks I will be ready to take on my own patrons soon." They came to a chamber at the far end of the corridor. Master Hardy followed the duchess and her children inside and waved to Anthony to wait outside.

They sat down on a bench near one of the windows, out of the way of the scurry of servants, and Kate could not think what to say. Just sitting there next to him made her feel as if she might burst.

"I have had no business so interesting as that you

brought me in January, Kate," he said. "For once I thought I could be truly useful."

Kate laughed wryly. "And rescuing drowning maidens from the Thames? Aye, I would say that was most useful, too."

Anthony laughed, too, a lovely, warm, springtime kind of sound that banished all those old, frozen memories. "I was certainly most happy to oblige with that. But I also meant when I found the information on the Dennis family in those old legal records, and you said it could be used to help the queen. Dusty old law ledgers are good for something, I suppose."

A thought suddenly occurred to Kate. Anthony could find documents where she could not go. He had discovered letters in law libraries before that helped lead her to a murderer. Perhaps he could do so again. "There might be something you could help me with now, Anthony. If you have time, of course. I cannot interfere with your business."

His expression sharpened with interest. "You have not found another dead body, have you?"

"Nay, no body at all, thanks be. But that is the strangeness of it." She quickly told him the old tale of Dr. Macey, Dr. Dee's old teacher, and his disappearance here at Nonsuch all those years before. Of the mysterious Lord Marchand, who had accused Macey of treason. She didn't speak of the cottage, though, or Master Constable and his quarrels. Not yet.

Anthony nodded thoughtfully. "I'm not sure where to begin looking, but there is certainly a tale to be found there, I would wager. Horoscopes and talking with spirits have long been an enthusiasm of those who speak about Dr. Dee. When I return to London, I will look into the old records. If this Macey had dealings with royalty, there should be much there if one digs deep enough. Is there some danger to the queen now in this business?"

Kate feared there might be, but it was only a gut feeling and she couldn't say for sure. As Sir Robert had said, the queen's enemies were always lurking. Was it spirits, or something more immediate? "I cannot say yet. But this house holds such oddness in its walls. It is so beautiful, yet so . . ."

"Haunting."

"Aye," she murmured, remembering Lady Anne's ghost stories. "Haunted."

"And you, Kate? How do you fare here at court this summer? Surely you have been busy as well."

"I do very well. Busy, aye, with much music for dancing and banquets. The queen has been in a merry-making mood, and someone must play for it."

He teasingly plucked at her blue silk skirt. "And be well paid for it, I hope. You are looking very fine."

Kate laughed. "The queen has been kind to me, as she is to all who serve her." Some more than others, like her Boleyn cousins, to the chagrin of the Seymours and their ilk.

"And has Her Majesty mayhap talked of a match for you yet?"

Surprised, Kate looked up at him to find his face tensely watchful. "Nay, she does not like to speak of marriage at all. Not for herself, or those around her."

He nodded, and she realized she wanted so much to know what he really thought. She had lived so long with courtly prevarication, and suddenly she was weary with it. Before Elizabeth became queen, Kate had thought she could say almost anything to Anthony. To laugh with him, confide in him.

Then things changed, so suddenly yet so softly she barely noticed at first. Then came that terrible night on the river. Anthony had saved her life that night, when she was kidnapped by a madman and taken onto the raging river in a boat. She had almost drowned, and

Anthony's arms around her made her feel safe again. Now she didn't know what to think at all. So much had changed between them.

"We hear talk of the royal court all the time in London," he said at last, with his old teasing smile. "Parties and dancing. Surely there must be many who woo you."

Kate laughed. "Nary a one, and if they did I would not believe them. Court gentlemen are ever full of pretty words, saying 'sweeting' this and 'darling' that. Life is all a pageant here, 'tis all. I hope I know better than to wager a farthing on such."

His smile deepened. "Kate—I hope you know that not all the world is so untrustworthy as that. Some of us do not live in a sonnet."

Kate studied him carefully, barely daring to breathe. "I— Yes, I do know that."

"There are things we must talk about, though I know now is not the time," he said, lighter now. "Can we walk in the garden tomorrow, if the rain will cease?"

She nodded. "I am meant to be composing a masque for Lord Arundel, but I'm sure I could get away for a time."

He opened his mouth to answer, but whatever he was going to say was lost as Master Hardy opened the duchess's door and summoned Anthony to his work. And Kate had to get to hers.

"We will speak later," he said once more, and she smiled. She did want to speak to him and wondered what he wanted to discuss, yet somehow she feared it as well.

She made her way down the stairs back to the great hall, deep in thought. In a quiet doorway, she glimpsed a couple standing close together, a blond head bent toward a dark one. For an instant, she thought it was Hertford and Catherine Grey again, growing ever more foolishly bold, but then she saw it was Violet and her once-disappointed suitor Master Longville.

He did not look so very disappointed now. Violet had tears in her eyes, as she had ever since Master Green had turned away from her at the queen's banquet. She nodded as he whispered in her ear, and he smiled triumphantly.

So many tangled romances. Kate had no time for such things.

Yet as she spun around to hurry away to find her work, she couldn't help but remember how it felt when Anthony touched her hand . . .

CHAPTER SEVEN

He was there again.
Kate paused as she hurried down the corridor outside the queen's apartments, caught by the sight of Master Constable hovering in the doorway. His dark robe and cap looked so stark against the carved paneling of the wall, and he seemed startled to see her passing by.

She remembered Robert Dudley saying Constable needed watching, and her own suspicions that it was true. Dr. Dee trusted Constable enough to work with him, but Kate couldn't help feeling a cold chill whenever she saw him. His clammy pale skin; the way his watery eyes seemed to shift to take in everything around him; the tremble of his hands. It all seemed most strange for a man purportedly learning how to harness the powers of the stars.

And now he was peering into the crowd of the queen's rooms again. Was he *spying*? For whom? What did he hope to discover?

"Mistress Haywood," someone called behind her. Startled, Kate spun around, her heart pounding. The workbasket she held fell from her hands, tumbling bundles of silk thread onto the inlaid floor.

She saw Mistress Ashley hurrying toward her. The Mistress of the Robes had her own hands full, bright, glossy satins that shimmered in the faint light. Her graying hair was escaping from her pearl-edged cap, and she looked most harried.

"There you are, Mistress Haywood. Did the queen send for you to play? Where is your lute? Oh, never mind," Mistress Ashley said quickly. "Come along now."

Kate had not actually been summoned by the queen, not that afternoon. She was merely fetching the workbox as a favor to Violet Roland. But she let herself be borne into the privy chamber along with Mistress Ashley. Perhaps it was a good chance to see what that strange Master Constable was looking for now.

He was caught up in Mistress Ashley's inexorable wake, too, though Kate noticed he tried to get away, his black sleeves flailing like a crow's wings. Two loitering ladies-in-waiting were also pushed into the room, and for a moment Kate lost sight of him in the crowd. She saw Master Roland playing cards with Master Longville amid all the tables of games, and ladies chattered behind their feathered fans. Catherine Grey laughed with some of her friends, sneaking glances at the queen.

Constable reappeared, his black cap bobbing over the heads of the shorter ladies around him. He seemed to take refuge near the large marble fireplace, his expression rather stunned.

Kate quickly found a quiet spot of her own, beside one of the open windows, where she could study the room. She couldn't immediately see anything that would be of obvious interest to someone like Constable. It seemed a normal enough day at court. People playing cards, sewing, chatting, whiling away the sunlit hours.

But the queen was there, which would always be of interest. Elizabeth sat at a small table near the other open window, the thin rays of sunlight glinting on her pale skin and the pearl-dotted loops of her red hair against the high collar of her golden gown. She bent her head over papers spread before her, a frown creasing her brow.

Beside her were Robert Dudley and Dr. Dee, with William Cecil peering over her shoulder. They were all looking most solemn.

She went up on tiptoe, trying to find Master Constable again. Why was he not with Dr. Dee now? Did his own teacher not entirely trust him? Yet surely whatever the queen talked of now with her closest advisers could not be so secret, or she wouldn't be doing it here in front of her whole court.

Kate looked around again and caught a sudden flash of a frown on Catherine Grey's face. Kate followed her gaze and saw that Lady Catherine watched Constable.

Kate crept closer to the queen, careful to keep close to the wall where she wouldn't be noticed. She managed to catch a glimpse of the documents spread in front of the queen and noticed they were not letters of state. It was a chart, drawn in a circle divided into sections and sketched with strange symbols and characters.

A horoscope.

"And this, Your Majesty, indicates the most auspicious time for a journey," Dr. Dee said, pointing to a section near the bottom.

"A journey for myself?" Elizabeth asked.

"It is hard to say, Your Majesty, but the signs seem doubtful for such a thing," Dr. Dee answered. "The position of these planets here and here seems to indicate rather a journey for someone near to you."

"Perhaps Archduke Charles shall come from Vienna?" Cecil said, a hopeful note in his voice.

Elizabeth shot him a glare. "Archduke Charles would do well to stay exactly where he is. Does it indicate a match there, Dr. Dee? Connected to this journey?"

Dr. Dee suddenly frowned and glanced up to study something above Kate's shoulder. She looked back to find Catherine Grey standing there, watching the queen with raw dislike on her pretty face. It was quickly banished in a bland smile.

Kate remembered how Lady Catherine had told Lord Hertford that Constable drew up her horoscope, as he had Violet's. Did that have something to do with what was in the queen's stars now? How were the two royal cousins connected in the stars?

"Not for yourself, Your Majesty," Dr. Dee said slowly. "For one that is near to you. Great change is coming for them, so great that it will affect you as well."

"Good change?" Elizabeth demanded.

Dr. Dee hesitated. "Greatly complicated, I fear. The moon disrupts the natural cycles here and wreaks great havoc. I would warn Your Majesty to look to your own family in the coming months, most closely."

The queen's family? Kate shivered. That could mean one of so many people, all with their own competing interests. Lord Hunsdon and his sister, the Greys, even Kate herself. All of them could be suspects in such a journey.

It seemed the queen felt the same. Her fist came down on the table, in the middle of the chart, and rattled the pens and instruments arrayed there. Dudley laid a gentle hand on her sleeve, and Dr. Dee stepped back.

"That is of no help!" Elizabeth cried. "I am cautious at all times, of everyone, but I have only two eyes and a family like a many-headed hydra. I need more specific directions."

Dr. Dee held up his hands. "The stars are often obscure, Your Majesty. We can only interpret their signs, their clues. But I can say, it would appear that someone near you has had their own charts drawn up recently—and the path of their stars is opposed to yours, whether they will it or not."

Elizabeth's face turned furious. She rose slowly to

her feet, her long, elegant fingers balled into fists. Robert Dudley touched her sleeve again, but she shook him away.

"Did *you* draw up another chart, Dr. Dee?" Elizabeth demanded.

"Indeed not, Your Majesty," he answered, his voice low and calm. "There are others who do not yet understand the dangers, I fear."

"I would hope it was not you, for I have given permission for no such thing!" Elizabeth said. "I must find out who close to me wishes me harm. Look closer there, Dr. Dee. Tell me more."

The queen pounded her fist on the chart again, her cheeks still streaked an alarming red. Dr. Dee drew closer, the only sign he might be at all concerned a small frown.

Kate glanced back at Catherine Grey again. Lady Catherine stood across the room now; Kate could barely see her through the shifting crowd. Kate caught a glimpse of her golden hair and moved to a better place where she could watch Lady Catherine.

She stood near the door, waving her hands as if she was arguing with someone. Her beautiful face was drawn into tense lines. The man who stood in front of her was Master Constable. His head was bent so Kate could not see his expression, but his shoulders were hunched.

Lady Catherine waved her hands again, wildly, much like the queen's own angry gestures when she was crossed.

Lady Catherine had told Lord Hertford that Constable drew up her horoscope. In secret? Was Lady Catherine the one the queen needed to be wary of now? The one who was soon to go on a journey? Perhaps that was why the queen had summoned the Duchess of Somerset?

Kate looked back at the queen, who had gone very still and watched Lady Catherine herself.

When Kate glanced back to Lady Catherine, she was being led away by Lord Hertford. Their two handsome heads were bent close together as he whispered something into her ear.

Constable was alone, his face paler than ever, but he didn't stand there solitary for long. Master Green, who was striding through the door with Violet's brother Master Roland, suddenly stopped and said something to Constable.

The astrologer's face went from white to flaming red in an instant. Green laughed, but there was no mirth in his expression. Roland drew him away, and Constable dashed out of the room.

Kate was rooted to her place, wondering what exactly she had just seen. She tried to run after Constable, but he had vanished down the corridor.

CHAPTER EIGHT

L ady Knollys's rooms were far from Kate's tiny shared chamber. Once Kate reached one of the fancifully carved towers of the palace, a liveried footman led her into an octagonal banqueting room, richly furnished with a round table surrounded by cushioned stools and cross-backed chairs. A tall buffet displayed silver and gold plate and saltcellars. Bright tapestries depicting a summer outdoor supper decorated the walls, and red-and-blue carpets were laid over the floor instead of plain rushes.

The windows were half-open to catch the cool evening breezes, and the scent of rain-fresh green grass and garden flowers filled the room, mixed with lavender-scented smoke from the censers in the corners. Chalky pale moonlight fell across the floor.

Kate hesitated inside the door and studied the gathered company. She knew who they all were, of course, and saw them often at court, but usually only as she played for the dancing or hurried past them on errands for the queen. They were all of high families, all of them old allies of the Boleyn family. In one corner, she glimpsed Violet's brother, Master Roland, and his handsome friend Master Green, and they gave her polite bows.

It was company she rarely saw without the shelter of her lute to hide behind, and tonight she had nothing.

She smoothed the skirt of her dark blue–and–silver silk gown, glad she had worn her best, with the embroidered silver sleeves and quilted white satin underskirt. She had her father's gift of the garnet earrings, and a pearl pendant the queen gave her for her last birthday. She knew she looked presentable, but even her richest belongings were nothing like the jewels and gold-embroidered velvets of the others.

"Mistress Haywood!" Lady Knollys called. Kate turned to see the hostess hurrying across the small, crowded room, her bejeweled hands held out. Lady Knollys wore the finest dark purple satin dress with a sleeveless Spanish robe of deep green over it, her dark hair bound with a pearl-studded caul. Her belly swelled gently under her kirtle, the signs of yet another little Knollys baby soon to arrive. This would be the twelfth, Kate thought.

She was followed by her favorite daughter, the beautiful Lady Lettice, who dazzled in pink-and-white silk, her red-gold hair loose in a shining wave down her back, and by her brother Lord Hunsdon's wife, Anne.

"I am so glad you could come," Lady Knollys said. Much to Kate's surprise, she took Kate's hand and drew her farther into the room. "It should be a most interesting evening, and one I am sure Her Majesty will want to hear about later."

Kate studied the people around them, even more curious now. What would the queen want to know about this casual gathering of friends? Why had she not come herself? Elizabeth often visited her cousin's lodgings. There was a palpable air of excitement in the room. "Should I have brought my lute?"

Lady Knollys and Lady Hunsdon laughed. "My dear Mistress Haywood," Lady Knollys said. "You must only enjoy yourself tonight. Keep a watch on events, mayhap. I fear one of our guests has yet to arrive. But there are refreshments, and you must have some of the Canary wine Her Majesty sent."

The door opened to admit more guests, and Lady Lettice said, "I will see to Mistress Haywood, Mama."

She, too, took Kate's hand, and drew her over to a long table by the windows, which was laden with platters of sweet delicacies of all sorts.

Lady Lettice chattered the whole time, flitting from one gossipy tidbit to another as she poured some of the sweet pale wine into a silver goblet and handed it to Kate. Lettice was very pretty indeed, Kate thought, and intelligent as well, full of observations about those around her and books she had read. Her dark eyes, much like the queen's, were too bright and alert for a young lady. Kate wondered if someone should keep a closer watch on her.

"Here, try one of the apricots in ginger syrup," Lady Lettice said, spearing one of the succulent fruits with a newfangled Italian fork. "They are quite luscious. As is Master Green over there, nay?" She pointed at Master Green with the fork. He stood across the chamber, still talking with Master Roland, the two of them observing everything around them as they talked together quietly. "But not as handsome as Sir Robert Dudley, I would say."

Lettice laughed, and even though her words were mildly scandalous (what would the queen say of another woman thinking her Robert "handsome"? Kate wondered), Kate found her too funny not to enjoy the conversation.

"I am so glad to have the chance to talk to you, Mistress Haywood," Lettice said as she sipped at her own wine.

"Are you, Lady Lettice?" Kate said.

"Oh, yes. I do adore music so much, and my uncle says you write your own compositions." Lettice suddenly leaned closer and whispered, "I am only allowed here tonight because Mama says only a few close friends are invited. I am too young to be much at court as of yet, though they say I will be betrothed very soon. And Uncle Hunsdon says we must be careful, you know."

Kate felt as if she had plunged back into the garden maze—she did not know which way Lady Lettice's words were going. "Careful, my lady?"

"Aye. My uncle says that now we are kin to the queen, we must not be seen to try to use powers that are not meant for mortals. But *you* are to be trusted, yes, Mistress Haywood? You would not gossip about our family."

"I do hope so, Lady Lettice," Kate murmured.

Lady Lettice was called away by her mother, and Kate wandered toward the round table at the very center of the room, turning the girl's words over in her mind. Lady Lettice leaped from subject to subject, but what did she mean when she said they had to be careful tonight? And why did she trust Kate so much? Did they know of her relation to them? They had never spoken of it.

Kate saw a clue to the first question when she examined what was displayed on the table. There was no food or wine there, but a most strange array of objects. Atop the snowy white damask cloth was a shallow black stone bowl set in a brass stand. It was lined with a silver mirror that showed the carved ceiling above in distorted waves. Next to the bowl was a large bell, inscribed along its edge with strange symbols, and on its other side was a large white horn, also inscribed with those unreadable symbols.

"A unicorn horn, to cast a circle of protection. Brought from the Indies," someone said behind her.

Kate spun around to find Lord Hunsdon watching her. He smiled behind his long red beard, but his dark eyes were cautious. "I am sorry. I did not mean to startle you."

"Unicorn horn, my lord?" Kate asked. She glanced back down at it, studying its smooth ivory white surface.

"It possesses great powers, they say. There are only a few in the world." He came to stand beside her and traced his fingertips in a circle around the horn. "There is a great web we cannot see with our own eyes, Mistress Haywood, a connection between heaven and earth that shows how celestial events will affect those in the world. People in our position cannot be too careful when it comes to protecting our family. We have been caught unaware before, and it nearly tore us apart."

Kate looked down into the mirrored bowl, half expecting to see spirits there. But she glimpsed only her own face, her own smooth dark hair under a beaded band, and her dark Boleyn eyes. "You mean . . ."

"My late aunt, Queen Anne, yes—and others. My own mother chose to retreat from the world, to hide in the country with my stepfather, but we have not that option now," he said solemnly. "We must use all the tools at our disposal."

Kate nodded, though she only half understood him. Lady Lettice's words made more sense now, the warning against using powers not meant to belong to mortals. The mirror, the bell—they were to summon otherworldly guidance tonight. She half wanted to flee, to avoid seeing whatever was about to happen, but her curiosity made her stay where she was.

That damnable curiosity that always led her into trouble when she should be at her most prudent.

The door opened again, and Lord Hunsdon glanced up. His kind smile vanished. "Ah, at last. We may begin."

Kate turned and saw Master Constable standing there. He wore his usual black robes, a silver box clutched in his arms, and he looked almost frightened as he stared around him. She remembered how he'd been creeping around the queen's chamber, and she wondered how he had come to be invited here.

Sir Robert was surely right to be concerned about the man.

She turned to say something to Lord Hunsdon, but he had already moved away.

"Master Constable," Lady Knollys said, hurrying forward to greet him.

"Forgive my tardiness, my lady," he said, giving her a low bow. He almost tripped on the hem of his long robe. "I was detained on an errand for my employer."

"'Tis of no matter. We are all gathered now," Lady Knollys said. "I am so happy you were able to come tonight. For it *must* be tonight, yes?"

"The spirits can only be called during certain phases of the moon, under the influence of a good planet," Master Constable answered solemnly. "Tonight shows ideal conditions."

Lady Knollys led him toward the table, and Kate hurried to a spot hidden behind the others, where she could watch without being noticed. Lord Hunsdon and his wife stood close to his sister at the other side of the table.

"Dr. Dee says you have the rare gifts of a scryer, which he sadly does not possess," Lord Hunsdon said. "I hope that you can help us with our questions."

"I shall do my best, my lord. My powers are but

newfound, and I have much to learn," Master Constable said. He looked nervous as he sat down on one of the chairs, fidgeting with his box, his long sleeves. "We must have as little light as possible in here."

Kate looked around to see that all the servants had vanished, and only the noble guests were left. Lady Knollys and her daughter put out all the fine wax candles themselves, until the only light was a lamp on the table.

Master Constable poured a small amount of water into the shallow bowl and took a handful of herbs from his box to sprinkle over the surface. He closed his eyes, and the room went very silent and still. Everyone seemed to be holding his or her breath.

Including Kate. Something fluttered deep inside of her, and she pressed her hand to her stomach to stop the sick feeling.

Suddenly, Master Constable spoke, and it made her jump. It was not his usual quiet, meek voice, but a deep, gravelly boom. He reached out and rang the bell.

"We show unto you the lower world," he said. "The governors that work and rule under God. Show us yourselves; tell us what only you can see, what we must know."

Master Constable leaned forward and peered into the bowl. Kate stood on tiptoe, trying to see it for herself, but all she could glimpse was the silvery, unrippled surface of the water.

There was an explosion, and Kate cried out as clouds of greenish smoke flew into the air above the bowl. She pressed her hand hard to her mouth, trying to suppress her fear.

"'Tis a dire warning," Master Constable cried. His voice was even deeper, and he no longer looked like himself. His face was waxen, almost yellow, his eyes blank. "Woe be unto the virgins of the earth if they be corrupted! Mercy and truth must meet if there is to be peace and justice in the land at last. The spirits say it can only be thus."

Kate saw Lord Hunsdon and Lady Knollys exchange worried glances. Lady Lettice clutched at her mother's hand as the plume of smoke shot higher in the air, swirling tighter and tighter until it was almost a column.

"The pure blood is tainted already—it must not be so any further," Master Constable intoned in a low, steady voice, as if he merely recited the terrible words. "The world shall be turned upside down and demons shall reign if the virgin disdains her virtue and becomes the concubine of Satan. Once, here at this very place, a high lady did the same, and paid in blood. It shall not happen again. No man must touch her, or all shall be drowned in the lake of blackest pitch. In the fire that dances next to water."

His face suddenly twisted beyond all recognition, and he stood to fling his arms up. "The Boleyn witches must be purified! Two queens have paid for their corruption already. There shall be no third," he screamed. "The king commands it."

Kate fell back a step in shock and grasped a handful of the tapestry to hold herself upright. Two dead queens, lakes of blood—Anne Boleyn and Catherine Howard? And the old accusations of witchcraft that had led them to the block . . .

"Varlet!" Lord Hunsdon shouted. He reached for the sword at his side, but his sister stayed his hand.

"'Tis not Master Constable who says this," Lady Knollys sobbed, tears running down her cheeks. "'Tis the spirits. Oh, by the saints, what are we to do?"

"The virgin must rule them now!" Master Constable said, his voice grown even rockier, rougher. "Born of the lecher and the witch, she shall make things whole again, shall wash away the old blood—if she remains pure. Then peace and plenty will shower over the land, and none may tear it apart."

Master Constable suddenly collapsed to the floor, as if all the bones in his body had gone out of him and he was a mere heap of black robes. The smoke swirled again and took on a form like a flaming sword—with bright red dripping from its tip.

Kate thought suddenly of Queen Anne and the French swordsman who had ended her life as she knelt before the block. One swipe of a bloody blade, and the queen's mother was no more. Kate had wanted to cover her eyes, but she could not look away.

The smoke collapsed, leaving not even a trace of scent behind, and everyone in the room screamed and ran.

Kate knew not how such trickery was done, how Master Constable managed to do such a thing, but she knew he could not just be left on the floor. While everyone else broke into hysterics, she hurried over to him and knelt down by his side. His box had tumbled from the table, scattering herbs and some strange grayish dust on the priceless carpet.

Among them was a small book, obviously old, water warped, bound in scarred brown leather, and tied with a loop of twine. Impulsively, she scooped it up and tucked it into the silk pouch tied at her sash. She had to find out how he had done this trickery tonight, so she could comfort Lady Knollys and assure her that the queen's blood would *not* wash over the land.

She pushed Master Constable over onto his back. He was heavier than he looked. The man was milk white, his face beaded with sweat, his eyes twitching wildly behind their closed lids.

"Master Constable, wake up!" she called, shaking him by the shoulders. "You must wake now, and tell us how you did this. What it all means."

He didn't open his eyes, and he shook lifelessly under her hand.

Suddenly, his eyes flew open and he stared up at her for one long, silent moment. His whole body went rigid, and Kate rocked back on her heels away from him.

"Boleyn witches!" he screamed, and collapsed back to the floor in a terrifying convulsive fit.

A gentle hand on her arm almost made her scream. She twisted around to see Master Green standing above her, his handsome face gentle and concerned as he looked at her.

"Come, Mistress Haywood; this is no place for a lady. Let us see you to your chamber," he said, quietly but firmly. "Dr. Dee has been sent for to fetch his apprentice."

She glanced past him to see that his friend Master Roland, Violet's brother, stood with him. His face was tight, as unsure of what to do as she was herself. "Aye, Mistress Haywood, you must come with us now." He glanced down at Constable with a grimace of disdain.

"Thank you, Master Green. Master Roland," she whispered. She let Master Green help her to her feet and lead her away from the frightening sight of Constable in his trance.

At the door, she glanced back to see Lord Hunsdon haul Master Constable to his feet. Constable's eyes were open now, and he no longer trembled violently, though he looked most dazed. Lady Knollys was soothing her rattled guests, and Lady Lettice was nowhere to be seen. Things were quieter already.

But Kate feared it would be a long time before she

could get the images of that night out of her mind. Would blood truly wash over England all over again? She was not a superstitious woman, but the thought of it filled her with a cold dread she couldn't quite shake away.

CHAPTER NINE

"And now comes Sir Trueheart, to defend the honor of his lady fair, the queen of all his heart!"

A wave of applause swept over the crowd gathered on the wooden stands overlooking Nonsuch's tournament grounds. The golden warmth of the sun, the soft wind that caught at the bright banners of green and gold seemed like a benediction, sweeping away the strange foreboding of the last few days.

No one basked in the light as much as the queen herself. Elizabeth sat on the highest dais, beneath an embroidered canopy on a velvet throne. Her gown was the same pale blue as the sky, sewn with the shimmer of pearls, her red-gold hair caught up in a crown of more pearls and diamonds shaped like twining flowers. All her ladies, gathered around her like the frilled lace of a May Day bouquet, wore real blossoms in their own loose hair, white like their gowns.

The rest of the court clustered in the stands, a rippling river of blue and silver and gold. Servants hurried among them with generously filled goblets of wine and cider and platters of sweetmeats, adding to the giddy market-day feeling of the day. Everyone was overjoyed to be freed from the chambers and corridors of indoors at last. It was as if no one had heard of the strange events in Lady Knollys's chamber at all.

A blast of silvery trumpets sounded, and the flower-bedecked gates of the joust field opened to let in Sir Trueheart, who sat astride his prancing white horse. The ladies all giggled and whispered behind their hands and their feathered fans, trying to decipher who he was behind his chased silver helm.

It could not be Robert Dudley, Kate decided as she studied the crowd. He sat beside the queen, the two of them sharing a bowl of strawberry sweets and laughing together. Nor could it be Lord Arundel, the architect of this tournament. Their host's jousting days were far behind him, and he watched the festivities with anxious eyes toward the queen's amusement—and an obvious curse for Dudley.

But Kate had to admit that Lord Arundel had been a most excellent host that day. The games had been arranged hastily to take advantage of the fine weather, yet there was no hint of shabbiness about them at all. Everything looked just like a tournament for King Arthur and his knights, down to the embroidered badges of the banners, just like the ones displayed at the banquet.

The riders and their richly caparisoned horses, the trumpets, the brilliant colors, the archers on the ramparts. It was all most romantic, with the competitors vying for the favors of their fair ladies, for the most applause, and for the greatest number of flowers tossed at their horses' hooves.

Against her will, Kate's attention strayed to where Anthony Elias sat with Master Hardy and the Duchess of Somerset's party behind the queen. Unlike the others, he had left behind his dark lawyer's robes and wore a new burgundy doublet, his brown, close-cropped hair and chiseled features handsome against the rich color.

She turned away quickly, but she feared the heat on her face was not just from the sun high overhead. Romance was everywhere at court in the summer, poetry and flowers and fine words. She had thought herself immune to its lure, buried in her music, but was she really?

What was real, and what was false? Just like the spirits Dr. Dee and Master Constable claimed to see, the secrets they saw in their stone. What she had seen herself in Lady Knollys's rooms. Kate could hardly know at all anymore.

She felt an odd prickling sensation on the back of her neck and glanced back over her shoulder at the tired wooden benches behind her. To her shock, she caught Master Constable watching her, his oddly pale eyes blazing in his damp white face. There was a shifting crowd between them, couriers gasping and laughing at the jousters and their feats, but he was unmistakably staring at *her*.

A vision flared in her mind—Master Constable falling to the floor amid the bright flash of the explosion, ladies screaming, Lord Hunsdon's fury, the sudden fear. She wished she could forget it, pretend it never happened at all, but she feared she would never forget it now. She would always hear the cryptic warnings of spirits she didn't want to believe in.

She knew William Cecil had questioned Master Constable about both the fight at the banquet and what happened in Lady Knollys's rooms. Surely he would not have let him go if there was any danger to the queen. Yet Kate did not like seeing him there now, remembering what happened.

She whipped back around to stare straight ahead of her, sightlessly. The two combatants on the field met in a great clash and clatter of splintered wood, nearly unhorsing one of them, but Kate couldn't see the gaudy spectacle of it all as everyone around her gasped. She still kept seeing that chaotic scene in Lady Knollys's room. She shivered, despite the heat of the sun.

"I know 'tis a bit frightening after the news earlier this summer from France," the man next to her said.

Kate was pulled back down into the day and the festive crowd around her. She looked over, remembering that Master Roland sat beside her, his sister, Violet, at his other side. He gave Kate a kind smile and offered her a goblet of chilled wine.

"Thank you," she murmured as she accepted it. "It is a very warm day, I fear. But I am sure nothing will happen here like what occurred in France." She had quite forgotten about King Henri, dying so horribly from the jousting lance that caught him in the eye, but it only added to the strange feeling that wouldn't let her go.

"The poor French king!" Violet cried. "And Monsieur Noailles, the French ambassador, does look rather green, does he not? Such a thing can't happen here, can it, Thomas?"

"Certainly not, sis. Such an accident is most rare, and I promise you Lord Arundel was very scrupulous about the arrangements for this tournament. I assisted with them myself," Master Roland said with a small flash of pride. "I saw the lances blunted and helped in drawing up the matches. His lordship trusts all his employees."

"It sounds as if Lord Arundel is an excellent master," Kate said, trying to forget about the darkness and see only the sunlit day. She took another deep sip of the wine.

"Indeed he is," Master Roland answered. "I was most fortunate to gain a place in his household and to have his trust. With his help, I hope to advance far at court, perhaps even one day gain a foreign post. There is no telling how far I might take my family with such a patron. Even find a high lord for *you* to wed, eh, Vi?"

His words were teasing, and Violet laughed in response, but Kate saw her friend's gaze shift away. Kate remembered Master Longville, his touch on Violet's arm—and the tenderness in her gaze when she looked at Master Green instead. "Oh, but I need no title! Just a cozy little home somewhere, some lovely babes . . ."

"As you say now, but there is no need for haste, Vi. Who knows what may happen for us soon enough?" For an instant, Master Roland frowned and his hands curled into fists, as if he caught a glimpse of something in the distance he could not yet quite grasp. But then he smiled again. "We need only have a bit of patience."

"How does your friend Master Green today, Master Roland?" Kate asked. "I have not yet seen him at the tournament."

Master Roland shrugged, but Violet suddenly looked at him closely. "I think he was sent on an errand by his master, Lord Hunsdon, Mistress Haywood, but I assure you he has recovered from that—business—at the banquet. It's a shock that a man such as Dr. Dee, with so very much in his favor, would keep such a man as Constable around him. We all know so little of him."

Kate felt again that prickling on the back of her neck, heard the unearthly cry. *Boleyn witches.* Before she could think of what to answer, Master Roland turned away to tease his blushing sister again.

"If you need no lordship for your husband, Vi, then what of Longville? He quite adores you, I think. He is always following you about. And I hear his house in Warwickshire is cozy indeed."

"Nay!" Violet cried. "I do not think I can like him."

Master Roland's smile darkened. "Has he bothered you?"

"Not *bother*. Just . . . I cannot like him that way, and I have told him so. He just does not yet believe me." Violet fussed with the folds of her pale lavender skirt. "Pray, brother, say no more about him. Oh, look, the silver knight has won! Who is he, do you think?"

The silver knight leaped gracefully from his saddle and knelt before the queen, sweeping off his plumed helmet just like a defender of Arthur's time. Sunlight gleamed on golden hair and a wide smile spread across his face as he looked up at the queen, who was laughing and applauding, much to Dudley's obvious dismay.

Kate, too, was shocked. For the silver knight who had won the tournament so handily was Rob Cartman. Her heart suddenly beat faster at the sight of him, so dashing, his smile so bright at his victory. He looked so very much like a knight in a poem, and she found that, no matter how much she might want to, she couldn't look away from him.

After the tournament, Lord Arundel had invited the court to explore his maze, and Kate had flocked with the rest of them to the labyrinthine paths. The garden maze felt like a different world, Kate thought, as she tilted back her head to gaze up at the square of blue sky above the walls of the sculpted hedges. The heels of her new shoes sank into the soft, rain-soaked earth, as if they were trying to hold her down so she couldn't fly away.

Voices and laughter were muffled, almost eerie, and she couldn't tell if they came from just beyond the wall beside her, or if they were very far away indeed.

Violet and Master Green, who had returned to see the last of the tournament, had been just ahead of her, Violet's lavender-colored brocade skirts a purple-plumage glow against all the shadowy green. They held hands, wrapped in their own moment, until they'd vanished around a corner.

For an instant, Kate felt as if she was completely alone in a world tossed upside down. Then she glanced back and saw Rob Cartman walking behind her.

He had washed after his victory in the tournament, and his damp golden hair appeared darker, his blue eyes shadowed. He had scored a great moment before the queen and all the court, surely impressing all the nobles he hoped to gain patronage from, yet he looked so serious. Was he not there to gain attention from someone, possibly Lord Hunsdon? Kate, on the other hand, felt anything but serious, just for a moment.

She smiled at him, feeling suddenly giddy in this world of sky and grass and summer laughter. It was as if the false romance of the tournament was reality for a moment. The darkness of the séance, Master Constable's scrying, and the horror of that faraway joust in France seemed far away. She wanted to hold on to that feeling as long as she could.

"So, Sir Silver Knight," she said. "You even had the queen smiling upon you today. Your trip to Nonsuch was never in vain."

He did finally smile at that, a quick, brilliant, concealing flash. "I could only see *your* smile, Kate. I never thought I could surprise you."

"How did you come to have such a place in the tournament? I didn't know you could ride like that."

"All actors must know how to ride. How to fight. How to be a chivalrous knight. Or a dark villain. Or the enchanter at the banquet putting the revelers under a spell."

Kate shook her head, thinking of the smoke, the screams, at Lady Knollys's gathering. Surely Nonsuch held enough enchanters. "And you have always wanted to be an actor," she said, remembering the tale he once told her when they first met at Hatfield House. His parents, simple farm folk; his uncle, the glamorous actor who took Rob away to teach him the trade. The years of wandering, hunger, hardship, passionate desire for art. She knew how such things felt.

"It was always within me," he answered simply. They walked slowly together down the winding path, close but not touching. "I knew I could never live in just one place, as my parents did, seeing the same people every day, talking of the same things over and over. I could never just be one person, when there were so many within me. Is it not the same with you, Kate? Is music not like many worlds in your heart?"

Kate was surprised he understood. So few people did. Her father; the queen, mayhap. Music was more than a dance. It was emotion contained in a sound. An escape. Just like helping Elizabeth was a sort of escape, going places she would never otherwise see, learning new things. "Aye, just so. But music has always been in my life, even before I was born, since it is everything to my father. I grew up not knowing anything else."

And also everything for the mother she had never known. Her Boleyn mother.

Rob reached out to pluck a stray twig from the hedge near her head. It was dark against his long, scarred fingers, and he turned it over in smooth, practiced movements. "My uncle once came to Nonsuch. Did you know?"

Kate remembered Rob's murdered uncle, his underhanded doings at Hatfield, which had led to his death. She was surprised, but she knew she should not be. Actors were always traveling, always meeting people of different sorts. Rob's uncle seemed to be a man with an eye to a profit all the time, an eye for a powerful patron.

Just like Rob? What would he do for his acting troupe?

"You seldom tell me much at all, Rob," she said. "Surely you know that. Yet I think you did mention such, there by the lake."

He laughed, but it was a rough, wry sound. "I let you see more of myself than most people, Kate, except for my uncle. I think of him much here, of what he must have been like when he was young and his troupe played here. Nonsuch seems to bring out such memories, does it not?"

Indeed it did, far too much. "Did he play for the old king?"

"Aye, when he was a young apprentice. King Henry loved a good play, especially one that glorified kings and romance. My uncle played the fair maiden then. He talked of the beauty of the palace, unfinished though it was then, and the beauty of poor Queen Catherine Howard. It sounded like a dream to me, but now that I see it myself, I know why it haunted him so."

Kate swallowed hard, thinking of the lost Dr. Macey, the ghosts that lingered at every turn of this fanciful place. "Yet that can all be more than a dream to you now, Rob. The queen has noticed you. As has her theater-loving cousin Lord Hunsdon—as you wished."

His expression sharpened as he looked down at her. The twig went still between his fingers. "You know Lord Hunsdon, then, Kate?"

Kate nodded warily. "Does not everyone know of the queen's cousin? She favors her relatives much now, and everyone says he enjoys a fine play. That he keeps players at his home. If he likes you—"

Suddenly, her words were drowned by a scream. It was a high, thin, terrified sound, a dagger slicing through the warm idyll of the summer's day. It sent the birds soaring from the maze.

"Violet," Kate gasped. Without thinking, she lifted the heavy hem of her gown and ran toward the corner where her friend had vanished. The soft mud snatched at her fine shoes, and her mind couldn't fathom what was happening around her. Yet she tumbled ever forward, headlong.

In the maze's square, sun-dappled center, Violet stood with her hands thrust out in front of her, as if she would push something away. Another scream escaped her lips as Master Green reached out to catch her arm and pull her back. His handsome face was frozen into a pale mask of disbelief.

In front of them, the ground was churned up in a froth of sandy brown mud mixed with grass and twigs like a tangled river, as if the days of rain had swept the ground itself away.

And tangled up with it was the stark, harsh white of bones. A flash of stained, shredded red cloth. A horrible grin from a skull that stared up at the deceivingly beautiful sky.

Lakes of blood. Kate pressed her hand hard to her mouth before a hysterical laugh could fly out. Master Constable had been right, even in his frenzy. Death had been lingering here at Nonsuch all along.

CHAPTER TEN

"Mistress Haywood! Mistress Haywood, wake up, I beg you."

Kate gasped as she fought her way up from the darkness of her nightmare, toward the sudden, shocking touch on her shoulder. It felt like creatures were clawing at her, trying to drag her back down into the humid world of night terrors. Memories of grinning skulls, white bones sticking up out of the mud, had haunted her sleep ever since she managed to close her eyes after the horrifying events earlier that day.

She sat straight up in bed, still gripped in raw fear, her mouth open to cry out.

"Nay, don't wake the others," someone said, that touch on her shoulder tightening.

Kate clutched the damp sheet closer and looked over to see that it was Kat Ashley, the queen's Mistress of the Robes, who knelt beside her bed. Mistress Ashley held a candle in her other hand, and in its flickering light she looked older, gaunter, far more fearful. In the daylight, the Mistress of the Robes ruled the queen's household with a crisp, iron efficiency; she was all remoteness and dark silks, not to be crossed.

Here, in the darkest part of the night, with her graying hair falling in a long braid over the shoulder of her bed robe and no fine pearls around her wrinkled throat, Mistress Ashley looked almost fragile—and afraid.

The thought of such fear made Kate clutch even tighter to the sheet. If even Mistress Ashley was unsettled here at Nonsuch tonight, made fearful by that skeleton in the garden, what hope was there for everyone else to stay calm?

Kate glanced quickly around the room. Violet and Anne still slept in their shadowed bed closer to the fire, holding on to each other against the force of their own nightmares. Violet had been unable to stop whimpering and shaking after her terrible discovery in the maze, until the queen's own physician dosed her with a strong cordial that made her fall into a fevered sleep as Anne murmured words of comfort to her.

"What is amiss?" Kate whispered. "Is the queen ill?"

Mistress Ashley shook her head. "Not—ill. Yet she cannot sleep. She keeps pacing her chamber, muttering about old curses. I thought I had best fetch you and see if you could play for her. Your songs do seem to soothe her."

Kate drew in a deep breath, gathering the real world around her against all the bad dreams, and she nodded. It was not the first time she had been summoned to play for the queen in the middle of the night. Elizabeth was often beset by dark thoughts that wouldn't let her sleep. Tonight the distraction seemed especially welcome, for Kate had no desire to lie in the silent chamber any longer, alone with the memory of that death's-head smile in the sunshine.

She quickly climbed out of bed and pulled on her own robe over her chemise. Her restless sleep had pulled her thick, straight dark hair from its braid, and she looped it up under a cap. Mistress Ashley took her lute from its stand in the corner and pressed it into her hands.

Kate ran her fingers over the initials carefully carved into the wood as she followed Mistress Ashley along the silent maze of corridors. *EH*, with a smaller *KH* beneath. Eleanor Haywood—the mother she had never known, who had once played, and loved, this same lute. *Boleyn witch*.

If only Eleanor *had* been a witch, Kate thought half desperately. Maybe then she could find a way to be with her daughter now.

They soon reached the doorway to the queen's bedchamber, and there the night was not quite so silent. Guards clustered close about the doors in the royal livery of green and white as well as Robert Dudley's scarlet.

It was Sir Robert who had reached the center of the maze first, drawn by Violet's screams, his sword in his hand and his men close behind him. He was ever ready for battle. He had surrounded Elizabeth with an unbreachable wall of his own guards, and no doubt was still on patrol outside the palace. None could ever gainsay him, not Lord Arundel or William Cecil, or even the queen herself.

"God's teeth, but am I to be a prisoner here, in this place my own father built for naught but pleasure?" Elizabeth shouted, her words thundering out from behind the closed door. "What can a rattling set of old bones do to *me*?"

Mistress Ashley pushed aside the hovering guards and hurried into the chamber, and Kate followed close behind her. Elizabeth's tower bedchamber was a blazing beacon of light against the impenetrable darkness of the night, a fire blazing in the large grate, candles lit in sconces and candelabra. Yet the windows were thrown open to let in the cool breeze.

On the great carved bed, set high on its dais, the velvet covers were thrown back, the feather pillows mounded up in an untidy heap. The curtains were looped back and tied with their gold-tasseled cords. One of the queen's little dogs, a greyhound sent by the Venetian ambassador, peeked out from the snowy linen sheets.

William Cecil, the queen's chief secretary, stood near the fireplace, still dressed in his black velvet doublet and robes, leaning heavily on his walking stick, as he tended to do when weary. Two ladies, Mary Sidney and Lady Catherine Grey, hovered behind him in their pale satin bed robes, holding on to each other as they stared out with wide, uncertain eyes. They were not good friends; once the Dudleys and the Greys had been closest allies, but no longer, not in this new world of uncertain alliances. But the hovering spirit of old death bound even two such different ladies together tonight.

The queen paced the polished length of the floor, as she was wont to do when the nights pressed in on her. She moved so fast, in such an agitated fashion, that the loose fall of her red-gold hair and the glossy scarlet of her brocade robe made her look like a moving flame. Her long, elegant pale hands twisted together.

"Until we are sure the danger is past, Your Majesty . . . ," Cecil said warily.

"Past?" Elizabeth cried. "'Twas clean-picked bones in that garden. How much more *past* can it be? I shall go riding tomorrow as planned. I cannot bear to be shut inside one more moment."

"But whose were those bones, Your Majesty?" Cecil said, in his usual calm, measured way. "Until we know, it would be wise to stay close. Or mayhap to leave Nonsuch altogether. We could return to Windsor early."

Elizabeth shook her head fiercely. "Nay, not Windsor. I can't bear that dank old place yet. It's still summer . . ." She squeezed her eyes closed, her long, pointed cat's face contorted as if in a flash of raw pain. "Do I not deserve a few more days of merriment?"

Cecil had served Elizabeth for many years, long

enough to know when to give in to her. He bowed his head. "If you will go well guarded, Your Majesty, and not ride away alone as last time. England needs you; you must have a care for yourself above all else."

Not go ride off alone—but for Robert Dudley. Even Kate could hear those unspoken words. The queen would often vanish on hunts with Dudley, the two of them returning flushed with laughter and followed by trails of gossip.

"I have given myself entirely to England, all my life," Elizabeth said wearily. "Surely she knows that."

The queen turned and saw Kate standing near the doorway. "Ah, Kate, very good. You have come to entertain me at last. Cecil, my dear, you should find your own bed. You, too, Mary, Lady Catherine. It will be dawn soon enough."

Cecil bowed and departed, his bearded face set in hard, weary lines. The two ladies followed him, and Elizabeth sat down in the cushioned chair beside the fire. Mistress Ashley went to pour a goblet of spiced wine, and Elizabeth gestured Kate to a low stool nearby.

"What shall I play tonight, Your Majesty?" Kate asked as she settled her lute on her lap and carefully tuned the strings. They were predictably responsive, something she understood, something she could control, and it calmed her as it always did.

Elizabeth stared into the fire, her white face looking older, more tired, thoughts hidden deep behind her dark Boleyn eyes. "Something old, I think. Something of my father's time. It seems appropriate on this night of ghosts, does it not?"

Kate had wanted to forget ghosts, but she nodded. She bent her head lower over the instrument, letting herself fall into it as she often did. It reminded her of another night of ghosts, of the Tower under a winter moon, and long-dead mothers hovering nearby. She started playing "Whereto should I express my inward heaviness," a sweet, sad old tune written by King Henry himself.

Elizabeth was quiet for long moments, her fingertips tapping on the carved arm of the chair. She stared deep into the fire, her forehead creased as if she saw things very far away indeed.

"You saw the bones today, did you not, Kate?" Elizabeth suddenly asked. She didn't turn to look at Kate, but kept her gaze steady on the fire.

Long hours of practice helped Kate not to falter in her song, even as an image of that grinning white skull in the brown mud flashed through her mind. "Only for an instant, Your Majesty, before Master Green pushed Violet and me away. He acted most quickly and calmly."

Elizabeth nodded. Robert Dudley had kept her away from the center of the maze, even as she loudly protested. He was surely the only one who could have prevented her. "What did they look like?"

Kate shivered. "Like—like bones, Your Majesty. All coming out of the mud, as if a river had flushed them free. The skull . . ." She swallowed hard, unable to go on.

Elizabeth nodded slowly, still watching the snap and dance of the fire. "They must have been there a very long time, to be only bones thus. The sight could have been more gruesome for you, I fear, Kate."

Kate thought of the boiled heads that always loomed above London Bridge, executed traitors doomed to stare down at the city until they fell into the river below. She also remembered the terrible, acrid smell of burning flesh that seemed to hang over everything when Mary was queen. Gruesome—aye, but no more so than everyday life could be. "Who could it have been?"

Elizabeth shrugged. "If the bones are as old as all that, I could not say. They must be of my father's time, or even earlier. He seldom used this house, you know. It was not even finished when he died. He meant it to impress my very pretty stepmother, who was barely older than me when he brought her to visit it." She gave a humorless little laugh. "Poor Cat Howard. It would have taken more than a fine house to hold *her* flighty interest. For all her prettiness, all her merry smiles, she drew death behind her wherever she went."

Kate took in a deep breath. She knew little of Queen Catherine Howard beyond her sad end, yet Nonsuch seemed to hold her as well as so many others. "What of Dr. Dee's old teacher, Dr. Macey?"

Elizabeth looked toward Kate, her eyes widening as if she suddenly had come back from the past. "The one who left here so long ago? Who told the horoscopes of my father and his court?"

"Aye. 'Twas said he was accused of treason and then vanished. Surely it is very possible. I saw a bit of muddy cloth with the skeleton, perhaps once red. If there is enough left to see the fashion of it . . ."

Elizabeth nodded, a thoughtful frown on her lips. "They took the bones to an unused room of the kitchen, I do think. Cecil would never let me go there to look, I am sure, but if you could . . ."

Kate swallowed again and nodded. In truth, she would rather not see that terrible deathly grin again. But Elizabeth was right. Kate could go where the queen could not, could take her time to observe without being observed herself. And it was true—there *could* be a more gruesome sight.

She felt the old curiosity, that old, terrible need to *know* that had taken her into trouble before, rise again.

"Should I go now?" Kate asked.

Elizabeth nodded. "Before anyone wakes. Then you can tell me if you find anything."

Kate carefully put aside her lute and drew her robe close around her before she hurried to the door.

"Kate," Elizabeth called as Kate reached for the door latch. Kate glanced back to find Elizabeth watching her closely, her face white and strained. She looked almost—afraid?

"Your Majesty?" Kate whispered.

The queen seemed uncharacteristically hesitant for a moment, her long fingers tense over the armrest. "My cousin Lady Knollys told me about what happened in her chamber with that strange Master Constable. She was most—overset."

"Boleyn witches?" Kate said, barely daring to voice the words.

Elizabeth bit her lip. "Do you remember that night in the Tower?" she said quietly, and Kate was startled the queen would speak of it. They never had; it was as if those moments were forgotten. The queen was always moving into the future, enjoying her glorious present. The past, made of pain and blood and fear, was gone.

Only here, in this place, the past didn't seem so far away.

"Of course I remember that night. And I will find out what is happening here, Your Majesty," Kate said. She was not at all sure she could keep that promise, but she would do her very best. For the queen. For their mothers.

Elizabeth nodded and looked back to the fire. Kate wondered what she saw there.

"Be careful, Kate. I can't lose you, too," the queen whispered.

Kate tiptoed down the cold stone stairs toward the small room tucked beneath the kitchens, deep underground. Unlike the warm, soft, bread-scented air above, this place felt chilly and dank. She pulled her robe closer around her and held her candle up higher.

As her slipper touched the bottom step, she thought she heard a sudden noise, quiet and muffled, far away. She froze, her chest aching as she held her breath in her lungs. She listened closely, trying to decipher if it was above her head or ahead of her in the darkness, in that room of death.

She heard nothing else, only the nighttime silence, which was thick enough to pierce with a sword, and slowly her breath moved again. She knew she had to move forward, always forward.

She slipped through an arched stone doorway into the small chamber. Surely it was usually used to keep butter or cheese, but tonight it was used for a much less pleasant purpose. Her candle cast its feeble light into the stone-lined space, and she tightened her other hand on the edge of her robe, bracing herself to look.

A sturdy wooden table was laid out against the far wall, and the bones that had been unearthed from the garden maze were arranged there in a semblance of a human form. Not every part was there; one foot and nearly one whole arm seemed to be missing.

Kate swallowed against a sudden sour rush of nausea and made herself tiptoe to the side of the table and look closer. A tuft of hair, mostly gray, clung to the skull, which still seemed to smile up at her. She could tell that whoever it was, they had not been very tall, but surely were prosperous, if the remains of the garment also laid out on the table were anything to go by.

It was a robe of finely woven wool, patches of red beneath crusted dirt, bits of tarnished metallic embroidery clinging to the edges.

"Who were you?" she whispered, studying the tiny

bones of the remaining hand. One finger seemed to have been broken and healed crookedly. "What were you doing in the queen's garden?"

Kate saw the gleam of something beneath the bones, as if it had fallen to the floor, and she steeled herself to look closer. It was a ring, but not just any ring. A large emerald set in wrought gold, with a cipher etched along one side. HRVIII. Henry VIII. The king's cipher! What was such a thing doing with the bones?

A sudden rustling sound echoed behind her, and Kate cried out. She instinctively swept the emerald into her pocket. Fear, and a dark, burning urge to fight rushed through her veins, and she whirled around, her candle held high like a weapon. Her glance frantically swept over the darkness along the stone walls.

"Who is there?" she called, trying to emulate the queen's confidence, her certainty that no one would dare harm her. Whether it was true or not. "Show yourself at once!"

A stooped, black-clad figure stepped out of the shadows and raised its face to her meager light. To her shock, she saw it was Dr. Dee who lurked there.

"Dr. Dee," she whispered. "I did not see you there."

"Forgive me for frightening you, Mistress Haywood," he said hoarsely. "I did not think anyone would be here so very late. But you found him in the garden, did you not?"

Kate glanced back at the bones. She thought of the old tales of Dr. Dee, of his studies of arts beyond human understanding. Of the mysterious Lord Marchand, who had once accused Dr. Macey of treason. "My friend did, aye. I was in the maze with her." Kate paused for a moment as she played back the doctor's last words. "Found *him*?"

Dr. Dee gave her a smile, a sad flicker behind his

thick beard. "'Tis my teacher Dr. Macey. Surely even a very young lady such as yourself has heard the old tale?"

He was right. Everyone knew gossip was rife at court; it was everyone's very lifeblood. And a disappearance among rumors of a queen's adultery and dark arts, here in this very palace—of course it was known. "I have heard it. I am sorry for it, Dr. Dee. But how do you know it is him, found at last?"

Dr. Dee gestured toward a small bowl on another table she hadn't yet noticed. A heavy gold ring set with a gleaming black stone, run through with shimmering veins, rested there. "That was found with the body. It was his. The stone—it is very rare, and he guarded it well."

Kate stared at the ring, thinking of its resemblance to the opalescent mirror that had shot sparks into the air of Lady Knollys's room. She didn't want to be afraid; she could *not* be afraid, not now. "When did you last see him?"

Dr. Dee gently took her arm and led her to the chair he had left against the wall. A strange, sweet smell clung about his black robes, like a growing green summer garden. "Please, sit, Mistress Haywood. It is bad enough we stand here in this damp place."

As Kate carefully lowered herself to the edge of the wooden seat, she noticed that Dr. Dee blocked her view of the body. Was he being courteous? Or was there something he did not want her to see?

"I last saw him before he came here, to Nonsuch, when we were in his chambers at Cambridge. We were going over an ancient manuscript he had just acquired," he said. In the meager light, his face looked gaunt, all harsh lines, and his eyes narrowed by long hours bent over ancient books. What had he learned in all those years? "King Henry was coming here on his summer progress, to see how his fantasy palace was taking shape. To show it to his pretty new queen. He wanted his own astrologer to come with him, to foretell the futures of them and this place."

"And you did not come with him?" Kate said. It sounded as if King Henry and his courtiers were much like Queen Elizabeth and hers, wanting to harness magic for their own uses. But magic would not be controlled, not always.

"Nay, I had my studies, and I was very young then, barely more than a child. I wish I had come with him, to try to help him. He was my teacher, and also my friend. I met him when I first went to school, fascinated by so many things that had no answers. I wanted to know about the stars, about the powers numbers have. The ancients knew things we are only now rediscovering, Mistress Haywood. Dr. Macey was also deep in such studies; he had been to the Continent and purchased many old manuscripts. We spent long evenings reading them together, trying to decipher their secrets. It was he who opened my eyes to the endless possibilities that linger all around us in this world. He knew that alchemy and mathematics were not for the perfection of mere metals, but for souls. For eternity."

Secrets that powerful people would pay much to possess? Kate thought of the book she had taken from Master Constable, which she'd hidden at the bottom of her clothes chest and hadn't gotten a chance to study yet. The bizarre symbols and nonsensical letters, like music. Music notes looked like scribbles to those who could not decipher them. Only people who had learned them could unlock the world of sound and emotion and truth contained in those little ink markings.

But the secret code of men like Dr. Dee, and Dr. Macey and Master Constable, revealed not just madrigals and motets, but life and death, and beyond death, too. Spirits and angels. Did *she* really want to know more of such things? After seeing what she had at Lady Knollys's, she wasn't sure at all.

Yet those secrets touched the queen and Kate's own family, as it seemed they had once touched King Henry and Queen Catherine Howard. And they touched Kate, too, and everything and everyone she loved.

Boleyn witches.

"What happened back then, here at Nonsuch?" she asked. "At least what you know of it."

Dr. Dee rubbed a trembling hand over his bearded face. "Dr. Macey was supposed to cast Queen Catherine's horoscope. Even I, young as I was then, was sure such an endeavor could not end well. Queen Catherine was so young, so flighty, always dancing, flitting from one friend to another. Her stars could not have been aligned yet. I begged him to put it off, to tell the king it could not be done until the planets were in agreement. But none could ever gainsay the old king. He was besotted with his wife, his rose without a thorn, and he would not be dissuaded. And Dr. Macey lived to serve the Tudors. As we all do."

Kate shivered as she remembered what had happened to the pretty, foolish Queen Catherine. The stars had indeed never aligned for her. She remembered, too, the tales of what Dr. Dee might have been doing while Mary was queen and Elizabeth her prisoner. Where did his loyalties lie? Where had Dr. Macey's?

"Is that why he died?" she asked quietly. "He displeased King Henry by telling what he truly saw in Catherine Howard's horoscope?"

A wry smile twisted Dr. Dee's lips behind his beard. "Dr. Macey never even cast her horoscope. If he had displeased King Henry, he would not have vanished and been tossed into a hidden grave. He would have been executed in full view of the public, as so very many were. Nay, he disappeared on a stormy night, before he even talked to the young queen. After he had a quarrel with another courtier, so I heard."

With Lord Marchand, whoever he was? Kate's thoughts raced with all the possibilities of what could have happened on that long-ago night, who could have been there. "Who saw him that night?"

That smiled faded, but he gave no sign he thought her questions strange. "One of his servants, Mistress Haywood, who came to talk with me after. It seems Dr. Macey was much preoccupied with something he was writing, something he would not show me or even speak of. He seemed agitated that night, pacing and muttering in his chamber, which was a small one near the attics. He left most abruptly, saying he had to meet someone. His servant feared for his safety, there was such lightning, the rain coming down so hard."

"And he did not follow?"

Dr. Dee laughed. "My dear Mistress Haywood. Court had opportunities the university did not. I am sure the servant had met a pretty maidservant that day. And he died soon after himself, so I could ask him no more."

A frown abruptly replaced that brief smile. "I have so often reproached myself for *not* following him here. I never saw him again after that, and I have searched for him in my studies so often."

"You could not have known. You were very young. Even with all your studies, surely you could not have seen his future. It sounds as if Dr. Macey was involved in a matter of some secrecy, and danger." Kate had a sudden, strange thought of Rob Cartman, the way he'd behaved by the lake. Even people one cared for could not always be known.

Dr. Dee shook his head. "I looked for him after, for many years. Both in the physical world and among the spirits, but he was nowhere to be found. Until you and your friend stumbled over him so abruptly. He was here all along."

Kate nodded, thinking of the cottage. Had he been searching for Dr. Macey there? "Perhaps he was waiting for you," she said carefully. "After all, you have returned to Nonsuch with your own student, to serve another Tudor monarch."

"Maybe there is something in what you say, Mistress Haywood. Are you perhaps a student of numbers, of the mystical arts, yourself?"

Kate shook her head. "I am only a musician, Dr. Dee."

"Music, too, has its own hidden code. You must know, Mistress Haywood, that when an alchemist or astronomer is not himself spiritually pure, he can never find success in any experiment. Inner harmony is the only way to find the ultimate harmony of the universe." Dr. Dee fell silent for a moment, and Kate noticed he turned a ring around his scarred finger. It was set with a clear opalescent stone, not black like Dr. Macey's. "I heard much of what happened with Master Constable, when Lady Knollys asked him to summon the spirits. Such matters should not be looked into by those who have not carefully studied them for long years."

Kate was sure that must be true, considering what happened. "Surely everyone at court has heard of that by now."

"I did warn him not to try such a thing. His studies are only just beginning, though I do sense great gifts in him. He must develop them carefully; they are too rough yet to try such things. Especially before such people."

"For Boleyns, you mean?" she blurted out on a spark of anger.

Dr. Dee's eyes widened as if he was surprised. "Aye, for Boleyns. They are too close to the queen, and they have deep powers of their own, though they may not know it."

"Anne Boleyn was no witch," Kate whispered.

"Nay, not as we think of them," Dr. Dee said slowly. He gave Kate a long, considering look, his eyes too dark and shining, and she had to resist the childish urge to squirm under that regard. "And, of course, Dr. Macey died long after Queen Anne was in her own grave. Can I tell you a secret, Mistress Haywood?"

The night seemed full of nothing but secrets. What was one more, surely? Kate nodded cautiously.

"I came with the queen to Nonsuch because she requested it, of course," he said. "But also to fulfill a promise I made Dr. Macey long ago, to make sure his son was taken care of."

Kate was shocked. This was a piece of gossip she had *not* heard. "He had a son? Here at Nonsuch?"

"In the village nearby. That was one reason why he wanted to come here then; he had a child with a seamstress there. I feared that was one of the reasons they say he was so agitated that night."

"You have no idea what happened to Dr. Macey?" Kate said urgently. "He had no enemies? No threats he faced then? What of Lord Marchand? Surely he did not like Dr. Macey."

If Dr. Dee was surprised she knew of Lord Marchand, he did not show it. He only smiled sadly. "Oh, my dear Mistress Haywood. We *all* have enemies. And Lord Marchand was a man not to be crossed. He had dangerous friends, like poor Queen Catherine's lover, Thomas Culpeper. But Dr. Macey surely had none who

would kill him thus. He knew how to be careful.
Marchand was just a drunken courtier like all the others. If I knew what Dr. Macey was working on then,
what he studied—if I could find his last writings . . ."

Kate thought of her hidden book, the one she could
not read because of the strange symbols. Was Dr. Macey's lost book like that one? "You search for it still?"

"Of course I do. I have learned much since then myself. I could decipher it now as I could not when I was
a mere student." He suddenly smiled. "Yet I know I am
not the only one who seeks the truth, Mistress Haywood. You, too, have your own gifts, I can see."

Kate stared up into his fathomless dark eyes for a
long moment. She felt terribly weary down deep in her
bones, and her head whirled with everything she had
seen. All she had heard. She carefully pushed herself to
her feet. There was little more she could do that night,
not until she had processed all she had learned.

"I will leave you to your vigil, Dr. Dee," she said.
"Thank you for confiding in me."

He gave her a small bow, and Kate felt his eyes on
her as she walked to the doorway. The only sound was
the hem of her robe brushing the cold cobbles of the
floor, yet she felt as if many eyes watched her.

"Mistress Haywood," Dr. Dee suddenly called. "I
have always been loyal to the queen. I must hope you
know that."

Kate glanced back at him. He looked like a ghost
himself, his black clothes blending into the darkness,
the terrible bones on the table behind him. He had lost
so many people, just as she had, just as the queen had.
What would a person do when faced with such a thing?
She no longer knew.

She finally nodded. At the top of the stairs, she
looked back one more time and found that he held Dr.
Macey's black stone ring in his hand. He turned it

around and around, as if he could see all the sinister secrets of the past in its depths.

She shivered and ran back toward the deceptive safety of the palace, which was just stirring to early-morning life. She had to show the queen King Henry's emerald and find out what the royal family had to do with Dr. Macey.

CHAPTER ELEVEN

"'Perchance I may prefer thee well, for wedlock I love best! It is the most honorable estate, it passes all the rest. I . . .' Oh, what is the next line?"

Kate made herself keep smiling as she watched Catherine Grey move across the makeshift stage in the great hall, surrounded by the other ladies assigned to be her goddess attendants. It was very clear that, honor or not, Lady Catherine was *not* happy to be assigned the lead role of Juno in the new masque, forced to stay indoors and rehearse while the rest of the court, including Lord Hertford, rode out to the hunt. Lady Catherine moved through her dances stiffly, the words of her song off-key and too quiet, even though Kate knew she had a lovely voice. Bess Martin, who played Diana, could scarce follow her meandering, and Lady Anne Godwin, who was meant to be the goddess's acolyte, had not shown up at all.

Kate sighed. She could rather sympathize with Lady Catherine, for once. It was a sunny, warm day outside, the perfect antidote to the suppressed fear that had descended like a gray cloud over everyone since the grisly discovery in the garden. She could barely keep the notes of the new songs in her own mind, and she had written them herself. It was so hard to think of goddesses and marriage, sylvan glades and romance, when so much real drama swirled around.

When she knew all too well what lay in that underground kitchen room somewhere beneath their feet.

On the other hand, this masque was meant to distract and amuse the queen, which was why they were all there in the first place. It would be a much easier task if they all worked together.

Kate signaled to the other musicians to pause in their song. "Lady Catherine," she said patiently. "In this moment, you are meant to feel a change of heart. That perhaps romance is possible, in fact a very good thing. You are meant to be light, happy. Pretty. Which we all know you are most capable of, more so than any other lady at court."

Kate almost choked on the flattery, but she knew it was necessary if they were to have the masque ready to perform so quickly. Lady Catherine would just have to forget her lovesickness for a few moments.

Lady Catherine shrugged and nodded, but it was still obvious her thoughts were very far away. She raised her arms, clad in the half-finished diaphanous sleeves of her costume, and sang a few more bars, much more expressive this time.

She was interrupted by the sounds of heavy hammer blows, as the servants sent from the Master of the Revels' office worked on the scenery of the large wooden moon and the towering papier-mâché trees behind her.

Lady Catherine whirled around, stamping her foot. "Be still, you varlets! Can you not see I must finish this song?"

Kate had to resist the urge to throw down her lute and have a little tantrum of her own. She was working with only an hour of sleep behind her, hard-won after her strange meeting with Dr. Dee and nightmares of skeletons dancing in gardens. But before she could lose her temper, Rob Cartman leaped lightly onto the stage. He had been leaning against the scenery above their heads, watching the rehearsal in silence, though Kate had been too aware of his presence ever since she arrived.

Unlike Kate, whose eyes were shadowed and hair disheveled, Rob looked as if he had stepped out of a play where he performed the part of a king or emperor. All golden hair and skin, his lean acrobat's body in a gold-embroidered purple doublet and black hose. The ladies all giggled at him, and Kate wanted more than ever to throw her lute at—someone.

At least he made Lady Catherine smile and forget her changeable Tudor temper for a moment. If he could only make her learn the song, too.

A blast of trumpets sounded from outside the open windows, and Kate leaned over to peer out the closest one to her stool. She was glad of the distraction from the spectacle of all the queen's maids of honor falling over themselves over Rob Cartman's handsome face.

Below her, Queen Elizabeth rode out for the day's hunt, despite her own sleepless night. She shimmered in her white-and-gold doublet and skirt, the white plumes of her hat waving jauntily in the breeze. She laughed as if she hadn't a care in the world, though Kate remembered well the shadow that had crossed the queen's face when she saw the emerald that had been with Dr. Macey's bones. She had only nodded and put it quickly away.

The queen's pages rode ahead with her falcon's-badge banners flying high, and Robert Dudley was beside her, as always. Lord Arundel rode at her other side, trying in vain to catch her attention, and Violet's brother, Master Roland, was behind him, the loyal attendant.

With the queen's pack of hounds baying at the horses' hooves, they took off at a gallop down the lane, Elizabeth and Dudley laughing together as if the bones in the palace were not there at all. As if the queen had not sat up all night, staring into the fire as if she saw ghosts dancing in the flames.

The rest of the court trailed behind her, a sea of green and gold and white and red, feathers and veils waving in the wind, laughter as bright as the sun above them.

Violet rode past, since she had no part in the masque. Kate's friend looked as delicate as an almond-paste sweetmeat in her pale lavender riding doublet, an embroidered and pearl-dotted cap on her blond hair. Master Green rode beside her, smiling down at her as she said something to him. It seemed he was forgiven for his brawl at the banquet, both by the queen and by Violet. Kate only hoped he would not do such a thing again, would not break Violet's sweet heart.

Kate remembered what Dr. Dee had said about Master Constable, that the younger man had great powers within him but could not yet control them. That seemed to be true of all young men at court, even if they possessed different powers. Charm, warrior instincts, good looks, ambition—magic. They were all dangerous.

"It is quite astonishing," a low, amused voice said at Kate's shoulder.

She glanced back to see Lady Bess Martin, a friend of Catherine Grey and of Lord Hertford's sister Lady Jane, as well as of Anne Godwin, watching the scene out the window. Lady Bess was the daughter of a very old family, once allied to the Seymours in their highest days of power under Edward VI. She was pretty, fashionably dainty, careful in her duties to the queen, but like everyone else she seemed to always be watching. Always smiling carefully, as if she knew many secrets.

In that she was no different from any other courtier.

Yet somehow Kate did not quite like the slant of her smile now.

"Astonishing, Lady Bess?" Kate said, careful to keep her voice most pleasant, most bland. She was meant to go unnoticed here at court. That was where her own power resided.

"Violet Roland and Master Green," Lady Bess said. "He is becoming one of the most sought-after gallants at court this summer, I do think. Yet he pays his greatest attentions to *her*."

Kate made herself keep smiling back. Surely Lady Bess knew that Violet was Kate's friend, that they shared a chamber. Anne Godwin was their mutual friend. Why would Lady Bess be gossiping with her now? "Mistress Roland is most amiable company for anyone, as I'm sure everyone must agree."

"Oh, I do think so! She is very sweet," Lady Bess said with a trilling laugh. "But her family . . ."

The Rolands? Kate thought quickly but realized she knew little of them. Violet's brother served Lord Arundel, of course, a very good position, and their parents lived quietly in the country. They were high enough for Violet to be given a much sought-after place among the queen's ladies. She merely kept looking at Lady Bess, something she had learned from the queen. Silence made people talk to fill it.

"The Rolands are in debt, or so I hear from my friends who live near them," Lady Bess whispered. "We all know a place at court pays little enough. Surely her parents, and her brother, hope that Mistress Violet marries very well indeed. But Master Green has no need of such a thing. Not when he could marry so choosily—"

"Bess! Bess, you must hear this," Lady Catherine called out, and Kate turned to see all the ladies still clustered around Rob, giggling at whatever he was saying. Lady Catherine waved to her friend, and Lady Bess waved back and hurried toward them, already laughing herself.

Kate looked back out the window just as the last of the hunting party vanished over the top of a hill. The trumpets and the baying of the dogs were fading, but her head ached. There were so many secrets, held by everyone around her, and she could not sort them all out. She suddenly missed her father, missed their quiet evenings by the fire talking of music, missed his smile, his gentle eyes.

And yet he, too, had kept secrets from her.

Kate turned resolutely away from the window and summoned everyone back to work. Once the rehearsal was over at long last, she dismissed the other musicians and made her way out of the great hall. She glimpsed Rob on the other side of the long, narrow room, still surrounded by Lady Catherine, Lady Bess, and their fluttering flock of white-clad friends. He tried to catch Kate's eye, but she turned away. She was much too confused for *him* right now.

She had much to consider.

Her own chamber was empty. Violet would be at the queen's hunt for hours yet, and Lady Anne was off on her own errands. She had been most secretive about her day that morning, claiming a vague "duty" she had to carry out, and Violet and Kate had been able to get no more out of her. But Kate was glad of the quiet moments now, the rare time when she could be alone.

She opened her clothes chest and knelt down to dig beneath the kirtles and sleeves, the embroidered chemises and slippers, to find the book she had hidden at the bottom. She drew it out, half-fearful to even look at it.

The volume did not look as if it held great secrets, secrets men like Dr. Dee would spend lifetimes traveling and studying to unearth. It was bound in plain brown leather, the spine worn, the vellum pages soft. She took a deep breath and opened it.

And found she could read almost nothing of it. There were lines and crosses, wavy letters, words in Latin. Drawings of strange beasts.

Boleyn witches.

A sudden noise outside the window startled Kate. She almost dropped the book, her heart pounding. She glanced up, surprised to see that sunlight still streamed in from the day outside. There were no thunder and lightning, no ghostly voices. Whatever was written in that book was still unknowable to her.

And perhaps she did not *want* to know. Not really. Yet still there was that curiosity within her that had long been her downfall. If she was told she could not know something, could not do something, it became all she wanted. Somehow she was sure this book held the answers to so many of those secrets. And there was only one place she could find them.

She knew where she had to go now.

Kate hid the book under her clothes again and caught up her cloak, even though the day was warm. She also hastily strapped a small, light dagger to her wrist, beneath her sleeve. There was still time before Queen Elizabeth returned from the hunt and the night's revelry began, but she had to hurry.

She rushed through the half-empty palace, past rooms where courtiers left behind for the day played at cards and on their lutes, talking together quietly. Servants rushed past her, intent on their own errands. She made her way through the kitchen, the only space still busy as the cooks prepared the food for that night's banquet. The Frenchman who created the sugar subtleties stood perched on a stool, barking orders at the pages who put the final touches on a fragile crystalline creation of a ship. Kate hurried past them, ignoring the steps that led down to the underground room.

She slipped out of the kitchen door into the warm breeze of the day, rushing down the pathways lined with fragrant herbs.

"Kate!" someone called.

She whirled around to find Anthony walking toward her from the knot garden at the side of the palace. He was smiling, as handsome as ever, with the wind tugging at his close-cropped dark hair and his austerely sculpted face set off by a plain dark-green doublet, but he seemed rather—wary.

"Anthony," she said. She felt so nervous when she looked at him, as she had ever since he arrived at Nonsuch. As if she was hiding something from him, which was absurd. He was her friend and had been for so many months, through the bleakest of times.

Her *friend*. That was all. She would never make a good lawyer's wife.

"Good morrow to you," she said, smiling, acting as if she was not hurrying off to anywhere.

"You don't join the hunt today?" he said, studying her closely, as if he could see what she was really doing. Really thinking.

She hoped he could not.

"Nay, I was rehearsing for a masquerade," she answered. "But the ladies grew too weary to continue."

His smile flashed brighter. "Or they wouldn't listen to direction any longer? I have seen the attention span of some of the queen's fair ladies. You might have more luck with some of Mary Sidney's lapdogs."

Kate had to laugh, thinking of Catherine Grey's pouts. "Aye, that is all too true. But what of you, Anthony? Is your work done for the day?"

His smile turned serious, and he suddenly looked every inch the lawyer. The respectable professional he would soon be. "Master Hardy is in counsel with the duchess. She is most overset by that sad discovery in the garden. She wished to speak to him alone."

Kate nodded. She could feel the concern in her own frown before she could conceal it, and she feared he saw it too. The whole court tried to pretend like the carefree summer spun onward as if nothing had happened, but a shadow had been cast over it that would not be easily banished. Was the duchess worried about her son? What could the Seymours have to do with Dr. Macey?

"It was most upsetting for everyone, I fear," she said. "The queen's summer has been very merry thus far, at Richmond and Eltham. But here at Nonsuch..."

Anthony studied the palace over his shoulder, and his frown deepened. She had the sense he saw what she did as he studied the glowing windows, the fanciful stonework, the plaster statues of gods and goddesses. A beautiful facade, with dark eyes peering out from behind, always watching.

"The sad bones in the garden would have nothing to do with why you're rushing off so suddenly, Kate?" he said, a hint of humor in his voice.

Kate felt her cheeks turn warm. She looked closely up into his face and remembered all the times she had confided in him, all the times he was so quietly understanding. The time he held her above the freezing river as she shivered and cried, so happy to be alive and so frightened.

Suddenly, she was so very tired of being alone with her thoughts all the time, alone with her worries. Of groping her way forward, alone, through a world she only half understood. Of never trusting anyone, never daring to believe what they said because they had proven her wrong so many times.

Anthony *had* helped her before. He had helped her

discover truths buried in old law books when she wouldn't have even known where to begin looking. He had shared her curiosity, her need to know what had happened, and he had patience and quiet sense she did not.

She *wanted* to trust now. She did not want to face that cottage alone.

She stepped closer to him, close enough to whisper. Even though it seemed no one else was near, she knew how deceptive that was. No one was ever alone at court.

Anthony bent his head down to listen, his expression never changing.

"It *does* have something to do with the bones," she said close into his ear. "There have been some—unusual events lately that make the queen most uneasy. Perhaps this old tale has naught to do with them, of course, but . . ."

"But you do not believe that?"

Kate shook her head. She heard Master Constable's words over and over in her mind, his mad wildness. *Boleyn witches*. That frantic look in his eyes, as if he was not really there at all.

Dr. Macey had once been involved with just such strange arts as Master Constable. What had he discovered all those years ago that had led him to that shallow grave in the maze?

"Kate," Anthony said, his voice calm and steady. "Are you in danger again?"

Danger? Everything at court was dangerous. But she shook her head. "I do not believe so, and I know now to always take care. But there is something I must do now. Can you come with me?"

"Of course. I would never let you go alone, if you would let me. But where are we going?"

"I must show you. I can't—can't really explain it."

Much to her relief, Anthony merely nodded as if he chased mad ladies across the countryside every day. He was always calm and steady; he would make an excellent lawyer to people such as the duchess and her ilk. He took her hand in his, and his fingers felt warm and strong.

She led him toward the gates of Nonsuch, out to the lane that twisted away from the grandeur of the palace and toward the little village and the hidden cottage beyond. As they hurried onward, Kate glimpsed two figures standing close together in the shadow of the tall stone wall that divided the fine gardens from the forest beyond, their heads bent close and their backs stiff, almost as if they argued. But their voices were too soft to carry on the wind.

To Kate's surprise, she saw it was Lady Anne Godwin and Master Roland, Violet's brother. They had not seemed to know each other well before, but now they were standing so close, speaking so intently. Kate remembered the rumors Lady Bess had told her, of the Rolands' debts.

She hurried onward before Anne could see her, before either of them had to make any awkward explanations. But she could not quite forget the angry, almost desperate look on Anne's face before she turned away.

In the daylight, the cottage was not as fearful as it had been in the mysteries of the night. It was still remote from the village, from any other homes, set back in its own half-concealing grove of trees and an overgrown garden, but the plastered walls and steep tiled roof were ordinary enough. Yet thick wooden shutters covered most of the windows, and smoke curled in dark gray tendrils out of the chimney, despite the warmth of the sunny day.

Kate leaned against the same tree that had shielded her that strange night, studying the cottage. It *did* seem ordinary, just a little, old-fashioned cottage. What had scared her so much before?

Why was she so nervous now?

"Tell me again who you saw here," Anthony said quietly.

Kate glanced over at him. He looked so intent as he studied the house, so calm and still. He steadied her, too. She had told him what she knew of the tale on their walk. Of Dr. Dee and his new pupil, Master Constable, of his search for Dr. Macey's son. Yet she could not quite bring herself to tell him all about that night in Lady Knollys's chamber.

She couldn't bear to see suspicion and coldness in his eyes, if he was to draw away from her at the mention of the Boleyns and their "witchcraft," the old tales from when Queen Elizabeth was a toddler. Not *him*.

"I followed a man here that night," she said. "I saw him from my window, and for some reason I had to know what was happening with him. It was Master Constable. I saw Dr. Dee here that night, and Robert Dudley, too. Men such as that have many secrets, of course, but after everything that has happened . . ."

After everything that had happened, Kate feared the queen was in danger. And the queen had to be protected at any price.

Anthony frowned. "You must not put yourself in danger thus, Kate," he said, almost fiercely. "After London last winter . . ."

Kate's fingers curled on the rough bark of the tree; she was half glad he felt protective of her, half scared that she felt glad. No one had ever worried about her before, except her father.

"Do you think I do not remember?" she said. "I am

as careful as I can be! I must learn how to make my own way through the court, with people who hide so much. I must be with the queen. She is . . ."

The queen—who was her cousin. The queen, so young and impetuous, so intent on her pleasure and freedom after so many years of fear and danger. The queen, who was the hope of everyone who longed for a safe, peaceful England, after the fires of Queen Mary.

Kate felt a flash of anger, yet she knew not toward what—or whom.

Anthony laid a gentle hand on her shoulder, and she felt a calm settle over her. She thought of the queen and her temper rages, and the way they quieted when Robert Dudley took her hand. "Kate, you are the bravest person I know. The most caring, too. I worry about you; that is all. Please, let me help you now, if I can. Don't go running about the countryside alone at night. Men like Dr. Dee—they know things, seek things, most of us dare not even think about. If you were in danger . . ."

Kate nodded. She didn't *want* to do things alone always, but she had learned that sometimes one had to jump alone into the darkness. Yet another thing Elizabeth had taught her.

But it was undeniably reassuring to have Anthony at her side now.

"I will take care, Anthony, I do promise," she said. "I have no desire to learn the secrets of the spirits." The living had enough secrets; the dead even more. She feared she would never be able to decipher either. "But the queen cares for Sir Robert. If he is involved in all this, in whatever happened to Dr. Macey . . ."

"Surely Robert Dudley was a child then."

Kate nodded. "But Dr. Dee was his tutor, and he has long shown an interest in the mathematical arts. Old loyalties are still strong." She saw that every day at court, the family groups, the friendships, the rivalries.

Old alliances still held from King Henry's time—and some were broken and healed and broken again.

Anthony's jaw tightened. "Aye. I know that well enough," he said, his voice hard, and she remembered his employer worked for the Duchess of Somerset—a Seymour, once allied with the Dudleys against the Boleyns. He redirected his gaze to the cottage. "What do you think they do here at this place?"

Kate studied the cottage again. So ordinary. "That is what I want to find out."

She felt Anthony watching her again, and she did not look at him. Her caution had returned.

"We need to find a way in," he said.

Kate thought of Master Hardy, of Anthony's career. He had worked for years to become a lawyer, to build a career where he could take care of his widowed mother, rise in the world. She could never have the ruination of that on her conscience. "I can't get you into trouble, Anthony."

He smiled, that sudden, almost rakish smile she so seldom saw. She could not quite trust it. "Who will ever know, if we're careful?"

Kate had to laugh. "It looks well secured, I fear, with all those shutters."

"Let us go around to the back and see if there's a kitchen, then. Mistress Hardy is always complaining of how distracted her cooks can be."

Kate thought of the unguarded kitchen at Nonsuch. She nodded, and they made their way carefully from behind the tree and around the low stone wall that surrounded the cottage. Beyond the roughly mortared border, the garden tangled and coiled over the gray rocks, a wild tumble of vines and white flowers. Yet, in the shadow of the house, Kate glimpsed a more orderly patch of what looked like herbs. Angelica, basil, rue, some strange, tall purple flowers.

She remembered the sweetish, greenish smell that seemed to cling to Dr. Dee and wondered if the herbs were part of whatever work went on here.

Anthony took her hand to help her over a low ditch running beneath the wall, and she was glad of his steady clasp. He didn't let her go as they found their way to the long, low kitchen extending from the back of the house. The door was securely latched, but after testing a few of the windows, they found one left open. Only a *slightly* careless cook, then.

The window was halfway up the wall, slightly above Kate's head, a narrow casement, but she was sure she could slip through. Despite all the grand food at the queen's banquets, she was usually too busy with her music to partake of much.

She tucked up the hem of her skirt. "Can you lift me up there?"

He gave the window a doubtful look. "Are you quite certain?"

"Of course. I can surely fit . . ." She eyed his broad, strong shoulders in the fine green wool of his doublet. "Though I fear you could not. I can make sure no one is around inside, and go open the door for you. I wouldn't be alone long."

He still looked doubtful. Finally, he gave a reluctant nod and held out his hands for her to rest her booted foot on them. He lifted her easily, and she had the fleeting, whimsical thought that hours with law ledgers had made him no less strong than a lean acrobat like Rob Cartman. She caught at the window ledge and pulled herself up and through.

She landed somewhat carefully and quietly, barely managing not to tumble into an ungraceful heap on the floor. She found herself in a kitchen that was blessedly deserted. The large fire was banked, so that wasn't the source of the smoke that could be seen outside. The faint smell of roasted meat hung in the air.

Kate held her breath for a moment, listening carefully. There was none of the usual bustle of a household; she could hear only a faint clanging sound from somewhere.

She leaned out of the window and waved to Anthony that she was safe. He nodded tersely and turned to make his way back to the front door.

Kate crept up the narrow stairs that led from the kitchen to the main part of the cottage. It was a rambling old place, with narrow corridors of uneven wooden floors, low ceilings, and many little rooms opening off the halls. The rooms were empty and sparsely furnished, the plastered walls bare of tapestries or painted cloths. She tried to tiptoe as the floor creaked beneath her, and she listened cautiously at every corner.

She encountered no one, no servants, not even a dog or cat. That faint metallic clanging noise still sounded somewhere overhead, but no voices or footsteps. She made it to the door without being confronted, but also without finding anything of interest at all.

What if Dr. Dee and Sir Robert Dudley had only used the cottage as a meeting place on that one occasion, and left nothing at all behind to help her decipher what was happening? She felt a pang of disappointment at the thought.

She released the bar at the door and let Anthony slip inside. At his raised brow, she shook her head and gestured toward the ceiling, where she heard that strange noise.

He nodded and took her hand again. They made their way through another series of narrow hallways until they found a winding staircase with another corridor stretching away at the top. It was quiet behind every closed door there, too, except for one. As Kate and Anthony got closer, the clanging noise became louder and louder.

Kate gave her free wrist a little shake, glad of the weight of the dagger strapped there. She had learned never to be without a weapon in the mucky lanes of Southwark last winter—thanks to the lessons in sword-play from William Cecil's man.

She pressed her ear to the wooden door and listened carefully. Her heart pounded in her ears, and she felt half-afraid, half-excited. Was that how soldiers felt be-fore battle began, when things were still quiet, uncer-tain?

Even through her exhilaration and fear, she noticed that the door was made of new, thick, polished wood, unlike everything else in the old house.

She could hear no voices, only the crackle of a fire and that steady metallic clink. She cautiously tested the door handle, and to her surprise it turned under her touch.

She felt Anthony close at her back, his hand on her arm as she peeked past the open crack of the door. There was no person there, but what she saw made her gasp, and his hand tightened as if he would pull her away. That sharp greenish smell she had noticed before stuck thick in her throat. It reminded her of Dr. Dee and the garden.

She pushed the door open and slipped inside. She had never seen anything like it before. It was not a large room, and the tightly closed shutters, which let in only cracks of daylight, made it feel even smaller. Ev-ery bit of space was filled.

The walls sloped gently up toward a slanted beamed ceiling, and shelves of books and rows of trunks fastened with strong padlocks lined each side of the room. Long tables held more stacks of books and ledgers, quills and inkpots, compasses, rulers. There were large, valuable globes in brass stands, and more strange metal instruments she could not recognize. On one table lay a spread of prosaic platters of half-eaten bread and cheese, a goblet of wine, and a pottery pitcher painted with blue flowers. A roaring fire in the large grate lit the entire scene.

All manner of glass vessels were arrayed before the fire, filled with liquids that bubbled and popped and shimmered. A large press stood to the side of the grate, and a pale greenish trickle slid into a bowl below it. The press was creating the strange clanking noise.

Alchemy? Was that what was happening here? She had read about such things; everyone had. Alchemy was the dream of every kingdom. Yet she had never seen it before.

Kate took a cautious breath. The smoke that emanated from the fireplace was an odd violet-gray color, and the smell Kate noticed, that cold, sharp metallic tinge, was stronger. It stung in her nose and throat.

"An alchemical lab," Anthony murmured. She glanced up at him and saw her own astonishment reflected in his green eyes.

"No wonder they keep it away from the court," she said. Despite the fact that Dr. Dee's horoscopes were so very fashionable, that Robert Dudley and his powerful friends favored the mathematician and studied astronomy and such themselves, there were those at court of a more staunchly religious mind who would never approve. Who would say the queen was not a true Protestant for encouraging such practices.

Boleyn witches.

Kate shivered despite the blasting heat from the fire. She turned away from the sight of all the strange, bubbling containers and scanned the books on the table. Volumes in Greek, Latin, German, all languages she knew not.

At the end of the table, its pages lying open and flat, she glimpsed something different. A ledger handwritten on stiff vellum, slightly yellowed with age.

There were circles and triangles, overlaid with strange letters that made no words she recognized. It seemed to be the same handwriting as that in the book hidden at the bottom of her clothes chest. She quickly scanned the letters and symbols, trying to commit them to memory so she could compare them later.

Something else caught her attention. A large, square stone set in a gold frame, weighing down a pile of close-written loose pages. It was deepest black, yet shimmering with faint, sparkling flecks, like the ring that had been taken from Dr. Macey's skeletal finger.

Kate's stomach clenched at the sight. What *was* that stone? She had never seen one like it before now, and here were two of them. Was it like that shew stone Master Constable had used for the séance—only even more powerful?

She felt compelled to reach for it, as if in a dream.

Suddenly, Anthony grabbed her arm. She gasped, feeling as if she had been indeed dragged abruptly from a deep sleep. She was shocked and afraid that she had lost control, even for an instant.

"Someone is coming," he whispered hoarsely in her ear.

Kate listened carefully, and indeed there was a heavy thudding sound of footsteps on the stairs outside. She felt even worse for not paying attention now, when it was so vital.

The footfalls were coming closer. She glanced around the room frantically. The shuttered windows were too small to go through, and too high up from the ground anyway. There were no concealing cloths on the tables.

But there *was* a large cupboard in the corner.

She grabbed Anthony's hand and dragged him behind her. There was no time to look for other concealment, no time even to think. She yanked open the cupboard doors, and luckily there were only more books piled there, and none of the luridly colored liquids or eerie black stones. She pushed the volumes aside and crowded in, drawing Anthony with her.

They pulled the doors closed behind them just in time. Whoever it was came into the room, and Kate heard the footsteps pause as the person seemed to look around. Kate dared not even breathe. Her lungs ached. She and Anthony were packed in close in the stuffy darkness, and she leaned against him, glad she was not alone.

She glimpsed a tiny beam of light coming through a knothole in the wood, flecks of dust sparkling as they floated past. Holding her breath, she leaned closer and peered through the ragged hole.

The room was distorted through the opening, narrowed to just one tiny slice of the book-laden table. A shadow fell across it.

Kate twisted her head around and pressed her eye closer. She glimpsed a man—tall, very thin, clad in a plain russet doublet, his back to them as he sorted through the piles of documents. He had pale reddish hair, overly long, straggling from beneath his cap.

She had a sudden, disturbing memory of the grayish red hair still clinging to Dr. Macey's skull, and she shivered.

His hand turned over a paper, and she gave a quickly stifled gasp. On his finger was a black stone ring, just like Dr. Macey's. Like the large one on the table.

Anthony's hand tightened on hers, and she bit her lip to keep silent. The man didn't seem to find what he sought among the papers, and he suddenly pounded his fist down on the table, making Kate jump.

"Blast it, Mother," he muttered. "I've told you not to clean in here."

Kate couldn't help but gasp at his sudden angry words. She clapped her hand over her mouth, but it was too late. Suddenly, he whirled around and jerked open the cabinet door. Kate fell back into Anthony with a cry, and he protectively pushed her behind him.

"Who are you?" the man shouted. His face, thin and pale, dotted with freckles, flamed orange-red to match his hair. "What are you doing here? If you think to find my secrets . . ."

Kate felt Anthony's shoulders tense, as if he would pounce on the man, and she knew a brawl would gain them nothing. She laid her hand on his arm, holding him still.

"We have come seeking no secrets," Kate said calmly, soothingly. "In fact, I believe it is *you* we have come to seek—Master Macey."

CHAPTER TWELVE

The man fell back a step, his mouth open in astonishment. "How do you know my name? Who are you? How did you get in here?"

"One question at a time, please." Kate eased herself past Anthony and out of the cupboard. Her legs ached after being shut in there, and she would have stumbled and fallen if Anthony hadn't caught her. "I was not *sure* you were Master Macey until you yourself confirmed it, but Dr. Dee said his old teacher Dr. Macey's son lived nearby. It would make sense you wished to continue your father's work."

Master Macey snatched a curved blade from the table and brandished it wildly in her direction. It appeared he possessed no instruction in swordsmanship, as all the noblemen at court did, but that blade looked wickedly sharp. Kate held her hands up.

"I vow I mean no harm," she said. "I merely want to talk to you. I am Kate Haywood, musician to Queen Elizabeth, and this is my friend Anthony Elias, a lawyer from London. I fear I was among those who found Dr. Macey in the maze at Nonsuch."

The blade lowered a bit, and the man's eyes widened. "You found my father?"

Kate nodded. She would have taken a step forward, but Anthony held tight to her arm. "I am sorry. I had no idea Dr. Macey had a son living near Nonsuch, until Dr. Dee told me."

He scowled, but the blade lowered even further. Kate hoped that was a good sign. "You spoke to Dr. Dee?"

She nodded. "He told me you were here to continue the important work your father began so long ago." That was not strictly true, of course, but surely it was easy for anyone to see that was what was going on here. The bubbling cauldrons, the glass vials, the strange books—what else could all this be? And it seemed to be such important work that even Robert Dudley was a part of it, mayhap its sponsor.

"You came from the court, from Dr. Dee, then?" Master Macey demanded.

Kate nodded again. "I haven't been able to forget your father. I—I just wanted to know more about him, to meet you."

Master Macey frowned suspiciously. "Why hide in the cupboard, then?"

Before Kate could answer, Anthony's hand tightened on her arm, and he said, "You had no servant to attend to your door. After what happened to your father, we were afraid something was amiss."

Anthony's tone was so firm, so confident and assured, that Master Macey nodded and lowered the blade even more. "I only have a cook here, and she does not come every day. My mother cleans, but not in here—not usually, anyway. We cannot be too careful."

"So I see." Kate took a slow step toward one of the tables, studying the two glass ewers resting in brass stands. One held a garnet-colored liquid, one pale green, and a slender tube ran between them. Master Macey watched her closely, but he made no move to stop her. "Was this your father's work, then? Alchemy?"

"Sorcery is against the law, you know," Anthony said.

Master Macey whirled around on him, his face reddening again. "My father was no sorcerer, and everything he did was in full knowledge of King Henry! It was the king who gave him the coin for his equipment. He had studied in Prague and in Amsterdam and knew all the newest theories. He was sure he was very close to success, if only he could find that one last key. The king had all faith in him. If he had not vanished—had not died . . ."

Master Macey's voice caught as if on a sob, and Kate gave him a gentle smile. "What happened when Lord Marchand accused your father of treason? Was it because of this work? What did King Henry say then?"

Master Macey shook his head fiercely, his face so red she almost feared he would faint. "Lord Marchand took back his foul accusation and left court! I know not why he said what he did—I was only a child then—but it must have been some personal reason. My father would never have betrayed the king. He could never have finished his studies without royal funds."

Kate thought of what she knew thus far of Lord Marchand, which was not much beyond the fact that he had dangerous friends such as Thomas Culpeper, and she decided she had to let the topic rest for now. "And your father perished soon after. Mayhap that is another reason why you are here, instead of taking your work far away? To find out what happened to him? I know Dr. Dee would very much like to discover the truth, and he is your master now, is he not?"

"I told you, I was a mere child then," Master Macey said between gritted teeth. "Whatever quarrels my father had were not important. My only task is to finish what he began here."

Kate studied the documents in front of her, the strange symbols like those in the book she now hid. She knew she should give it over to Master Macey, or to Dr.

Dee, but she could not. Not yet, not until she knew more. "Dr. Dee said if an alchemist is not spiritually pure, he can never find success in any experiment. That inner harmony is the only way to find the ultimate harmony of the universe."

Master Macey gave a cautious nod. "That is true. It's one of the first things any student of the celestial arts must learn."

Kate glanced back at Anthony, who stood nearby with his arms crossed over his chest. Like any good lawyer, he kept his expression unreadable. "Could your father have been doing other—work?" she asked. "Perhaps something for the king? Something that would prevent the complete purity of these experiments?"

Master Macey's fist tightened on the hilt of the knife. "I told you—my father was no dark sorcerer! He would have had no congress with demons, for any purpose."

"Nay," Kate said quickly. "Not demons. Dr. Dee would surely never have learned from anyone such as that. But something more earthly, perhaps. King Henry's court held many dangers."

Master Macey looked slightly mollified. He nodded. "I could not say. I told you, I was only a small child then, and my mother could read very little herself. But she did say . . ." He paused, looking away hesitantly.

"She did say what?" Kate urged. "Please, Master Macey. Any small bit of information could help us find out what happened to your father—and stop it from happening to anyone else."

Master Macey's jaw tightened. "My mother said my father had been given a most important commission, one that was meant to be complete by the time King Henry arrived at Nonsuch. He was to draw up the horoscope of Queen Catherine Howard, so the king could present it to her at a grand banquet."

The horoscope of a doomed queen? It sounded like

a most dangerous proposition indeed, just as Dr. Dee had said. "And then what happened?"

"He never finished it, or perhaps never even began it. Such a horoscope was never found among his things. My mother did fear it led to my father's disappearance, especially after what happened to the poor queen. My mother is a simple soul and thought it was dark spirits. She now refuses to speak of it."

"Meddling in the affairs of kings can indeed be a dangerous folly," Kate murmured. She thought of the queen, of all the enemies around her.

"And of angels and spirits, if one does not yet understand their ways," Master Macey said, his tone dark, sad.

Kate glanced up at him, surprised at the tears that suddenly shimmered in his eyes. "Do you speak of Master Constable? Does he not understand the ways of the universe?"

Master Macey gave her a grim nod. "I heard what happened when he went to the queen's cousin. Dr. Dee has often warned him away from such doings. To foretell the fortunes of monarchs is indeed treason."

Kate well remembered what had happened in Lady Knollys's room, and she thought Master Constable had probably not meant what he said then. Dr. Dee said his apprentice had not yet learned to harness his spiritual powers, whatever they might be. And he had obviously not harnessed his courtly skills, either. "And perhaps, too, his soul is not pure enough to balance the humors of the heavens?"

"Master Constable should have a care," Master Macey said. "I hope he has learned that now. Dr. Dee insists that both he and Master Constable work with me. Dr. Dee is a connection to my father, and I could not do without him. But Master Constable . . . Well, I allow him so I can work with Dr. Dee."

"And all you wish to do is finish your father's work," Kate said. Was that not what they all did? She with her music, Master Macey with his experiments—the queen and her father's unsteady throne.

Master Macey looked away, his eyes bleak. "It is all I have of him, mistress."

Kate thought of her mother, of the lute with Eleanor Haywood's initials carved into its wood. She nodded. "I will leave you to this work, then, Master Macey. But please know the queen herself has asked me to look into these matters. I wish only to see things made right."

"Only the heavens themselves can do that." Master Macey gave her an abrupt nod and turned away to reach for another book. It was obvious he had said all he meant to.

Kate knew there was nothing left there for her to discover—yet. She took one last glance at the strange room, taking in the bubbling vials, the clouds of steam. Surely the key to understanding Dr. Macey's writings was there somewhere, but it was not yet in her grasp.

She left the house—by the front door this time—with Anthony close beside her.

"Did you find what you sought there, Kate?" he asked as they turned down the lane. The country breeze felt warm and clean after the smoke of the cottage.

"Not yet," she said. "But soon, I hope. I think there is someplace else I must look . . ."

CHAPTER THIRTEEN

"I told you—these matters are very delicate. They take time. The spirits have their own methods . . ." Master Constable felt the cold, prickling trickle of sweat inch its way down the back of his neck. He feared it showed on his brow as well, and if there was one thing he'd learned in Dr. Dee's employ, and among people such as this, it was to *never* show fear or doubt. Even here, in the presumed sanctuary of their alchemical laboratory.

And especially to this person. Constable had already taken the coin. Already spent it. At first it had seemed so very easy. Dr. Dee seemed the deepest fool for not doing such simple tasks himself. But now Constable saw there was naught easy about it.

Everything had gone horribly wrong, and he could see no way to make it right. Whatever he did, one powerful force or another would be angered.

How had he dug himself into such a morass? Why had he ever come to court at all?

But he knew too well why. Greed, ambition. The burning need for something beyond his parents' country hovel. And a certain lady's blue eyes. Eyes that never even saw him. Not when she looked only at that silver-tongued varlet, Green.

Fear burned through his veins like quicksilver. Constable buried his face in his hands, unable to look at the person across the table from him. The person who had seemed a savior at first, the answer to all his troubles. Now he saw that this person opened a world of troubles beyond any other he had ever known.

A pile of books went flying from the table with one swipe of a gloved fist. They clattered to the floor, crashed against the wall, delicate leather spines cracking. Constable shrank down lower on the bench, sure his own spine would be next.

"The spirits be damned! I made no bargain with them. 'Twas *you* who took my money, you who knew your task. It was a simple one, and you bungled it." The person leaned over the table, and behind Constable's tightly closed eyes it seemed a devil loomed there, a dark, winged shadow that blotted out the sky. "I do not deal kindly with swindlers; nor does my master."

Constable cringed. Indeed he had heard tales of what happened to lower sorts who meddled in matters too high for them. Look what happened to Dr. Macey— bones in the mud of the garden.

Had he been as stupid as Constable?

"I—I shall make it right," he said, trying to sound confident, placating. Not a pleading, powerless little mouse. "What happened in Lady Knollys's chamber was beyond my control. But the queen does not leave Nonsuch for several days. There is time . . ."

"There is no time." The fist pounded down on the table again. "You will do what you were paid to do. Now."

"I— Perhaps I can pay you in something else. Something far more valuable!"

The menacing figure paused, and Constable felt a wild hope rise in him. "More valuable?"

"Aye—a . . ." Constable thought quickly, his thoughts racing as they never had before. "A book! A recipe for the secrets of alchemy, written by Dr. Macey himself long ago. No one else knows of its existence."

And nor would he, if he had not found it in its secret hole within these very walls. No one needed to know he had quickly lost it, though. He would surely find it again. He *had* to find it again.

He squeezed his eyes shut and prayed silently, desperately.

"Perhaps we could renegotiate," his tormentor said. "But only after I see the book. Bring it to me. Soon."

Constable opened his eyes just in time to see a swirl of dark cloak, the door slamming behind his tormentor. Constable was alone again, yet it seemed as if creatures swirled above his head, pointing, laughing. Just as those demon boys always had at the village school.

He buried his face in his hands again, panic squeezing through him like an ice-cold vise. When Dr. Dee had taken him on as a pupil, when he found himself at the queen's own court, he was sure those days were gone. That he would return home rich and powerful, a beautiful lady at his side, and they would all be sorry.

But he was the one who was a fool. He had gone too far, and now he would pay for it, just as Dr. Macey had. Unless he could act quickly—yet he did not even know where to start.

His frantic gaze fell on Dr. Dee's precious shew stone, resting on its brass stand, all calm, clear opalescence. Not at all like it had been that night he secretly borrowed it.

It was true, what he had said. What happened that night at Lady Knollys's had been beyond his control. He didn't know what had happened, no matter how many times he went over it, in the dark of sleepless nights. He was set on his task, the simple action he had to take in exchange for the payment. And then . . .

Then everything went black in his mind. He had no

control of his body, his words. Dr. Dee had warned him many times of such things, of the incomprehensible forces that lurked all around, waiting, watching for any chance to enter the mortal world once again. They sensed any vulnerability.

That night descended into chaos, and he had lost his chance. The chance to get his paid message to the queen, through the cousin she trusted. How would he find another chance? The Boleyns would surely never speak to him again. . . .

A sudden thought came to him like the pinprick light of a star through a dark night. Lady Knollys and Lord Hunsdon were surely not the *only* ones Queen Elizabeth trusted. There had to be someone else who would listen.

He frantically tried to remember who had been there on that terrible night, who had watched what happened. The faces were all a blur.

But he remembered the musician girl, who had been staring down at him with large, dark eyes as he came back into himself. Amid all those screams and cries, she was the one still point. Her eyes—surely he had seen them before, or ones very like them. But where?

Constable shook his head. It mattered not. What mattered was that the girl often played for the queen, was often in the royal company. Perhaps she could be persuaded to murmur a word or two for him? To help him redeem himself, and earn that coin?

He frowned, remembering how she had seen him that day he so foolishly tried to creep into the queen's bedchamber. Desperation had made him think he could find something there to help him in his task, or a place to leave something that would persuade the queen. He should have known it would be too well guarded, even when the queen was gone, but he had felt compelled to try anyway.

Mayhap the musician girl had forgotten? He tried hard to remember, to picture her that day. Had she been distracted with her own tasks? He could barely recall. Surely it would be worth it to try to talk to her.

He would try anything now, anything to make it right. And then he would never meddle in such matters again.

He thought of Dr. Macey's raw bones, dumped in the mud, and he shuddered. Perhaps he would even give up his studies and go home to learn to farm. But he knew, even in the clammy grip of terror, that he was not yet *that* desperate.

He still had time to fix things.

The door suddenly opened, and he bolted upright in fear. Surely his tormentor could not yet have returned! No one could expect him to have acted so quickly . . .

Yet it was Dr. Dee who stood there. Dr. Dee, who had gone to work in their hidden laboratory before the sun even appeared. Constable's master looked tired, gray faced beneath his black skullcap, his beard tangled.

He closed the door quietly behind him, watching Constable closely. Dr. Dee always did seem to see far too much. It was one reason why Constable had worked so hard to become Dr. Dee's apprentice. He wanted to know his secrets.

But he did not want to share his own.

Constable slowly sat back down, struggling to push down his fear, to seem normal. As normal as he could on any such day, anyway, with Dr. Macey's body lying somewhere below them and the rehearsal for a lavish royal masquerade going on as if naught had happened.

"How do your studies progress?" Dr. Dee asked calmly. He went and poured himself a goblet of ale from the tray a maidservant had left that morning. He cast a cool glance at the books scattered so violently on the floor. "Not well?"

"I— Forgive me, Dr. Dee," Constable stammered. He hastily knelt down to gather up the volumes. "A mishap only. My studies progress well enough. How did you fare with your work this morning?"

Dr. Dee shrugged. "It is slow still, I confess. Timothy Macey is sure we shall soon see a change, but we need Dr. Macey's notebook. Without it . . ." His gaze, so dark and inscrutable, sharpened on Constable. "Are you sure you have not yet come across it? It may not be apparent what it is at first glance, you know."

Constable felt his face turn hot at the memory of that book, with its indecipherable symbols and brittle old pages. The one he had so foolishly taken with him to Lady Knollys's, and which had then vanished. Another matter he had to take care of before it spiraled beyond his control entirely.

If it had not already.

"Not—not as of yet, Dr. Dee," he said. "I am sure one of the maids merely put it in the wrong place among all these volumes. We have so many books, and when we travel . . ."

Books maidservants so often refused to touch, even to dust, for fear of what they contained. So few people would ever be capable of deciphering Dr. Macey's work. Constable himself was only just beginning to learn. It was one of the things that had led him into such trouble.

Dr. Dee nodded. "Keep looking, then, as I shall. We must find it, soon."

"Of course." Constable ducked his head as he gathered the fallen books. He had to solve *all* of this, and very soon. The musician girl was a desperate hope, but surely a hope nonetheless. He had to find a way to talk to her. And there was only one thing he was good at . . .

*   *   *

The stupid hedgepig! Why was everyone at the queen's court so simpleminded? Were they not supposed to be quick, ambitious, witty? Yet they bungled everything, at every moment. Even supposed magicians were hopeless.

The cloaked figure paused at the top of the hill, near the fantasy of a banquet hall that had been built to please a seemingly unpleaseable queen. The small window of the tower where that imbecile Constable lodged could just be glimpsed. *That* was the biggest disappointment of all. It had seemed so easy—pay the man off to do a simple task.

But it had all gone so wrong, and Master Constable had brought unwanted attention down on all their heads. It would make the task all the harder now. And yet, just perhaps, it could make the reward all the sweeter.

"Father was right," the figure whispered. If one wanted something done, one had to do it alone. The whole family could be ruined now.

Or one could turn the mistakes of others to a rare advantage. Was that not what everyone at court did anyway? Boleyns, Seymours, Dudleys, Greys. The world was always turning, one family up, one down.

When would it be *their* family's turn?

Soon. Very soon indeed. And if that bungler Constable, or anyone else, got in the way, they would be very sorry.

What was Master Constable doing?

Kate caught a glimpse of the strange man as she made her way down the corridor toward the stairs leading to her chamber. He was scurrying along, looking to neither the right nor the left. He didn't even seem to notice when he nearly bumped into a group of peacock-plumed courtiers who shouted after him. He dashed around a corner, his black robes flying out behind him.

Kate hurried after him, trying to keep him in her sights. Robert Dudley had said the man bore watching, and she had to agree with him. First he had been loitering around the queen's rooms, and now this. It could be entirely innocent, of course. She herself was often distracted when working on a new piece of music; perhaps he had some experiment that preoccupied him. But could it really be so distracting all the time?

The man seemed oddly—haunted.

She turned the corner just in time to see him dash through a doorway. She followed, but by the time she got there he had vanished. It was a crowded room, with nothing odd about it that she could see. Why would he go this way? She frowned as she studied the gathered courtiers, nodding at those she knew, such as Master Green. He, too, seemed distracted.

Kate frowned. Ever since they had come to Nonsuch, everything seemed so odd! She couldn't make sense of it.

"Kate! There you are. Violet and I have been looking for you everywhere."

Kate glanced back to see Lady Anne Godwin hurrying toward her. Anne smiled, but even that looked strained to Kate's now suspicious eyes. Anne took her arm and led her back toward the doorway.

"We are meant to play primero this afternoon, remember?" Anne said with a laugh. "Where are you running off to so quickly? Has the queen sent you on another errand?"

"Nay, I—Anne, did you happen to see Master Constable when you came in?"

Anne gave her a puzzled glance. "Dr. Dee's pupil? The fishy-looking pale one? Nay, not at all. But I daresay I wouldn't notice him if I had. Whyever would you be looking for *him*?"

Kate looked again at all the faces around them. Everyone watching everyone else. "No reason at all. He just seems rather—suspicious, I think."

Anne laughed. "Him? I don't know why you would worry about him at all. Now, come, the cards await . . ."

CHAPTER FOURTEEN

"My brother would like me to marry Master Longville, you know. He has quite changed his mind about him," Violet said as she and Kate strolled through the garden. Her tone was casual, light, as if she commented on the fine blue sky overhead.

But when Kate glanced at her, startled by the sudden words, she saw that Violet's pretty face looked pale and tight, her eyes just a bit too wide, too shimmery. She held a yellow rose between her fingers, and she had twisted the stem into a knot.

Kate looked toward Master Longville, where he walked ahead on the gravel pathway with the Duchess of Somerset and her daughter Lady Jane. The duchess's walking stick made emphatic taps on the stones. Longville seemed to be in earnest conversation with her, his somber dark doublet blending in with her usual black gown and veil. He was good-looking enough, surely, with his sandy brown hair and earnest eyes, and he did seem to like Violet very much. He was always near her, it seemed, and had been since before the court left on the summer progress.

And yet there was something about him that made Kate feel a twinge of disquiet she could not quite decipher. Romance and marriage were far beyond her knowledge.

"I am quite sure your brother wishes only for your happiness," Kate said carefully.

Violet gave a harsh laugh that contrasted too roughly with the merriment emanating from the grassy hillside nearby, where the queen and some of her courtiers played at blindman's buff. Queen Elizabeth, shining all in white and silver, her loose hair bound back with the silk blindfold, twirled in a circle, laughing, reaching out to catch at the people swirling around her.

"My brother is fond of me, I daresay," Violet said. "But since he has come to serve Lord Arundel, it seems he has changed."

Families were another thing Kate knew little about. She and her father had always been their own small family, never needing to speak much to know what the other was thinking. "Changed in what way?"

Violet shrugged. "When we were younger, he was so lighthearted. He would always include me in his games, would tease me, make me laugh—which he still does, of course. But now he seems so serious, so worried and preoccupied all the time. Our family always lived a quiet life when Mary was queen, as so many did who followed the 'new faith.' I realize now I liked it that way. I used to dream of court, of banquets and dancing, but in reality life at home was finer. But not my brother. He has so many ideas to raise us in the world."

Kate thought of Lady Bess Martin's tidbit of gossip, that Master Roland was in some debt. Life at court was vastly expensive. Even with a position with Lord Arundel, one of the wealthiest men in England, it would be an easy thing for an ambitious young man with a sister as maid of honor to the queen to overset his finances.

But what sort of debt was it? And to whom?

"How would marrying you to Master Longville do that?" Kate asked. She tried to recall all that she knew about the man, but it was not much. He came from a deeply Protestant family, one that had once been loyal to Queen Anne Boleyn. They had gone abroad when Mary was queen, as Lord Hunsdon, Lady Knollys, and the other Boleyn families had.

"He has many manors, one of which is near to my parents' home. They would like to adjoin the estates, I think," Violet said. "And he is of the Protestant faith, just as my parents are. My brother also likes that. He is devout, no matter what appearances may say."

Violet gestured toward Master Longville and the duchess. "My parents were once friends of the Seymours, and I think my brother would like to renew that connection. He believes that Lady Catherine Grey may one day be the queen's heir, and perhaps Lord Hertford her consort. Though that is a secret, of course," Violet said carelessly, as if talking of such dangerous matters was as nothing. She looked angry, distant, so different from the sweet, merry friend Kate had come to care for.

"But you do not agree with him," Kate said. "You do not like Master Longville?"

"Oh, Kate!" Violet gasped. She pressed her trembling hands to her face, and Kate reached out to touch her shoulders, concerned at such strange behavior. "It is just—I like someone else so very much. Too much."

Kate shook her head, afraid for Violet. "Master Green?"

Violet nodded, gasping as if she would try to keep down the tears. Hide her feelings, as a courtier should. "Aye. He is so wonderful, and I think—I hope—he also cares for me. I can think of no one else when he is near."

Kate's concern grew. It was true Master Green was handsome and charming, but he had also become embroiled in that fight with Master Constable. And so many ladies seemed to enjoy his company. "Has he declared himself to you? To your brother? And has your brother rejected Master Green's suit in favor of Master Longville? But he and Master Green seem like such good friends." That would surely explain Violet's strange behavior today, if her brother had suddenly become so changeable.

Violet shook her head. "He hasn't, yet I fear if he did my brother would just send him away. I think they have quarreled. It's as if working for Lord Arundel has put a plan in his mind, and he won't be turned from it. Somehow Master Longville is part of that plan, and I don't know why." Her voice rose on a wail, and Kate tightened her grasp on Violet's arm, trying to calm her. "What has happened to my family, Kate? Why can I not be happy as others are in their marriages?"

Kate pulled her friend into her arms and murmured quiet, soothing words into her ear. Over Violet's shoulder, she stared at the merry game on the hillside, the spinning giddiness of the silks and satins. Lady Catherine Grey stood near Lord Hertford, the two of them laughing, their hands nearly touching as if they forgot where they were. Then skidding away when they remembered. If others gossiped about Lady Catherine being the queen's heir and Hertford being her intended, did they know?

The queen reached out and curled her long white fingers into a velvet sleeve that belonged to Sir Robert Dudley. Sir Robert laughed down at her, so dark and piratical, so handsome. The perfect counterpart to her gold-and-white beauty.

She drew him closer, tracing her fingertips over his face in soft, gentle caresses. The arch of his nose, his lips, his close-cropped beard. She snatched off the blindfold to stare up into his eyes. For an instant, it was as if they were the only two people there.

Why can I not be happy as others are?

For an instant, Kate felt an unfamiliar longing in her own heart, the longing to feel thus and have someone look at her in that way. Yet look at what happened when love vanished, as it always did in one way or another. Queen Anne Boleyn was killed when her husband tired of her, as was Queen Catherine Howard, not long after her golden days here at this very palace. Kate's own mother had died, leaving her father heartbroken. Work was all there really was. All that could be relied upon.

She closed her eyes, thinking of Anthony and how he had helped her break in to the cottage. Of Rob Cartman and the ambition that was always burning in his eyes.

Violet was right. Why *could* they not all be happy, as normal people should? But serving a queen was not normal at all.

"I am sure all is not so bleak as that, Vi," Kate said. "Have you spoken to your brother, told him what you have told me? Surely Master Green would be just as good a match as Master Longville. He and your brother could patch up their friendship. If he knew your feelings . . ."

Violet shook her head again, but Kate could see a faint hope slowly kindling in her eyes. "Yes! Yes, I will speak to him, and surely he must listen. He shouted at me last time I tried to make him see that I must be happy, but he is my brother. A brother should consider his sister's happiness. Aye. I will speak to him right now . . ."

But the next time Kate saw Violet, she found her facedown on her bed, sobbing and kicking her velvet shoes into the counterpane. Her brother was not, after all, so concerned with her happiness, and insisted she would marry whom he said. Violet would not be comforted, no matter what Kate or Lady Anne said.

Perhaps she had been mercifully saved from families after all, Kate thought with a wry laugh. She had left a distraught Violet with Lady Anne Godwin, who would surely be a good one for hatching a plan for the next volley against Master Roland's plans for his sister, and gone out for a short walk. Her head was spinning, and she desperately needed to clear it if she was to be of any more help to Violet.

Aye, she thought, families could surely be a curse instead of a blessing. When she was younger, she had longed for siblings, for aunts, uncles, cousins. It was only her father and herself. Now her mind was full of Violet and her quarrel with her brother, of Lady Knollys and all her children, of the tribe of Boleyns. Where did duty to family end and duty to oneself begin?

The raucous games on the hillside had settled into a more sedate picnic under the shade of several bright green spreading trees. The ladies looked like flowers on the grass, their skirts spread around them, with their gallant suitors offering tidbits and wine. The queen held out a morsel for Robert Dudley, laughing as he took it from her fingers with his lips.

Master Longville sat on a stone bench with the Duchess of Somerset, still deep in conversation with her. What did they have to talk about so seriously?

Did Master Longville truly love Violet? Kate wondered. Or was there another reason he was so intent on the match? She thought of what Master Roland had said about the value of old connections, and she knew she needed to find out more about what he meant.

Kate turned a corner on the gravel pathway and found herself facing the green hedge walls of the maze. She froze for an instant, transfixed by the memory of what had happened the last time she was there. Screams, bones. The mud. Red cloth. Had she missed anything that day, any clue she should have paid more attention to?

Dared she go in now? She knew she should look closer, but still it made her shiver.

"Mistress Haywood!" someone called, and she was glad of the excuse not to step into those leafy shadows just yet. She turned to see a maidservant hurrying toward her. "I was asked to give this to you, mistress, as soon as possible."

Kate took the rolled and sealed scroll the girl held out. It looked much too formal to be a quick message. Had the queen sent it? "Who gave it to you?"

"Master Constable, mistress, Dr. Dee's man. He said you should have it urgently."

Master Constable? What could he possibly have to tell her? "Thank you," she murmured absently, her thoughts racing. The girl hurried away, leaving Kate alone again, staring down at the scroll in her hand as if it were a serpent that would come to life and bite her.

She glanced back, just barely able to glimpse the queen's picnic. The laughter and bright colors, the flirtations—they all seemed a million miles away.

She plunged into the maze, suddenly sure she needed to be alone to read the message. The dark-green walls closed in around her, cool and lush, smelling of the fresh, damp earth. It seemed to be a place that could hold so many secrets, so many whispers from the past. It could hold hers, too, if she would let it. The deeper she went, the more it seemed to surround her.

So deep was she in her own thoughts that it took her a moment to realize she was not entirely alone in the maze. She heard footsteps, steady, deliberate, crunching on the fine gravel, somewhere beyond the hedge wall.

That was not unexpected, of course. The maze was part of the garden, open to everyone on that fine day. But something deep inside of her seemed to seize, as if in warning. A sense that something was not right. When she'd had those feelings before, she had ended up almost drowning.

She shoved the documents quickly into the pouch at her belt. She hurried her steps until she was nearly running around the next corner.

No one was there on that new path, but the footsteps were even louder behind her, getting closer and closer, and she couldn't tell from which direction they came. She ran on, her skirts tangling around her legs, hobbling her. She reached a dead end, nothing in front of her but a thicket of green branches, unbreachable. She had to turn back; it was the only way.

But before she could spin around, she heard a sudden strange *whooshing* noise, like a hundred wings descending. Someone shoved her hard from behind, and she tumbled down onto the muddy ground. A heavy weight landed on the back of her head, and as a red-hot rush of pain hit her, everything went blurry.

Kate struggled to keep from falling down into darkness, to keep from giving in to the blinding explosion in her head. She shoved herself up from the ground with her torn palms and twisted around. All she could see through the haze was the swirl of a black cloak, vanishing around the corner of the maze. She screamed as loud as she could—and then everything went black.

"Oh, Kate! You poor, poor girl. Are you still in pain? Do you need another bolster? Here, let me get you more wine . . ."

Kate had to laugh at Violet's fussing, her fluttering around their small chamber to fetch blankets and mix up possets. It felt good to know someone cared, that someone was there to help her when she needed it. Ever since her screams in the maze summoned running guards who had carried her to her chamber, she had barely been alone for a moment. She'd had to send everyone away for a few moments, claiming she needed to use the chamber pot, just to have time to hide the paper Constable had given her. Thank the stars no one had tried to change her clothes before she did that.

The queen sent her own physician, as well as spiced wine and sweetmeats. Mistress Ashley insisted on making her own recipe for a strong, healing posset, and Violet and Lady Anne never left her bedside. Lord Arundel kept sending messengers to make sure the masque would be able to go forward. And Anthony, who was barred from the room by the ladies, sent bouquets of white roses.

Violet and Anne kept up a steady chatter, but neither of them talked of their romantic woes now. Violet seemed determined to forget the disquieting scene from earlier, to deny that she might indeed have to forget Master Green and marry Master Longville. And Anne didn't speak of Master Roland at all. Kate began to think she had imagined the two of them talking together so intently near Dr. Dee's cottage. Perhaps it had been merely a casual encounter between acquaintances.

But she knew very well she had *not* imagined what happened in the maze. Every time she shifted against the pillows, she felt the ache of bruises, remembered the raw fear of those strong hands shoving at her back. She saw again the black cloak swirling away, like the giant ravens at the Tower.

She shuddered. It was too much like when she had tumbled down the stairs at the Spanish embassy last winter, the raw panic, the cold flash of certainty she was going to die.

And yet—surely the fact that someone had gone to all the trouble to chase her through the maze, to frighten her, meant she was close to discovering something. But *what*? How could whatever happened to Dr. Macey so long ago threaten anyone now?

As Violet tucked a blanket closer around her, Kate shut her eyes tightly and went over what she had learned lately, little as it seemed.

None of it seemed to fit together, like a poor hand of cards at primero. She couldn't slot all the disparate suits into place, and it made her want to scream with frustration. She needed to get out of that bed and talk to more people!

She curled her fists tight into the velvet counterpane, crushing the fine fabric, to keep from shouting out one of the queen's favorite oaths. Lady Anne glanced up from her embroidery and frowned.

"Are you in pain, Kate?" she asked. "Shall we find another of Mistress Ashley's possets?"

Kate shook her head. That was the *last* thing she needed. Kat Ashley's herbal possets, which she distributed most enthusiastically whenever anyone was ill, were much too potent. They made Kate feel fuzzy and dazed, when she most needed to think clearly.

"I am well enough," Kate said. "Perhaps I should just rest for a while."

"I could read to you," Violet said. "Some of those new poems from Florence! They are so very romantic . . ."

She suddenly pouted, as if she remembered how romance was going so sour in her life just then. But she smiled, determined and bright, a mask like everyone wore at court.

"Perhaps we should leave Kate alone to sleep for a time," Lady Anne said, setting aside her sewing and rising from her stool. "Come, Vi, we will walk in the garden for a time."

Violet looked most uncertain. "But what if Kate should be seized with illness again, and be too dizzy to call for help?"

"I will be very well," Kate hastened to say. She would be glad of an hour alone with her thoughts. "There are servants walking past in the corridor all the time; someone would be sure to hear if I called out."

Lady Anne at last persuaded Violet to leave for a while, and Kate was finally alone. She carefully eased herself out of bed and went to open the window, longing for a breath of fresh air. One of Mistress Ashley's nursing dictates was that a fire must burn at all times, the windows firmly closed against any noxious breezes. It was most stifling on a warm summer's day.

Kate glimpsed the queen walking in the garden, her crimson gown and bright hair a splash of brilliant color against the green hedges and gray stone path. Only two ladies followed her, Mary Sidney and Lady Bess Martin, and next to her was not Robert Dudley, but the somber brown-clad figure of William Cecil. He spoke closely in the queen's ear, and she scowled but did not answer.

It must be a most solemn discussion of state matters, then, Kate decided. The real world hardly ever intruded on the dream of Nonsuch.

Kate could hear nothing from so far away. She left the window to fetch a shawl to wrap over her chemise and tidied away the ewers of wine and half-empty goblets. She went to tuck Lady Anne's abandoned sewing back into her workbox, and as she did so she noticed the half-formed monogram worked on the snowy linen. Entwined *A* and *R*.

Anne . . . Roland? Was that what she meant to stitch there?

Kate could not solve all her friends' romantic dilemmas, she thought as she replaced the embroidery where she had found it. She could hardly make sense of her own. But she was learning, ever learning, there at court.

She returned to her bed and felt around beneath the bolster until she found what she had hidden there—the scroll Master Constable had sent her. There had been no moment alone to look at it, and she was aching with curiosity to know what it might be.

She brushed off some of the dried mud and broke the seal to unroll it. She found it was not one page but two, a smaller wrapped inside a larger. The vellum was newer, whiter, on the larger one, the ink dark and fresh. She found to her chagrin that she could read neither of them.

Yet she *did* recognize what they were. She had seen such things among the queen's papers and in Lady Knollys's chamber. There were twelve equal sections, divided into a wheeled chart, each section covered in tiny writing, strange symbols like lines and circles and squiggles. They were horoscope charts. She carefully studied them, even though she knew she would need to find a guide to decipher them.

The older one had a date at the top, *July 1523, the Year of the Bleeding Moon*. The signature at the bottom was *TR Macey*, with the year 1541. The year Catherine Howard came to Nonsuch with the king.

The year Macey had vanished. Perhaps this was one of the last horoscopes he had ever drawn up. But for whom? For the queen herself, as Master Macey said his father was meant to do? She carefully studied the signs again, and something about them made her feel cold. Maybe he had never even given it to the subject? Why did Master Constable have it now? And why would he give it to her?

Kate set it aside to study the newer document. There

was a date at the top. *January 11, 1540*. She gasped in surprise. That was her birthday. The day her mother died.

There were strange, crooked lines and ominous-looking Latin words. Yet there was nothing at all to tell her what it meant. If this was indeed her own horoscope, how could she know what it was telling her?

Then again, she remembered how wrong Master Constable's horoscope for Violet sounded. How he told her she was of a "melancholic" nature and had to marry immediately to keep the unhappiness at bay and the humors in balance. She also remembered how beyond all control he seemed at Lady Knollys's séance. What *were* his powers, if any? Could she trust this at all?

She had to find someone who could help her read these charts. Yet who could be trusted to keep them a secret? She needed time to think about it all, yet she sensed that was one luxury she did not have. The court would not be at Nonsuch long. She had to find out what Constable wanted in giving these to her, of all people.

She started to carefully reroll the two horoscopes and suddenly noticed tiny black letters on the back of the smaller one, almost too small to be seen. *Boleyn, Beware.*

Kate clapped her hand to her mouth to hold back a cry. Surely these were part of the reason she had been attacked! No Boleyn was safe now, it seemed. Did her attacker know her true lineage?

A knock suddenly sounded at the door, making her drop the papers. She hastily shoved them under her bolster again and crawled back beneath the blankets. She tried to look fragile and ill, as if she had heeded all warnings and would be meek and biddable from then on.

But if she *was* a Boleyn, she feared there was no chance of that.

"Enter," she called.

To her surprise, it was not a servant or a doctor, or Mistress Ashley with more of her possets, but Rob Cartman. He looked uncertain as he stepped inside, almost wary.

"I heard that you had a fall, Kate," he said quietly. He crossed his arms over his chest, staying near the door.

Kate nodded. That was the tale the queen had given out, that Kate had tripped and fallen in the garden, suddenly seized in a faint. She didn't know who would believe it, not after Dr. Macey was found in the same maze, but none dared question the queen.

"I will recover soon," she said. "We will have Lord Arundel's masque as planned—and Lord Hunsdon will see your theatrical skills on full display. That is what you came here for, aye? To find a new patron?"

He looked surprised, but he covered it very quickly with a smile. "That is not the only reason I came here, Kate. I wanted to see you again."

To see her? After so long with no word? Kate could not believe it. "Why? I have heard naught from you in many months."

"But you saved my life, when I was trapped in gaol. I can never forget that. Never forget how brave you were, how . . ." Rob broke off on a growl and raked his hand through his hair. The golden strands stuck straight up, and somehow it made him even more handsome.

Yet was he acting, as Kate feared he always was?

"We must all earn our bread in the world," he said quietly. "I am responsible for my uncle's troupe now, and the only way I can do that now is by finding a patron any way I can—or else tramp along the roads in all seasons. I know you understand. You must work just the same."

Kate nodded. She had no dowry, no fine family—at least none that could be anything but a deeply buried secret. She had her music, loved serving the queen. But sometimes . . .

She closed her eyes. *Nay.* Some things could not be changed. She had a fine life, all on her own, and she was fortunate for it. She didn't need to be thinking of love or marriage.

"I will help you finish the masque," she said. "I should be well enough tomorrow."

He nodded, but his expression shifted from wariness to—what? She couldn't read his eyes now. "Kate—was it truly only a fall? You are not the sort to be clumsy."

Did he care? She couldn't hope for that. Not now. She forced herself to laugh. "Everyone trips over obstacles sometimes, do they not? I am well, I promise."

"I do hope that you are being careful here at court, since your father is away," he said quietly. "You need someone to protect you."

Kate gave a wry laugh. She was learning how to protect herself now. She had to. "You are one to talk about being *careful*, Rob Cartman. You have been in danger every moment I have known you."

He laughed, too, and suddenly he looked like the man she had first known at Hatfield. Young, impetuous, almost arrogant. Fun. "It does come with being an actor. But I would not wish such a life on *you*. I had no choice in the matter; I had to be an actor like my uncle. But you have a choice."

He looked as if he wanted to say more, and Kate remembered that he had said his uncle once came to Nonsuch, too, to play for the old king. His uncle had fallen into a deadly fate. Surely Rob would not do the same?

He suddenly turned and left the chamber, the door

clicking shut behind him, and Kate was alone again. She slipped her fingertips under the bolster and touched the horoscopes hidden there. If she could read them, would they tell her what she should do? Because she feared she would always be unsure of where to turn next.

CHAPTER FIFTEEN

"I cannot bear to talk of such things today! My head aches," Queen Elizabeth cried. "Why must we speak of this now? I am to meet Sir Robert at the stables to look at a new mare. He is Master of the Horse and most careful of his position."

"And that is exactly why we must speak now, Your Majesty," William Cecil answered. His tone was quiet, careful, but taut, as if his patience was close to snapping. "Because of the great amount of time you have been spending lately with Dudley."

Kate bent her head lower over her lute, trying to play as quietly as possible while still having the song as an excuse to stay in Elizabeth's bedchamber. Trying to shrink farther back into the window seat so she would be forgotten. She had stayed in bed for only a day, but she had insisted on getting up to attend the queen that morning. She couldn't lie alone thinking anymore.

It was a beautiful summer afternoon, the light peachy golden outside the window, the breeze smelling of sweet roses. Outside the tents, tables were laid out for games of primero, and there were plenty of goblets of wine and platters of fruit for a lazy afternoon. Couples rowed on the lake or lingered in the shade of the Grecian temples. But Elizabeth was still in her chamber, still dressed in a lace-trimmed bed robe with her hair loose over her shoulders. Only Kat Ashley and William Cecil attended her. She had sent everyone else away.

Except for Kate, half-hidden behind the heavy brocade drapery.

Elizabeth leaped to her feet, nearly toppling over her chair. Her cheeks were a hectic pink, her eyes blazing. "How dare you, Cecil! I am the queen. I shall have friendships where I choose. Robert Dudley and his family have long been most loyal to me, to the Protestant faith."

Kat Ashley reached out as if to touch Elizabeth's arm, to soothe her, but the queen shook her away. The lush Turkish carpets muffled each of her steps as she paced back and forth, and Cecil simply watched her silently from where he stood near the door, leaning on his ever-present walking stick. His lined, bearded face looked weary and resigned, yet calm.

"No one questions Sir Robert's faith, Your Majesty," he said. "Yet it is because you *are* queen that I must speak to you thus. Surely you remember the dangers of the road that brought us here? The dangers still around?"

Elizabeth's head whipped around, her hair like a rope. "No one needs to remind me of what it took to claim my rightful throne," she shouted.

"Then you know that Philip of Spain would love nothing more than to gain a foothold in this land again," Cecil said. "That Mary of Scotland is now Queen of France and claims to be the rightful queen of England as well. A scandal now could be ruinous, not just here but in courts all over Europe. Sir Robert Dudley is married, Your Majesty, no matter how ill his wife might be. If it was thought you were . . . romantically entangled . . ."

Elizabeth's hands shot up, her long fingers curled

into fists, only to crash down on a table. Silver goblets clattered to the floor, spilling wine on the priceless carpets. "What care I for gossips? They will always say whatever they choose, no matter what I do. Sir Robert is my friend. I spent too long without friends, too long being careful of every step, every word. Cut off from everyone I cared for." Her angry shout faded to a hoarse murmur, deeply sad. "Do I not deserve to enjoy my life now? Just for this summer?"

Cecil's mouth tightened. "You have an entire kingdom to think of now, Your Majesty. And it is in danger. You must marry and give your subjects an heir, if we are not to return to life as it was under your sister's rule."

Elizabeth dropped down onto a stool, shaking her head. But there was no denial, even for her. "My reign is but new. There is time for such things later."

Cecil shook his head impatiently. "There is no such time! Not any longer. Mary of Scotland will not wait to press her advantage. You must choose a suitor. Soon. It should have been finished months ago."

Elizabeth waved her hand as if she would push away his words. "Have I not always had a care for my people, at every moment? I care for them now, and they love me. I saw it on the journey here, as did you. I do have time, just for a little longer."

"There is Archduke Charles of Austria," Cecil pressed on. "A most suitable choice. A younger son, so he would reside here in England. Young and vigorous, they do say."

"I will marry no Catholic!" Elizabeth cried. "Look what happened when my sister married one."

"Then Eric of Sweden," Cecil said. "Or the Duke of Casimir. Or Lord Maitland of Scotland, who is on his way to visit your court even as we speak. Or even an Englishman of some suitable rank, if you must. But it must be very soon, Your Majesty."

"I told you—I need no one to tell me of my duty to England," Elizabeth said through gritted teeth. At least it was no longer shouting. "I will look at every candidate most closely, Cecil, I promise you. But I will not be bartered off like a cartful of turnips, locked away to be a mere broodmare to some foreign lord."

"Then will you at least meet with the privy council tomorrow, Your Majesty?" Cecil said. "There are many matters to discuss, marriage only one of them, and you have not sat with them in weeks. The papers that must be signed are barely looked at."

"It is summer, Cecil," Elizabeth said, her fingers tapping a frantic pattern on the wooden arm of her chair. "We are on progress, meeting our own people, enjoying the fair weather, the peaceful days. There is to be another hunt tomorrow, I think, and a masque."

Cecil bowed his head, but even Kate could see the stony set of his expression.

Elizabeth sighed. "Very well. I shall meet with the privy council in the morning. Now I am tired. I must rest before tonight's banquet."

Cecil nodded at this dismissal and turned to leave the chamber. Through all his years of serving Elizabeth, and her father and siblings before her, he knew when to press and when to retreat. When to let the queen turn matters over in her own mind and reach her own decisions.

As he passed Kate's window seat, he leaned close for a moment and murmured, "Shall we speak soon, Mistress Haywood? I have heard it has been some time since you had a lesson in reading codes. We need all the help we can find now, I think."

Kate could only nod mutely, her lute going silent in her hands. She, too, had missed the brief lessons she took from his men after the coronation, and she wanted to be of help in any way she could now.

As the door closed behind him, Kate turned back to look at the queen. Elizabeth raged silently, throwing books to the floor, her cheeks flaming a hectic, fevered red. Kate longed to run to her, but she knew she could not. Not now, when the queen was caught in the grip of a temper. Kate knew too well the feeling of being trapped by circumstances not of her own making, a family too complicated to fathom. Even Kat Ashley stood back, watching Elizabeth with tears in her faded eyes.

"My lovey," Kat said sadly. "You do know what he says is true. We have all waited so long for this time, for when you would be queen. We have worked and sacrificed for it, for *you*, so you could fulfill your destiny. Robert Dudley is not worth the ruination of all that."

"Enough!" Elizabeth screamed. "I will hear no more of it, not even from you, Kat. Do you understand? No more!" And she snatched up a heavy glass perfume bottle from her table and sent it crashing against the wall.

Kat Ashley retreated, her face buried in her hands. Elizabeth collapsed to the carpet.

Kate had never been more uncertain of what to do next. The queen at last sat huddled on the floor, her hands clutched in her loose hair, as still and pale as one of the marble statues in the garden. Kate knew Elizabeth would never want anyone to see her thus, so vulnerable.

But neither could Kate bring herself to leave Elizabeth alone. She had seen the queen merry, laughing, dancing, angry, furious. But not so sad—not since Hatfield, when Mary was queen and everything was so dangerously uncertain.

At last, Elizabeth pushed herself to her feet. She moved slowly, carefully, as if she was much older than her twenty-six years.

Elizabeth shook back her hair and sat down again on

her abandoned seat. She smoothed the satin of her robe with her hands, and her dark eyes stared ahead into something surely no one else could fathom. Slowly, the sounds of the day outside trickled back into the chamber, the laughter, the voices.

Kate was sure the queen had forgotten she was still there. She started to back away, to leave Elizabeth to her haunted thoughts, but the queen suddenly turned sharply to look right at her. Her cheeks were still a feverish pink, her eyes burning.

"Do *you* also say I should marry, Kate?" she said, her voice hard, old.

Kate shook her head. "I say Your Majesty is the only one who can say what is the right action for you to take."

Elizabeth sighed, and her shoulders slumped. Her posture was usually so perfect, so regal, but now she fell back in her chair as if she was unutterably weary.

"You remember what it was like at Hatfield, I know," Elizabeth said. "Every moment so uncertain, so full of fear. Now . . . now I just wanted to know what it was like to be free. But the bars of the cage are closer than ever."

Kate swallowed hard. She did not know what to say, how to comfort the queen, a woman whose entire life had been one of uncertainty and danger, ever since her mother died when she was three. She was now the most powerful person, man or woman, in the land, yet she was still surrounded by terrible risk.

"Robert Dudley is one of my oldest friends," Elizabeth said softly, musingly, almost as if she was alone and speaking to herself. "We were in the Tower at the same time when my sister was queen, and he has always served me well. Always been one of the few people I could speak to honestly, as a person, a woman, not a princess. And I worry about him, about us. I do. And he's so worried about my safety and now this mess with Dr. Dee, about what was found in the garden maze. Dr. Dee was his tutor once, and they've often corresponded over the years . . ." Elizabeth's voice trailed off. "I do have hopes the hunt and masque tomorrow will distract him. You will help me with that, won't you, Kate?"

Kate slowly nodded. "I will always help you, Your Majesty. I hope you do know that." But Kate feared she could do only so much for the queen she loved. Maybe Master Constable had been right. The stars would never align for them now.

But then again—the stars could only predict. Humans themselves had the power to change events, and Kate intended to find her power now. She had to, for all their sakes.

CHAPTER SIXTEEN

"'Perchance I may prefer thee well, for wedlock I love best! It is the most honorable estate, it passes all the rest.'"

Lady Catherine Grey was much improved in her role as the goddess Juno, Kate was relieved to see, as the flock of her goddess acolytes danced across the stage amid clouds of white silk. She had learned her lines and even seemed rather enthusiastic as she waved her arms gracefully over her head and sang of the joys of relinquishing a single state for romance and marriage. Maybe she hoped, as Lord Arundel did with this masque, to persuade Queen Elizabeth of the benefits of marriage.

Or perhaps her smiles had to do with the crowds of courtiers who had gathered outside the open windows of the great hall to watch the rehearsal—including Lord Hertford, who had escaped from his mother. When Kate glanced at him over her lute, she saw that he observed Lady Catherine with a moonstruck smile on his handsome face. A smile that only widened as she spun around so fast her frothy white skirts swirled up to reveal her satin shoes and fine silk stockings.

Kate sighed. At that point in the rushed rehearsals, she could hardly care *why* Lady Catherine had learned her role so well, only that she had done it. Lord Arundel wished for the queen to see the masque that night, after the banquet, before she left Nonsuch, and there was still much to be done.

As Kate started to play her lute, she studied the scenery that was almost in place, the outline of the spires of the goddess's temple in the background, the sylvan, nighttime glade where Juno and Diana met. Workmen hurried around to hang up the last of the sparkling stars among the clouds of white cheesecloth, guided by Rob Cartman. She hadn't been able to speak to Rob about anything but the play, which suited her well. She wasn't sure what to say to him when she was so confused.

But she had to admit—he was all too handsome, laughing in his loosened russet doublet, his white linen shirt half-unlaced. And too many of the other ladies noticed, too.

Kate quickly turned her attention back to the play. Everyone seemed to be learning their parts well, all most eager to impress the queen. Yet Kate feared she was the one distracted today. She couldn't forget Roland and Green, their former friendship seemingly forgotten for some mysterious reason, and Violet's tears when she was so sure she would be forced by her brother to marry Master Longville.

She glanced over at a group who sat near the open doors to the hall. Violet was with Longville today, yet she seemed most distracted when he tried to talk to her. Green was nowhere to be found. But she knew she should not concern herself with romances now. The queen was upset, and Kate found herself nervous about making her way around the palace alone. Every corner seemed to hold some shadow, dark places that could hide an unseen villain ready to hit her over the head. The mysterious symbols on those unreadable horoscopes kept flashing through her mind.

She needed to find time to speak to Master Constable.

She looked back to the large crescent moon that hung over the stage, the shimmery silver symbol of the goddess Diana and her virginity. The carpenters of the Office of the Master of the Revels had done a splendid job with it. It was large and smooth, glowing as if lit from within.

Kate frowned as she glimpsed a small flaw in the glossy silver surface. A dark smear along the curve of the crescent, making the perfect line of it uneven. She kept on with her playing as the ladies danced, half listening to Lady Catherine, and told herself to remember to have the carpenters lower the moon and fix it.

Yet when she looked again, the dark mark had become even larger. It spread slowly over the bright silver, like a lurking shadow or a slithering snake.

A terrible memory flashed through Kate's mind as she stared up at the moon, a vision of Rob Cartman's uncle sprawled dead in a grassy meadow at Hatfield before Elizabeth was queen. The dark crimson, almost black, blood that had oozed from his arrow wound. Slow, steady, and horrible.

Almost as if time itself had seized and slowed, the room around Kate turned blurry. She didn't hear the song, only a faint, distant humming sound, and the colors of the people around her and the elaborate scenery of the stage all swirled together. But that spreading line of red was vivid and clear. As she stared at it, her whole body felt as if it was turned to ice. As cold as the bones of old Dr. Macey.

And slowly, slowly, a scarlet drop slid from the tip of the moon and dripped down onto the stage below.

Then, like a shot from a cannon shattering a stone wall, everything sped up. More of the red flowed down from the moon and splashed over the draped white muslin and satin gown of Lady Bess Martin. Lady Bess shrieked and frantically shook her arm, making everyone spin toward her.

Lady Catherine Grey's delicate face contorted with anger. "How dare you interrupt my song, Bess!" she shouted, only to break off on a shriek of her own when she saw the stain on her friend's sleeve.

All the other ladies broke into screams, the scene onstage descending into madness as they pushed and tripped over one another, toppling painted trees and ripping down swaths of cheesecloth meant to be meadow mist. Even the watchers outside the windows, who didn't know what was happening, were shouting.

Lord Arundel, who saw his glorious masque crumbling around him just like his hopes for a royal match, jumped up from his seat in the gallery overhead, yelling incoherent words.

"It's the moon," Kate said. She could have sworn she screamed the words, that they were torn from her throat, but in reality they barely escaped her lips.

Her lute hung from her limp hand, and someone grabbed her arm, yet she couldn't turn away from that awful moon. It was like something from one of Mistress Ashley's posset-induced fever dreams, too fast and too slow all at the same time, unreal. She longed to escape, to open her eyes, leap up from bed, free herself. But this was *real*. Too real.

"What is happening, Kate?" Violet screamed, and Kate realized it was Violet who held on to her arm. Violet who shivered so hard her trembling whipped through Kate like a winter storm wind. Kate took Violet's hand, but she still couldn't look away from the stage.

The moon began to sway, slowly at first, then faster, faster, whirling on the heavy chain that suspended it from the ceiling.

Sir Robert Dudley leaped onto the stage, closely followed by his ever-present guardsmen. "Move, everyone, now!" he shouted. He scooped Lady Catherine into his arms and practically tossed her to one of his men. The other ladies jumped down onto the floor, just in time.

The moon broke free from the chain that held it to the beamed, gilded ceiling and crashed onto the stage. The planks of the temporary dais splintered, the false trees shattering.

And caught just behind the edge of the crescent, in the raw wood hidden by the coat of silver paint, was a crumpled, red-stained doll.

Nay, Kate thought numbly as she stared at the horrible scene being enacted right in front of her. Not a doll. A body, stiff with death, splashed with blood. Real blood, not stagecraft.

A cold, clammy, sick feeling seized her, and she clutched at her stomach. She forced herself to swallow back that sour, sick taste and peer closer. She had learned much in the last few months, first at Hatfield and then at the queen's coronation, and one thing she remembered was to always, always notice details, even if they were most trivial.

Even when what she *really* wanted to do was flee, screaming, as everyone else was.

The body was that of a man, clad in a crimson-stained shirt and dark hose, the hair tangled and matted over a face turned away. The clothes were what blinded her for a moment, made her fail to recognize him at first, for she had seen him only in astrologer's black robes before.

But as she made herself look at the face, at the

twisted features, the eyes frozen wide with fear, she saw it was Master Constable. She would never be able to speak to him now.

And surely it was not the spirits who had killed him and stuffed him inside that wooden moon, but someone all too human.

CHAPTER SEVENTEEN

"He did not do this, Kate! I am sure of it. He never would," Violet sobbed against Kate's shoulder.

"Hush, now. All will be well," Kate murmured, wrapping her arms around her friend. She was far from believing her own words, though. After the terrifying scene in Nonsuch's great hall, someone would have to pay for this crime so order could be restored to the queen's court—soon. She had to hold Violet up now, but she also needed to find out more about this horrible murder. She couldn't do that locked away in the palace with the queen's hysterical ladies.

And Master Green had certainly been seen to quarrel with Master Constable, in front of everyone. Who better to blame for the man's murder?

That was why she stood in the village lane with Violet now, watching as Lord Arundel himself locked Master Green away in the gaol. Nonsuch was too small and built for pleasure, not for dungeons, so Green was to be kept there until he could be hauled to London. Arundel's jowled face was red and furious at having his wondrous house thus befouled and his marital chances with the queen spoiled.

Master Roland stood beside his employer, his face granite hard and unreadable as he watched his friend being accused of a heinous crime. The houses along the narrow lanes were locked up tight, as they had been ever since the royal retinue arrived with the prisoner, though Kate could see curious eyes behind shutters.

"Violet, you need to go back to the palace," Master Roland told his sister, not looking at her. "Now."

"Nay, I will not!" Violet cried. "He is your friend, brother. Surely you cannot believe this of him."

It was Lord Arundel who answered. "He brawled with Master Constable in front of everyone, Mistress Roland. Surely he had some deep grudge against the man. Who else could it have been?"

Who else indeed? Kate remembered everyone at that scene in Lady Knollys's chamber, the fury and fear. All the people whose horoscopes he had drawn up. Who knew what was in those? What the man had done in London, or before he had come under the tutelage of Dr. Dee?

But Lord Arundel was right. Master Green was known to have a bit of a temper, and he *had* shown his hatred for Master Constable, though no one seemed to know what the quarrel was about.

"Surely *you* believe me, Kate?" Violet said. She spun back to Kate, her hand surprisingly strong as she clutched at Kate's arm. Violet's face was wet with tears, her eyes frantic as she searched Kate's face for confirmation.

Kate remembered Violet's confidences, her love for Green, her determination not to be parted from him, not to marry Master Longville. Now it seemed something much more terrible than marriage to another man would come between them, and Kate's heart ached for her friend.

"He *was* seen arguing with the . . ." The victim. Kate couldn't bear to say the word, and she shuddered to think of that hideous sight, of Master Constable's bloodied body stuffed behind that moon. She had not liked the man, but surely he had done nothing so hideous as to deserve that.

Had he? She thought again of the shouts and fear of that séance, his wild words, and of that day she saw him creeping around the queen's empty bedchamber. Of that strange cottage full of secrets. Who knew what secrets a man like that held inside?

Yet only Master Green had been foolish enough, aleshot enough, to show his anger in front of everyone.

"Arguing with Master Constable," she finished weakly.

"But he was only angry! He forgot about it quickly, as men always do, and thought no more about it," Violet said, hope and fear warring on her face.

"What was the quarrel about, then?" Kate asked.

"It was—" Violet broke off, her expression turning confused. "I—I know not, but it was over and done. I am sure of it."

"Vi." Master Roland came to his sister and gently took her hand in his. Kate saw how tender his eyes were as he looked down at her. "He is my friend, but I also know he is a man of most uncertain temper. That was why I warned you against marrying him when I saw how serious your intent was becoming. I would not wish such a husband for my sister. And now it seems I was right."

"Nay!" Violet cried. She shoved her brother's chest hard, sending him stumbling away. She looked most wild, her eyes wide, her hair escaping its caul, while her brother looked resigned. "You have turned against him now because it is easy for you, but I will not."

"Violet, be reasonable—," Master Roland began. He was interrupted by the loud rumble of a coach making its way down the narrow, rutted lane, accompanied by the thunder of many horses' hooves.

Everyone in the small village, the hamlet that had replaced old Cuddington after King Henry tore it down to make way for his palace, had taken refuge behind their closed doors when Lord Arundel and his retinue appeared. Word that something terrible had happened at court seemed to have spread quickly there. But now they peeked out, cautious eyes between shutters and door cracks, to see who appeared so grandly in their midst.

The coach lurched to a halt. It was not the queen's luxurious conveyance of gold, white, and silver, but a dark-painted, solemn vehicle. It was as if it meant to be unobtrusive, but no carriage so costly and rare could ever be so. Especially not when accompanied by a half dozen liveried outriders, their swords on display.

It was William Cecil who climbed down from the coach, his face contorted with discomfort at the bumpy ride, his walking stick clutched in his ink-stained fingers. Kate was most surprised to see him, as he did not like to travel even a short distance when he did not have to.

"Lord Arundel, you have handled this unfortunate matter masterfully, but Her Majesty has requested that I speak to the prisoner myself," Cecil said.

Lord Arundel scowled, but everyone knew that Cecil was the queen's chief adviser. "Of course. Shall I accompany you inside? My men are assisting the village gaoler with guard duties until Green can be moved to London for further questioning and proper punishment."

"Nay!" Violet screamed. "He is innocent, I tell you. He would never have done this."

"Master Roland, perhaps you would take your sister back to the palace and calm her," Cecil said, his voice weary. "Her Majesty needs all her ladies around her now."

"Of course, Sir William," Master Roland said quickly. He took Violet's arm and led her away from the gaol. She tried to resist at first, but then her whole body seemed to wilt, and she followed her brother toward their waiting horses.

As he lifted her into the saddle, she suddenly spun around to look at Kate. Her expression was fierce and pleading all at the same time.

"*You* believe me, don't you, Kate?" she said. "Someone must believe me!"

Kate could only nod. She found she couldn't bear to add to her friend's sorrow at all. It did look very bad for Master Green. Too bad? Was it all simply too easy?

Violet and her brother rode away, and Cecil turned back to Lord Arundel.

"There is no need for your lordship to stay," Cecil said. "You surely have much to attend to now at your house."

"But this varlet had the temerity to commit his foul crime in *my* house!" Lord Arundel argued. "I should question him myself."

"The queen will certainly wish for a diversion this evening," Cecil said. "You must surely be the one to provide it."

Cecil spoke calmly but most firmly, and Arundel nodded. The queen *would* need to be entertained, distracted, and Arundel would have another chance to impress her—if he could. He departed with much of his retinue, leaving the street slightly less crowded.

Cecil sighed and rubbed his hand over his bearded jaw. "I thought *that* would get rid of the man. Mistress Haywood, perhaps you would accompany me inside? A village gaol is no place for a fine lady, true, as my wife, Mildred, would remind me. But I would like your thoughts on what this Green has to say."

Kate laughed. "I am no fine lady, Sir William." And she had seen foul gaols before.

"Ah, but you are. Even the queen sees that." He offered her his arm, and she took it as he led her inside, his guards following, their swords clanking and boots thudding on the packed mud of the lane.

Cecil leaned slightly on her arm, something she was sure he would not want his own men to see—or for any rumors of weakness to get back to the ears of people like Robert Dudley. Kate was sure the weight of his tasks, such as persuading the queen to marry and making sure her many enemies did not come close, weighed on him. A murder, in addition to all that, could surely make him long for retirement.

But the queen, and the country, needed him.

The village gaoler—a thin, hollow-eyed, graybearded man who had surely not dealt with such serious matters, and important people, in a very long time—bowed low as Cecil ducked his head past the low doorframe and stepped into the small antechamber.

"I fear we have but a small space here, my lord," he said in a whining tone. "We have our own matters to consider, and the queen's safety—"

"I assure you, my good man, that you need not worry about these matters much longer," Cecil told him. "I wish to speak to the prisoner, alone, for a few moments."

"Sir William, are you certain?" one of his men said cautiously. "Green could be of a dangerous temper now."

"I doubt that very much," Cecil answered wryly. "And if he is, you are just here outside the door. Mistress Haywood will accompany me."

Cecil gestured to the gaoler to open the cell door, which he hastened to do, his heavy keys clanking. Cecil stepped inside, Kate still on his arm, and the door closed heavily behind them.

The man who sat on the roughly hewn bench against the damp stone wall didn't even look like the Master Green Kate knew from court. The handsome, flirtatious gentleman who charmed all the ladies with his music had vanished.

In his place sat a slumped figure, his elbows on his knees and his face hidden in his hands. His hair was tangled, darkened, his fine embroidered doublet unlaced and his white shirt streaked with dirt.

Kate couldn't help but feel a pang of pity for him, and for Violet, too. Matters here did appear hopeless indeed.

He glanced up at the sound of the door and leaped to his feet when he saw it was Cecil who stood there.

"Have they come to take me away already?" Green asked hoarsely. He laughed, a half-wild sound Kate had heard from others before, people who were backed into desperate corners and liable to leap any way at all.

"We have only come to talk to you for a moment, young man. I am sure your employer, Lord Hunsdon, will have much to say before you are sent away," Cecil said. "A few moments is all these old bones can bear of this place. But we must find out what happened to Master Constable, and you are one of the only ones who can help us."

"I know not what happened to the man, and I vow that is the truth," Green said. "I have not spoken with him since the queen's banquet."

The banquet where he had drunkenly quarreled with Constable. Kate studied Master Green's face, but she only saw deeply etched lines of confusion and fear. Fear that he had been falsely accused—or that he had been caught? For she knew that was not the last time he had spoken to Constable.

"Yet you did argue with him," Cecil said, still so calm. So affable. "We all saw you there at the banquet."

Green slumped back down onto the bench, shaking his head. "I had too much strong wine that night. I should never have gone near him. But this thought in my mind had been eating at me . . ."

"Was it about Violet Roland?" Kate asked.

He glanced up, his lovely blue eyes, now rimmed with red, wide with surprise. It was as if he hadn't noticed she was there until that moment. "You are Violet's friend Mistress Haywood."

"Aye, I am. And she said that when Master Constable cast her horoscope, he said she should not marry a sign that would render her more melancholic. Is that you?"

Master Green laughed harshly. "She had been fretting about it, afraid that it meant we should never marry. I told her that was arrant nonsense, that Master Constable was no true astrologer, but still she worried." That was why they had brawled.

Kate frowned. Violet had seemed rather concerned about her horoscope when they were on their way to Nonsuch, but now her biggest fear seemed to be that her brother had turned against his friend and would make her marry Master Longville. It was not implausible, though, that she would tell Green she was so worried about the stars, for Violet was of a romantical mind.

Yet something told Kate that was not all there was to the quarrel with Master Constable. Green would not quite look at her now, staring instead at the dirty straw on the floor or the small barred window overhead. His fingers tightened into a fist over and over on his knee.

"So you *do* wish to marry Violet?" Kate said.

"Of course I do!" Green cried. "I love her, and she loves me. I thought we were all but betrothed earlier."

"Until Master Constable's horoscope got in your way," Cecil said dryly.

Green shook his head. "Nay, because her brother seems to think I am not good enough for her now."

"Why is that?" Kate asked. "Does he think you would not treat his sister well?"

"Why would he think that?" Green said, his voice fierce. "I have long been friends with Roland. We shared tutors when we were boys. Our families knew each other, shared a faith even during the days of Queen Mary. My family is not wondrously wealthy, but we are most comfortable. And the position I have with Lord Hunsdon . . ." His face twisted, and he shook his head again. "*Had*, I suppose. My position could have raised both myself and my wife. Roland had no reason to suddenly turn away my suit."

"Unless he decided he preferred Master Longville," Kate murmured.

Green snorted. "Longville. That varlet. Why should Roland prefer *him* as a brother-in-law?"

"Because his horoscope aligns with Mistress Violet's?" Cecil said.

Green shrugged, and his shoulders slumped again, as if a sudden wave of hopelessness washed over him. "The Longvilles' fortune cannot be much greater than mine."

Kate listened as Cecil asked Green where he had been for the last several hours and discovered Green had been on a walk alone in the forest of Nonsuch, thinking about Violet and their future. He didn't think anyone had seen him, for they had all been watching the masque rehearsal or with the queen in her chamber. He could only protest his innocence again.

As Cecil turned to knock on the door for their gaoler

to let them out, Green suddenly reached out and grasped Kate's hand, much to her shock. She looked down at him, at his desperate eyes, and remembered too well what it was to feel such fear.

"Please, Mistress Haywood," he whispered fiercely. "Tell Violet I vow I am innocent of this and that I love her most truly. That I will prove it and find a way for us to be together."

Kate could only nod, for her throat was so tight she could not speak.

"Mistress Haywood, we must return to the queen," Cecil said, and she went with him out of the small cell. The door closed and locked behind them, and as Cecil consulted with the gaoler, Kate studied the antechamber. The small table by the fire, with its official-looking ledgers, the tray of congealing food and puddled ale left from the gaoler's supper. Beside it was a small pottery jug painted with blue flowers, one she realized she had seen before, or one very like it. At Master Macey's cottage.

They left the prisoner in the charge of Cecil's guards, and Cecil handed Kate up into his coach to return to Nonsuch just as another horseman arrived. She saw it was Lord Hunsdon, come to see his employee at last. The man's face was reddened and angry above his beard, and he did no more than nod at Cecil before he stormed into the gaol.

Kate sat back on the velvet cushions as the carriage lurched into motion. It was a beautiful vehicle, luxurious with fine carpet and a gilded ceiling, glass windows looking out at the passing scenery. She had never ridden in a coach before, but she could not enjoy it, for her thoughts raced to keep up with the chain of events.

"Well, Mistress Haywood," Cecil said. He leaned his head back on the velvet cushions of his coach, his face weary. He was not an old man in years, Kate knew, but worry and work had put gray in his dark beard and made him walk with a stick already. "Is he the murderer?"

Kate shook her head. "I am not sure he did it. Surely Violet Roland's concerns about her horoscope would not have kept them apart."

"But a romantical young man deep into his cups might not be thinking so rationally."

Kate laughed, thinking of all the young men Cecil and his wife, Mildred, had fostered over the years, young lords who tore through life with swords waving. She had met plenty of them at court herself. "Nay. But men do quarrel all the time, especially young ones who are hotheaded and passionate. Green did not kill Constable that night at the banquet when he was angry. Surely once he had sobered he would not be so inclined to violence. He doesn't seem the sort to plan such things methodically, and surely he would know that being clapped in gaol wouldn't help his suit with Violet. I don't think he did it."

"But it would not be an easy thing to show he did not."

Kate sighed. "I fear he must have been the only person at court alone just then."

"And one of those who would have been strong enough to move the body and hoist it up into that moon."

"Yet not the only one." Kate thought of the men at the joust, wielding lances and swords. Such as Rob Cartman, the silver knight. Everyone at court was connected in some way, but sometimes the ties were hard to trace. "What know you of Lord Marchand, Sir William?"

Cecil looked surprised at the sudden change of topic. What had Lord Marchand to do with these events? Even Kate hardly knew where she went with such a question. "He is not an old man, but his health keeps him from court. He lives in Sussex. They do say he is a scholar of sorts, interested in philosophy. He often orders books from abroad, but no one can find any illegal works in his shipments. He is unmarried. He inherited the title from his great-uncle."

"And this uncle was the one who served King Henry when he came here to Nonsuch?"

Cecil's weary expression sharpened. "Ah—you think of that unfortunate business with poor Dr. Macey."

"They say Lord Marchand accused Dr. Macey of some kind of treasonous activity," Kate said. "And now Dr. Macey has been found, and another astrologer is dead."

"You think they are connected? After all this time?"

Kate thought they surely had to be, but she could not think how. Not yet. "Not that I can see right now. What happened to old Lord Marchand?"

Cecil shrugged. "He died, though I know not how. He was lucky to escape that trouble over Catherine Howard. Marchand was friends with Culpeper, and we all know how he ended up."

He fell silent, as did Kate, as the gravelly road passed beneath the coach's wheels. She turned over all the people in her mind—Macey and Marchand and their heirs, Green, the Rolands, Longville, Catherine Grey and Lord Hertford, Dudley and Arundel. How did they all fit together?

The coach jolted to a halt before the doors of Nonsuch. The pretty house was quiet behind its courtyards and gardens, a strange occurrence after so many hours of frantic merriment. The queen had to be resting, or mayhap strolling somewhere with Robert Dudley.

"I am also inclined to think Master Green did not do this," Cecil said suddenly. "He seems the sort who appears brash and fearless, but whose guilt would eat away at his heart until he collapsed and confessed all. I have seen such many times."

Kate thought of Violet and all her tears, her certainty her swain could not be a murderer. "Then how do we find the real killer, Sir William? Before he strikes again at the queen's court?"

Cecil gave a rueful laugh as he painfully climbed down from his fine, inconvenient coach. "Ah, Mistress Haywood. If one only knew where to start . . ."

CHAPTER EIGHTEEN

"London," Queen Elizabeth said decisively as she strolled briskly down the corridor, leaving Kate and Cecil to scramble after her. She had been told everything they learned at the gaol, and she made her pronouncement. "That is where you must go, Kate, as soon as possible, to look into Master Green's affairs there, and see if anything can be discovered about what happened to Dr. Macey here so long ago. Whatever can be found out. There is no one else I could send who would not attract too much attention. No one I can trust. But of course you cannot go alone. We will think on a possible escort for you. Perhaps your friend young Master Elias? He seems a most responsible sort . . ."

With that, she turned a corner and was gone, Cecil still holding out documents for her signature, even after their quarrel in her chamber. The queen was still the queen and would answer to none.

Kate had to learn from her example. Surrey seemed to hold only dead ends, like in the garden maze itself. Perhaps there would be more to discover in the crowded streets of London.

She whirled around on her heel and hurried toward her own chamber to begin packing and thinking of where to search first once she reached the city. She also had to find Violet, tell her of Master Green's message, and try to comfort her. But she stopped when she glimpsed a black robe and black cap in the gallery ahead of her.

"Dr. Dee!" Kate called after the dark figure. "I wonder if I might ask you something."

He turned and gave her a distracted smile. "Of course, Mistress Haywood. Is it concerning Dr. Macey? Or Master Constable? If there is anything more I can tell you that would help, I would be only too happy. I must go and write his poor parents soon."

Kate thought of the papers Constable had sent to her before his death, the ones she knew she could never decipher on her own. "I confess I am not sure what exactly it is. I am exceedingly puzzled about something."

Dr. Dee merely nodded and followed as she led him to her chamber. Luckily, Violet was not there and the room was quiet. Kate quickly found the two horoscopes in her chest and held them out to the astrologer.

"Are these what I think they are? Horoscopes?" she asked. "This one seems to bear my own birth date."

Dr. Dee studied them closely, frowning, and Kate saw he was not so old as his bearing and clothes would mark him, though he still seemed fearsomely wise. His finger traced the spoke of the lines, the strange symbols. "If this is indeed yours, Mistress Haywood, you are a true winter sign—you care for others and feel responsible for them, possibly too much. You are proud, and very lonely perhaps. You long for family—see this sign here? But family can also be your downfall. You must be careful of them. They leave you a very mixed legacy. Intelligence, ambition, but also perhaps blindness to some matters that one should best beware of? Romance could prove most dangerous to such a one."

Boleyn witches. The Boleyns were her family, were they not? And none had been more undone by their ambition than Boleyns. Yet she knew she could not worry about herself now, not when everyone else was in such danger. "But what of this one?" she asked, pointing to the age-lined document.

Dr. Dee's frown deepened. "I fear whomever this horoscope was drawn for could not have ended well, or at a great age. They were much too concerned with gaining attention, with a merry time in the sunshine, as all Leos are, but that makes a person vulnerable. They forget to be cautious. Most alarming."

"Is it—is it Queen Catherine Howard's?" Kate whispered. It did sound like the young queen, who was said to have been one for dancing and laughter—and for flirtation.

Dr. Dee traced the tip of his finger over the line that looked a bit like a horseshoe. "I fear it might have been. This looks like Dr. Macey's hand. If this is what he saw in that poor young queen's future, I do not wonder he chose not to give it to her. I had some papers secured that Dr. Macey sent me once, yet I never looked at them. But where did *you* get it, Mistress Haywood?"

"Master Constable sent both of these to me, or so the messenger said. But I know not why. To warn me of something?"

"'Boleyn Beware,'" Dr. Dee muttered, peering at the back of Kate's chart.

"Why would Master Constable do such a thing?" she demanded, all her confusion making her as frustrated and angry as the queen in one of her rages. She forced herself to take a deep breath. Only a cool head could puzzle this out. "Why give them to me? We hardly knew each other, and what I did see of him did not incline me to trust him. Do you know what he could have been hiding, along with these strange papers?"

Dr. Dee slowly rubbed his hand over his face. He

looked weary, just as Cecil did, with all the terrible events that had been wearing at all of their minds of late. "Perhaps he was in need of money. He must have stolen them from my locked chest. He said nothing to me, but his family are simple people. They do not have much in the way of fortune."

"He must have been in great trouble with someone here at court," she said. "Owing debts, or possibly someone did not care for their horoscope." Just as Master Green had not cared for Violet Roland's. But killing the bearer of bad news could not change one's stars.

Or perhaps it was not a horoscope at all, but something else about Master Constable and his work. She closed her eyes and envisioned that room at the cottage, the bubbling cauldrons and open books, the shock on young Macey's face at finding her there.

Alchemy was a dangerous thing to dabble in, to be sure. What if Constable had planned to double-cross Dr. Macey's son? What if he had promised some powerful courtier far more than he could deliver? If he came from a simple family, it would be easy enough to fall into such trouble at court.

She opened her eyes and looked up at Dr. Dee. That was his work, as well, all that was happening in that strange, smoky room. She feared he, too, knew more than he would say.

"Master Constable's family did not have much fortune, 'tis true," he said. "I took him on as a pupil because I saw much promise in him, many gifts he needed to learn to control. But his parents were simple farmers. I am sure life at court might easily have dazzled such a boy, led him astray. Many spend more than they can afford on such a life."

Kate nodded, thinking of fine clothes, bribes required to find information, wine and food and horses. But what need had someone like Constable of such things? Surely what happened at Lady Knollys's chamber was orchestrated for someone's benefit. "Do you know of anyone who might have bribed him in some way?"

Dr. Dee studied the floor, seemingly deep in thought. "He would not confide in me of such things, but I must say I sensed he was hiding something in recent days. He was quiet, distracted at his lessons. Perhaps in giving you these, he sought your help."

"Do you think he was being blackmailed, then?"

"I could not say, Mistress Haywood. All I can suggest is we all must be cautious now. Especially if this horoscope is your own. You must be very careful indeed."

Kate took a deep breath and nodded. Dr. Dee was a powerful man, obviously most adept at hiding his thoughts, but she was desperate to learn what was happening before someone else got hurt.

As the door closed behind Dr. Dee, Kate spun around to look out the window. The queen walked in the courtyard below, listening as Mary Sidney read from a volume of poetry. Perhaps once Queen Catherine Howard had walked in the same place, with her own ladies, before her world shattered. The same could not happen with this queen.

Kate knew Elizabeth was right. She was the only one who knew where to look for more answers now. But there was still one more place she needed to search while at Nonsuch.

She quickly hid the horoscopes in her chest with the old book and hurried out of her chamber. There was to be dancing that night, a banquet to distract everyone from the canceled masque and the terrible reasons for it, so she had to hurry.

She left by the kitchen door again, so as not to be seen by the queen's ladies gathered in the courtyard.

She made her way as quickly as she could back to the village, almost running at times. She turned at the lane that led toward the cluster of shops and houses, marked by a pile of stones left from the demolished old town of Cuddington, and rushed toward the hidden cottage.

She stopped at the gate and tried to catch her breath. There was no smoke at the chimney, no greenish sweet smell in the air. The windows were tightly shuttered, as before, yet there hung about the place an air of stale neglect. If she hadn't been there only days before, hadn't seen the wonders hidden behind those ordinary plaster walls, she wouldn't have given the place a second look.

But today she sensed something missing.

Kate shoved open the gate and ran up the overgrown walkway. Even as she pounded on the door, she feared no one would answer.

"Master Macey," she called. "'Tis me, Mistress Haywood. From the queen. I must talk to you."

There was only silence. She hurried around to the back, only to find the kitchen window she had slid through before firmly latched. She tilted back her head to look up at the tiled roof, the crooked chimney. No smoke there, either.

No alchemist would let their fire go out. She knew she had to find Master Macey, but where would he have gone? She thought of those pitchers, the blue flowers on the white pottery, and knew where to start.

Kate knocked on the door of the tiny cottage, hoping it was the right place, that this woman could indeed lead her to Master Macey. It was where the gaoler said the woman lived who brought him his meals, the woman who left flower-painted pottery behind—just like at Master Macey's cottage. She couldn't stop the persistent whisper in her mind that insisted he was in trouble, that whoever had killed Master Constable was surely after magical secrets and would come after Master Macey next.

Unless *he* was the one who killed Constable in the first place, which was of course a great possibility. And he would not take kindly to being found.

Kate remembered being pushed into the mud of the maze, the feeling of hard hands shoving at her back— the fear that a dagger would land next. But then she remembered Violet's tears, Master Green's protests of innocence, and she knew she had to try.

She knocked again at the door. No one answered, but she thought she glimpsed a whisper of movement behind the one small window.

"Please, madam, I mean you no harm! I only need to speak to you for a moment. It is most urgent," Kate called. She held up her hands to show she carried no weapons. "It concerns young Master Macey."

The movement fell back from the window in a blur, and Kate waited, holding her breath. At last there was the clatter of a bar being dislodged, and the door opened a couple of inches.

A woman peered out, scowling. Her face was deeply lined, sun-browned, the wisps of hair that escaped from her cap gray streaked, but there was a glimpse of old beauty in her eyes, in her long neck. Beauty that was enough to captivate a king's astrologer? Kate wasn't sure.

Kate peeked past her to see a small sitting room, sparsely furnished with only a stool and two tables. A row of pottery, painted with small blue flowers, was lined up on one of them.

"What do you want to know of him?" she demanded, her voice hoarse.

"I know you deliver meals to him, as you do to the gaol and much of the village," Kate said.

"Aye, so I do. What of it?"

"He has gone, and I must speak to him most urgently. I was hoping perhaps he had told you where he might be going."

The woman's suspicious expression crumpled into something terribly like despair. "I had hoped *you* were coming to tell me where he was."

Kate was confused. "You thought *I* would know where he was?"

"Aye. You are from the queen's court, are you not?" She gestured to Kate's finely cut gown. "I saw you in the village with that grand queen's man Cecil."

"Then you know what happened at Nonsuch?"

The woman almost spat on the floor. "That cursed place! It has held naught but wickedness since the first stone was set. First it took Timothy, and now . . ." She choked off the last words, and her thin, twisted fingers clutched at the doorframe.

So this *was* Dr. Macey's mistress, the woman Dr. Dee said was left behind at Nonsuch when he had vanished. "And now your son. Aye? Master Macey is your son?"

A smile touched her face. "That he is. My name is Amelia Macey, as I call myself now. I raised him myself after his father vanished without a word. Dr. Dee sent money later, so I could find him tutors to teach him what I could not. I knew his father would have wanted it thus, even as I knew I shouldn't let such wickedness into our lives again. Better he should have been an honest digger of ditches than end up like Timothy! And now look what has happened. I was right."

Kate glanced back over her shoulder to see the curious glances of the people who passed by the tiny cottage. "Perhaps you should let me inside, Mistress Macey, so we may talk further. I promise, I wish only to help you and your son. That is the queen's wish as well."

Mistress Macey sniffled and frowned, but she did open the door wider to let Kate slip inside. The cottage was small and spare but spotlessly clean, scented with summer flowers in those pottery pitchers. No hint of alchemy.

"Then you know the work your son does at his cottage?" Kate said. "And that was why you thought I might know where he is, since I came from the court?"

Mistress Macey's face crumpled again. She looked almost as gray as her linen cap. "Aye, he's been working for high-up men, dangerous men. I've warned him time and again that it's most perilous to meddle with such matters. Look what happened to his . . . his father."

Aye, look what happened to Dr. Macey. Look what could happen to anyone at court if this killer was not found. "I only want to find Master Macey, to talk to him on the queen's behalf. So many people are in danger now, including him. Do you have any idea at all where he might have gone, if he wished to hide for a time?" Or if he intended to flee justice . . .

Mistress Macey scowled. "He does have a wife in London."

Kate was surprised. She had heard no hint of other Macey family before. "A wife?"

Mistress Macey gave a distinctly disdainful snort. "Aye, a strumpet who worked in one of those Southwark brothels. I told him not to marry the likes of her, but he never listens to his old mother. He might have gone to her, I daresay."

"Where does this wife live in London?"

Mistress Macey shook her head, closing her eyes as if she could not bear the matter for another moment. "How should I know? 'Tis the devil's lair, London. But my son needs to be saved from its evils, if he still can. I was so happy when he said some nobleman was setting him up for his studies here in the country. I was so sure he would move back for good . . ."

Was this nobleman Sir Robert Dudley, then, who had been at the cottage the night Kate followed Constable to its door? Why, then, would he want her following Constable? She pushed down her impatience. It was obvious she would learn little more from old Mistress Macey. But she knew exactly where she might find a former Southwark whore who had married an alchemist.

"I will look there, then," Kate said. "Thank you for your help, Mistress Macey. The queen will be most grateful."

She turned toward the door, but Mistress Macey suddenly grasped her sleeve. Her grip was surprisingly strong, the light in her faded eyes desperate.

"Just find my boy; I beg you, my lady," Mistress Macey said. "He is all I have left. His soul is still redeemable, I am sure. Please, find him!"

Kate swallowed hard. She had seen so much desperation lately. For love. For too much loss. "I will find him, Mistress Macey, I promise."

She just hoped neither of them would regret what they learned when she did.

CHAPTER NINETEEN

"Nearly there now, Kate," Anthony said. "Aldgate is just ahead."

Kate nodded eagerly. Her backside, even seated on the padded Spanish saddle and through the layers of her wool riding skirt and petticoats, ached terribly. Even though she had long lived in the country while Elizabeth, an avid horsewoman, was a princess in exile, Kate had never quite trusted horses. They seemed large, unpredictable creatures. Riding so quickly from Surrey to London, without the leisurely pace of the queen's court, hadn't made the journey any more comfortable.

But Anthony had. She'd told him all she had learned of the old tale of Dr. Macey and the new one of his son, and everything she still puzzled over. He told her tales of Master Hardy's more colorful patrons and of his life in London, which made her laugh as the rutted country lanes fell behind them.

His life and budding career sounded interesting, useful, and one day she was sure he would be more prosperous, with many influential patrons.

Now the roads, which had been nearly empty for so long, with nothing to see but hedgerows and gates to distant houses, grew crowded. More and more people, on foot, in carts, and on horseback, joined in the steady streams flowing toward London, the center of the king-dom. Their shouts and cries, the clatter of their wheels, pounded at her ears in a tangled cacophony like no other music she knew.

She felt the excitement growing within her as the walls of the city came into sight. She glanced over at Anthony just as he smiled at her, and she saw he felt it, too, the love of life in the city. The pulse of life all around them.

The river of humanity narrowed through the gate, past the guards that patrolled the city walls, and then rushed onward, everyone intent on their own business, just as Kate and Anthony were.

They turned their horses down a narrow lane, and the hazy sunlight grew even dimmer by the tall, close-packed houses of timber and plaster. The peaked roof-lines nearly touched above their heads, and at eye level the shop windows were open and the counters spread with fine wares.

Ribbons of every color, embroidered kid gloves, glinting gold and silver jewelry wrought in shapes of flowers and birds, beautiful leather-bound books. Kate was tempted to stop and look, to admire the beautiful artistry, but she knew there were far more vital errands to be done that day.

She urged her tired horse to follow Anthony's a bit quicker, but the crowd on the street was too thick. She drew in a deep breath—and choked. Weeks in the clear country air had made her forget quite how London re-ally smelled, especially in summer! The latrine ditch along the middle of the street was nearly full, with the miasma of rotting vegetables, horse droppings, and waste buckets tossed from the open upper windows, combined with the rich sweetness of roasting meats and sugared cakes at the taverns, cider and ladies' per-fumes. Beggars pressed in close to the side of her horse, drawn by her fine clothes, only to be pushed back by Anthony, who had slowed his horse and rode protectively near her.

It was almost too much to take in, like a piece of music she had not quite deciphered, whose notes escaped her grasp.

They soon reached Master Hardy's fine house in Cheapside, where they were to lodge while Kate looked for a clue. It seemed Master Hardy's messenger had arrived ahead of them, for as Anthony lifted her down from the saddle in the stable courtyard behind the tall house, the door opened and Mistress Hardy herself appeared.

She was a lady beyond middle age now, but lovely still, with bright blue eyes, fine white skin, and graying pale curls peeking from beneath her lace cap. She wore a stylish dark blue silk gown that went with her pretty house, a ring of heavy keys at her belt and a smile on her lips.

"My dear Mistress Haywood!" she cried, bustling forward in a rustle of silk skirts and the rattle of the household keys at her waist. She took Kate's arm and led her toward the house. "How very tired you must be after such a rushed journey. Men can be so very ridiculous sometimes. Come inside at once; have a goblet of wine and sit by the fire. Though it *is* a warm day, is it not? Perhaps you would prefer a lemon ice—it is quite the newest thing here in London . . ."

Kate had to laugh as Mistress Hardy bore her into the house, found her a cushioned chair, and poured her a goblet of light wine as she asked after Kate's father and all the merriment at court. It was an hour before she left to see to the supper preparations and Kate could speak again to Anthony.

"Are you certain you won't wait until tomorrow to begin such a search?" he asked cautiously, ever the lawyer even now. "Mistress Hardy is quite right; you must be tired."

"Indeed not." And Kate found to her surprise that she was not. Instead, she felt a new energy coursing through her. Surely the answers to her questions had to be near now. "We have no time to lose now. And I think I know where to begin. . . . "

Kate strode across London Bridge, moving through the dark shadows cast by the tall houses quickly in her borrowed boy's clothes. She'd long ago learned that in a doublet and hose, with her hair tucked up tightly beneath a cap, she could go places unnoticed as she never could in skirts. It was also much easier to dodge around puddles and avoid the worst muck of the streets.

Anthony had only laughed when she appeared in her manly garments, when she had been afraid she might shock her respectable lawyer friend. They had secretly left the Hardys' house and now strode together over the crowded bridge.

But he still insisted on moving along the outside of the walkway, protecting her from any falling chamber pots, which secretly made her want to smile.

The last time Kate had crossed London Bridge, it was winter, with ice clogging the river below and snowflakes drifting down over the masses of people who had gathered to celebrate the new queen's coronation.

Now the sun had crept from behind the clouds to beat warmth onto the stone and timber thoroughfare, and the heat intensified the smells. The sour tang of the water, the smell of spicy ginger cakes from the bakeshops, and the thick woodsmoke from the blacksmiths' chimneys made the air feel like a thick, damp blanket.

Everywhere people jostled and shouted, merchants crying out their wares from the open windows, the whole city hurrying on their never-ending business as Kate had to go about hers.

They soon passed under the arch of the bridge that led to the river's south bank. There were only a few traitors' heads on the pikes high above, staring down endlessly at the city with their empty eye sockets. The queen's reign of many months had been peaceful thus far—but Kate well remembered Cecil's warnings of Elizabeth's circling enemies, just like the black-winged birds wheeling over the river now.

She thought of Master Green waiting in the Tower and shivered despite the heat of the sun. Would there soon be yet another head up there?

Kate led Anthony along the narrow path beside the river, past the wherrymen waiting for passengers to row back to the north bank or downriver to the grand houses of the Strand, past women doing their washing in the waves and mud-lark children searching for tidbits they could sell. Though it had been months since she had gone that way, she still remembered the direction.

They turned onto a narrow, muddy walkway between the leaning, close-packed buildings that lined the water stairs. Anthony's handsome face looked doubtful, yet still he followed her as they emerged into an open lane.

As it was still afternoon, Southwark was much quieter than the bridge and the more respectable streets around the Hardy house. The streets of Bankside wouldn't truly come alive until dark, as Kate remembered, when the bear pits, taverns, and brothels opened and patrons poured across the river searching for such illicit pleasures.

Right now, most of the shutters were closed up tight. An old woman drove along a flock of shrieking chickens, and a rickety cart rolled past. A young maidservant fetched water from the public fountain, yawning into her apron. Kate went past them all and turned down Carter Lane, where a cluster of old, precarious-looking buildings huddled around a small courtyard.

It was somewhat above the lowest order of Bankside bawdy houses, with the midden of the house's trash out of sight behind the building, but the sign swinging in the slow, hot breeze left no doubt of the structure's real purpose.

The Cardinal's Hat, read the painted letters, below a distinctly phallic depiction of that scarlet headgear. One of the windows above was open, and a woman's pale face stared out as she lazily combed her bright yellow hair.

An enormous dragon of a man guarded the front door, his beefy arms clad only in stained shirtsleeves crossed over his burly chest. His head was bald, closely shaved to only a dark shadow of stubble, and he stared out over the quiet street with blank eyes.

Mad Henry was still at his post, then, Kate thought. She could only hope Madame Celine was as well. Celine knew what happened with people of every sort throughout London.

"This is the place," she said. She took a step toward the Cardinal's Hat, but Anthony's hand on her arm stopped her.

"You know people here?" he asked, his voice shocked.

Kate suddenly wondered if he knew the Cardinal's Hat in some . . . intimate way. She found she did not like that thought at all, but there was no time to dwell on it now. She would simply have to ask him later. In a subtle way.

"I have a friend here," she said. "She helped me in some matters for the queen last winter. I am sure she can help us find what we seek now." She shook away Anthony's restraining hand and hurried to the door, waving at the burly guard. "How do you do, Mad Henry?"

"Back again, then, are you?" Mad Henry said, as if Kate had been there only a day before and not months. He didn't uncross his arms, but his eyes, black and bottomless under bushy brows, sparkled. "Celine'll be right glad to see you again. She says she never thanked you enough for finding out who killed our Bess and Nell during the queen's coronation."

"If it wasn't for Celine's help, I never would have," Kate answered. She still shivered to remember those days, when someone marred the celebration of the queen's ascension to the throne by cruelly murdering red-haired women. Bess and Nell had lived there at the Cardinal's Hat. Nell was Rob's mistress. "I am glad to see you and Celine are still here."

"Where would we go? Countryside is too quiet for the likes of us." Mad Henry glanced past her to Anthony, who stood silently at her shoulder. "Haven't seen him here before."

Kate felt an unaccountable satisfaction that Anthony probably did not frequent brothels. "This is my friend Anthony. He is helping me look into a matter for a—a friend, and I have hopes Celine might be able to help us again."

"She'll be glad enough to pay you back." Mad Henry pulled open the heavy door and shouted, "You, lad! Come show these important guests to Madame, and be right quick about it!"

A page boy scrambled up from his place by the front hearth and sketched them a quick, awkward bow. Kate and Anthony followed him up a narrow, creaking wooden staircase and along the winding corridors of the Cardinal's Hat. The doors to the many chambers were closed and all was quiet within as without. The warm, stuffy air smelled of cheap tallow candles, stale perfume, and sweat.

From behind one door came a moan and a giggle, but everyone else seemed to be sleeping. Except Celine herself, the owner of the Cardinal's Hat, who never seemed to sleep.

"Mad 'enry says important guests for you!" the boy cried as he threw open a door at the end of the hall.

"I got no time for such things now," a disgruntled voice said. "Not until tonight."

Kate stepped into the room, a small closet that held only a writing table and a few stools but was more luxurious than the rest of the space, with cushions and yellow draperies. Two open windows let in the hot breeze as the woman laboring over ledgers at the table glanced up.

Celine looked no different than she had in January. Her face, only lightly creased with age, was free of white paint and kohl at that hour, and her improbably orange-red hair sat braided atop her head. She wore a loose green gown over her stays and petticoat and held a quill pen in her hand. She gave a fearsome scowl as she looked up, but just as Mad Henry's had, it turned to a smile.

"Mistress Haywood!" she cried. "Back again, are you? I would have thought you far from London in such a foul season. Boy, go fetch some wine for our guests; don't just stand there staring!"

"I am only here for a few days," Kate answered as Celine came over to urge her to a stool. "My friend Anthony and I are here to make inquiries about some new trouble, I fear."

"Aye, there's trouble enough to go around all the time," Celine said, giving Anthony a sweeping, appreciative glance. He stood protectively behind Kate as she sat down across from Celine's table. "But little enough here of late, praise be. We owe you much for what you did last winter. Tell me how I can help now."

Kate quickly told Madame Celine what she had come to discover—how to find Master Macey's wife in the great tangle of London.

Celine listened carefully, her beringed fingers tapping at her desk. She frowned a bit, seeming to run through every bit of gossip in her head, every person she knew in Southwark. Information could make all the difference in a bawdy house's fortunes, and Celine was a shrewd businesswoman indeed.

"I do have a friend who owns the White Swan, over in Blackman Street," Celine said. "Long Madge. We came to London about the same time when we were mere green slips of girls; we help each other when we can. Though I must say she doesn't keep her house in as sharp an order as should be. Always having to find new wenches, since hers leave so fast." She gave a sniff. "Madge was complaining just a few months ago that one of her prettiest girls was leaving to marry a magician."

A magician? Surely there could not be very many Southwark geese married to such men. But "magician" could mean many things—astrologers, dealers in amulets and powders, scholars. She glanced at Anthony and raised her brow. He frowned doubtfully. "A magician?" Kate said.

Celine scowled. "Aye. Bawds leave the trade to marry often enough, but usually to some farmer or blacksmith. I remember this tale because it sounded so odd. A magician? I wouldn't let any of my girls mess about with things like that."

"Did Madge say anything about who this man was? Where he took his new wife?" Kate asked.

"I remember she said she warned Bett about it all,

but the silly girl was determined, said her man loved her and would never be mixed up in any demon arts. Madge told her he would never be prosperous, unless he was fortune-teller to the queen herself, but Bett left anyway."

"And this was recently?"

Celine shrugged, the emerald satin of her gown rippling off her powdered shoulders. "Madge told me of it a few months ago. We can go talk to her, if you like. It won't be busy at the White Swan for a few hours yet."

Kate nodded eagerly. She felt as if she was getting just a tiny bit closer to Master Macey, one little step at a time. "That would be most kind of her to speak with me. I do need to find this Bett, I think."

Celine's eyes widened. "Is she in some trouble, then, Mistress Haywood?"

"I am not sure yet. But her husband has disappeared and left behind some rather vital work he seems most devoted to."

"These girls!" Celine said, half-angry, half-despairing. "Haven't the sense of a goat, most of the time, especially when it comes to men. You would think they would learn prudence, as I had to."

Kate glanced up at Anthony, and he gave her a nod. In his eyes, she could see the same worry she herself felt for Bett Macey. They both feared whoever took or killed Macey would come for his wife next.

Celine stood up and reached for a large shawl, wrapping it over her chemise. "If we're going to talk to Madge, we should go now. Mad Henry! Where are you?"

Anthony took Kate's arm and leaned down to whisper in her ear, "I told my friend at the Episcopal Courts I would call on him this afternoon to look into Lord Marchand's records. Perhaps we should visit this, er, Long Madge tomorrow."

He looked most concerned, and Kate bit her lip, suddenly uncertain. She did have a tendency to leap forward without looking, just as her horoscope warned. She needed to learn prudence, just like Celine's girls. But what if Bett was in danger?

Celine laughed. "Worried about your fine lady, are you, young sir? Most gallant of you. The world needs more like you, indeed. But I think she can take care of herself better than most men I know."

"I only seek to protect her, madam," Anthony said quietly.

Celine's face softened. "Aye. But Mad Henry can look after her, bring her safe back to your house when she's done with her business."

As if to reaffirm her words, the door opened and Mad Henry appeared, as large and muscled as a prize bull.

Kate took Anthony's hand tightly in hers. "I will be well, Anthony, I promise. We do need to know what can be found about Lord Marchand, and you are the only one who can do that. I will not leave Celine and Henry."

He seemed most reluctant, but at last he nodded, and they parted at the door of the Cardinal's Hat. Celine and Mad Henry led Kate out into the twisting puzzle of Southwark alleyways, heading even farther from the river. The streets were more crowded as the day went on. They passed a few gentlemen in fine doublets, with giggling women hanging on their arms, and merchants trying to sell the last bits of fruit or spiced ale from their carts before they could go home.

The White Swan was not as large or well kept as the Cardinal's Hat, but it was by no means the lowest of stews, either. The walls were plastered, some of the windows were glass, and the sign that hung above the door was well lettered. The midden was hidden back behind, not piled by the entrance.

A window on the top floor swung open, and a

woman leaned over so far Kate feared she might topple out. She looked to be about Celine's age, her face lightly lined under her paint, her hair suspiciously black. She wore a fine purple gown trimmed in yellow tinsel.

"Celine!" she called. "Come to call on me again so soon? And I see you brought a young, fair sir to be entertained. None of your pretty geese could satisfy him, could they?" She laughed raucously.

Kate glanced over her shoulder to make sure Anthony hadn't followed but had to laugh, too, as she remembered her own strange appearance. She'd forgotten she wore lads' clothes.

"I fear you don't have what would satisfy *this* caller, Madge," Celine called back. "We need to talk to you. Can we come up?"

"Of course," Madge answered. "I just got some new wine from a customer; you can try it with me." Madge ducked back into the house, pulling the window shut.

There was no Mad Henry guarding the White Swan's door. Celine led them right in and down a corridor toward a sitting room. Some of the girls they passed, lazily lounging about in their shifts and loose robes, called out greetings to her. Mad Henry stayed just inside the door, his arms crossed over his chest, watching over it all.

Madge was already pouring out the wine. She studied Kate as she passed the whiteware goblets, and she gave a hearty laugh. "I see Celine was right—I don't have what might satisfy you, young miss. Though we do get ladies of an unusual persuasion from time to time. . . ."

Kate felt her cheeks turn embarrassingly warm, and she took a quick gulp of wine.

"No teasing, now, Madge," Celine chided. "Mistress Haywood comes from the queen's court, and she's looking most urgently for someone you might know."

"Aye, now?" Madge said, all serious now. "How would I know anyone from the queen's own court?"

"Celine tells me you had a girl, Bett, who left to marry some sort of magician," Kate said quickly. "Do you remember his name, or anything about him? What he looked like?"

"His name was Miniver or Mattingly, something like that," Madge said. "Nay, I recall now! 'Twas Macey. An unusual enough name. I heard tell his father once served at the royal court. So Bett said anyway, so who knows if that's true."

Kate nodded, satisfied that Bett must be married to the right "magician." "I must find her and her husband. Do you have any idea where she lives now?"

Madge frowned thoughtfully over her wine. "Ah, yes. Silly Bett. I did warn her. I only saw the man once or twice myself, but he seemed most distracted. Plainly dressed, too. Most of those scryers don't have two coins to rub together, and what they do have they spend in the St. Paul's book stalls. But she insisted. I don't know where she is now, but she was good friends with Rosie. She might know."

Madge pulled open the sitting room door and shouted for someone to fetch Rosie. The girl quickly appeared, haphazardly lacing a red-striped bodice over her chemise. She looked very young under her paint, her brown hair pulled hastily back, her eyes nervous. "Aye, Madame Madge?" she said.

"This lady is looking for Bett," Madge said. "Do you know where she's gone, then?"

"I . . ." Rosie swallowed, her eyes widening even more as her gaze darted between Madge and Kate. "Is she in trouble, then? I was so afeared . . ."

"Nothing of the sort," Kate said quickly. "I merely want to ask her about her husband, Master Macey."

Rosie nodded, looking a tiny bit more relieved.

"Want your horoscope drawn up, then? Master Macey was always good at that, and doesn't charge much, either. We all went to him when we had saved up enough to hear our fortunes. That's how Bett met him."

"When was the last time you saw Bett?" Kate asked. Rosie hesitated.

"Go on, then," Madge urged.

" 'Twas just yesterday," Rosie said. "I went to her lodgings at Coleman Street over the river, to see the baby. But Bett wasn't herself."

"Not herself in what way?" Kate asked.

"Bett is usually full of jests, but that day she seemed—nervous. Kept jumping up to look out the window," Rosie said, shuffling her stockinged feet. "She said she hadn't seen her husband in a few weeks, but she was scared someone had followed her to market. Someone in a dark cloak, even though the day was hot."

Kate remembered the swirl of a black cloak in the maze, and her worry for Mistress Macey grew. "Did this person try to speak to her?"

"I don't think so. She didn't tell me anything more, miss," Rosie said. Her voice was rising, as if she might start crying. "Is she in trouble?"

Madge laid a gentle hand on Rosie's shaking shoulder. "Aye, miss. Is Bett in danger? I did warn her when she married, she didn't know what she was getting herself into. But she's really a good girl."

Kate nodded. "I am sure she is." Once it became clear that Rosie could tell her nothing more but the address where Bett Macey lodged, Kate left the White Swan. As Mad Henry escorted her back across the river to the Hardys' house, she couldn't quit thinking about a poor young mother, trailed by a cloaked figure, and Master Macey's empty cottage.

"You won't do anything foolish, now, will you, Mistress Haywood?" Mad Henry said sternly as he left her at the back garden gate.

Kate shook her head, but even as she sent Henry away, she very much feared she was about to be foolish indeed.

CHAPTER TWENTY

"Why would you want to be looking at these dusty old things, Anthony? Dull as tombs, they must be, if you can read the old writing at all. Most of it is so faded, and they obviously had no tutor to beat neatness into them as we did." Thomas Overbury, an old friend of Anthony's from their grammar school days in Hatfield village, led him up a winding staircase to the rooms above that held all the ledgers of old wills probated long ago.

Tom had begun studying to enter the church and worked as clerk to a bishop high up in the Episcopal Courts. If a deceased person held property in more than one diocese, as Lord Marchand had, his or her will would sometimes be proved in the prerogative court at Canterbury, but as he had once had a large London house, Anthony hoped to find something in this local archdeacon's court. If it was there, Tom would have access to help him find it, and hopefully there would be some clue there as to what had happened at Nonsuch all those years ago.

Anthony laughed as Tom put down his lamp on a table that was indeed very dusty. "Master Parker was a stern teacher, to be sure, and most exacting about penmanship. But his tutelage seems to have done us good in the end."

Tom grinned. Despite his dark churchly clothes, he

was still full of laughter. "So it has. I am for the church, and you will soon have a thriving law practice of your own. Then you can make more useless papers for poor apprentices to bind and store." He heaved a large volume onto the middle of the table, sending up a great plume of choking gray dust.

Anthony studied the shelves rising around them on all sides, stretching up into the dark shadows of the ceiling, all of them stacked with ledgers and boxes. It was clear he had a large task before him, but he would happily do it for Kate.

He would do anything for her. If only she would accept it from him. But what could he give her now that would compare with life at court?

He remembered how worried she had looked when they parted in Southwark, how reluctant he was to leave her in such a place, but he had learned that when it came to protecting those she loved, Kate would always do as she wanted, no matter what anyone said. It was maddening, but it was also one of the things about her he liked most.

He had to hurry his task and get back to her, quickly.

"Not entirely useless," Anthony said. He pushed up the sleeves of his doublet and shirt to save them from the worst of the grime and reached for the first ledger.

"You want to see the will of a Lord Marchand, who had a house at the far end of the Strand, yes?" Tom said, climbing up one of the perilous-looking ladders to pull down another volume. "In what year did he die?"

"The same as poor Queen Catherine Howard, I think—1542 or '43?"

"If he had property in the country, it might not be here at all, of course. But worth a look." Tom grabbed a few more bound ledgers and handed them down. "The London courts want their share whenever a lordship dies. Is this a case for your Master Hardy, then?"

"Something of the sort," Anthony muttered. He did indeed have much to do for Master Hardy, with his employer attending on the Duchess of Somerset at court, but Kate came first now.

Tom shot him a shrewd, narrow-eyed glance as he left all the books on the table, piled high. "Moving ahead, then, eh, Anthony? You always were the clever one. Well, good fortune with your search. Shout if you need anything else."

Tom left Anthony alone with the mountain of documents and not much time to go through them. The warm, musty-smelling dimness closed in around him, and he bent close over the old pages.

There was nothing for anyone named Marchand in 1541 or '42, and nothing about Dr. Macey, either, only a few mentions of horoscopes drawn up for King Henry's courtiers. But halfway through a ledger dated 1543, he found exactly what he sought.

> *17th June, 1543, in the reign of King Henry the VIII, Lord William Marchand Bequeaths his Soul to Almighty God and to the company of Heaven. . . .*

It seemed Lord Marchand had no children, but *To my good wife half the manner of House* was left. *And to my closest relation, my cousin and executor, Master Edward Longville . . .*

"Longville," Anthony muttered. That was the name of the suitor of Kate's friend Mistress Violet, the one the lady rejected most heartily. Surely the Longvilles of today were somehow bound to the Marchands, if there were any left. But Anthony could see no way that would lead to the murder of two astrologers, decades apart.

He read further in the documents associated with the will, bound in with them in the ledger, and found an inventory of the Marchand town house. It was not complete, but amid the plate and carpets, he found a listing for a carved prie-dieu, a prayer bench, "brought from France," left to Lady Marchand.

Were the Marchands of the old religion, then? Could that have been what led to the dispute between Lord Marchand and Dr. Macey?

Anthony knew he needed to look further into the matter, check records of different courts, but first he had to tell Kate what he had found. He wanted to hear her thoughts on the matter, for her mind was always one step ahead.

He pushed the ledgers back into a neat pile and snatched up his cap. He met Tom halfway down the winding staircase.

"I found something else about this Lord Marchand I thought was most interesting, Anthony," Tom said, holding up a thin, twine-tied book. "I thought the name sounded a bit familiar, so I dug through a crate of old Westminster Palace records that were brought here and forgotten. Those are always the most interesting, of course, things one shouldn't look at."

It did not look like much, with that rough binding, but Tom was right—that was often the best information of all. Anthony reached for it eagerly. "That was good of you to take time away from your own duties, Tom."

Tom laughed. "Makes a change from church matters, doesn't it? Rather intriguing. But I don't think we should take too long over this one, forgotten or not. It wouldn't do for our employers to know we were looking at such things. Unless this is for Master Hardy, of course . . ."

Anthony was puzzled. Wills were usually dry things, not very dangerous to one's employment. But when he laid it carefully on the table and studied the faded lines of writing, he could see what Tom meant.

This was no ordinary court report. According to the stamp at the top of the crackling old vellum, it was from the Star Chamber.

Star Chamber sessions, judged by royal privy councilors along with judges, were used only for prominent people questioned in important matters. The sessions were held in secret, all evidence kept in writing. Why was it there?

Anthony frowned as he read it, sure Tom was right. They should not be seeing it. But he was glad they were.

The papers were dated December 1541 and concerned the testimony of several associates of none other than Thomas Culpeper, the doomed lover of Queen Catherine Howard. And one of those men was Lord Marchand.

Surely if he was known to be a friend to Culpeper, they had been associated on the visit to Nonsuch, when the queen's friends would surely have made merry. Would Marchand have killed to protect his friend? Accused an astrologer of treason to conceal his own?

Fortunately for Marchand, it seemed it was found by the court that he had no culpability in the matter of the queen's treason, and he was released to go on to live for a little longer. There seemed to be nothing else heard of him until that will.

Anthony rubbed his hand over his jaw. If this was a royal matter, even one decades old, Kate needed to be warned. Immediately.

"Anthony," Tom said, his tone most serious for once. "Why exactly are you looking into all of this? I know the Culpeper matter ended long ago, but still . . ."

But still—meddling in the doings of monarchs was a most perilous business.

"It is for a friend," he said shortly.

Tom nodded. "I hope you will warn him, then."

Anthony frowned. He would warn her—but he also knew she would not listen. Not if someone else was in danger and she could help. "Thank you for your help, Tom. You can hide this again."

He left the darkness of the court building for the fading day and hurried toward the Hardy house, his thoughts in a shadowed blur. He knew only that he had to find Kate, to talk to her about what he had found.

"Oh, nay, Master Elias," the maidservant said as she took his cap. "Mistress Haywood has not yet returned . . ."

CHAPTER TWENTY-ONE

Kate stared up at the house Rosie had directed her to. This had to be it. It seemed quite unremarkable in every way. A quiet street of artisan families going about their business, paying no heed to anyone else. Kate knocked at the door loudly, three times, but there was no answer.

Yet this was where Celine's friend said Timothy Macey lived, where all the women went to have their horoscopes drawn up when they had saved their pennies, and where they went to have a gossip with the new Mistress Macey. Surely this was the same place his mother spoke of, where he kept his small family when he was not trying to finish his father's lost work?

No smoke rose from the chimney, and all the doors and lower windows were tightly closed and shuttered. Yet an upper window hung partially open, and a cry suddenly rang out from beyond its swaying frame. Kate knew the house was not so deserted after all.

A cold panic rushed through her as she pounded again on the door. "Let me in!" she cried. "I've come to help you." But there was no answer. She remembered the open kitchen door at the cottage and ran around to the back of the row of houses.

The door did indeed stand open, but it didn't appear to be from any servant's neglect. The latch was broken off, the wood panels scarred. Mud was tracked over the threshold.

Kate heard another cry from inside, and she ran into the narrow hall. Once in the shadowed house, she followed the sounds of voices—a woman's high-pitched plea, a baby's sob—up the stairs to an open loft above the warren of kitchens and sitting rooms.

The space was large, low ceilinged, dark. Kate smelled that familiar sweet, greenish, smoky odor, the same as that of the cottage, and there was the same clutter of books and glass vials everywhere. The rest of the scene was chaos.

Glass lay shattered on the floor, crystalline and shining in the faint light from the open window. Documents were scattered everywhere.

At the far end of the room, huddled by the empty fireplace, a woman clutched a baby to her shoulder. She was young, with long, loose dark hair and a simple white-and-yellow gown, and her face might have been pretty if it wasn't streaked with tears and contorted with fear.

A figure in a dark cloak, much too heavy for the warm day, blocked the woman in by the hearth. His back was to Kate, and the hood drawn up so she couldn't see his face. What she *could* see, all too well, was the gleam of a dagger in a gloved hand.

She remembered being shoved down into the mud of the Nonsuch maze, the swirl of a dark cloak like raven's wings. It seemed she had stumbled onto her attacker again, but this time he had a true weapon.

Luckily, so did Kate. She quickly grasped the hilt of her own blade where it was strapped above her wrist, behind the cuff of her doublet, and she drew it down into her palm. She'd been neglecting her lessons with Cecil's men of late and couldn't wield a blade with much skill yet, but its steely heft still felt reassuring.

"Nay, please," the young mother begged. "I know not what you speak of. I can't even read, so I don't know what my husband's books are."

The blade waved wildly in front of her face, making the baby howl. The cloaked figure looked tense, coiled as if to leap on them, and Kate knew she had to act.

"Leave them alone!" Kate shouted. There was no time now to be afraid. She had to be like the queen when Elizabeth faced her enemies. Cool, calm, unmovable.

The mother shrieked again, and the cloaked figure spun around. The hood fell back, and Kate almost gasped aloud in shock. It was not a man at all. It was Lady Anne Godwin who stared back at her, Lady Anne who threatened the woman and her child. She looked little like the stylish, coolly smiling lady who shared lodgings with Kate and Violet, but Kate saw to her shock that it was indeed she.

Anne's face was white, strained, her hair straggling over her brow, completely unlike the court lady Kate knew her as.

"Kate!" she shouted, her voice shaking as hard as the dagger. "What are *you* doing here? This has naught to do with you!"

Kate's blood raced with fear for Mistress Macey and her child, fear for herself, but she knew she couldn't let it affect her now, couldn't let it show on her face. "But it does. You made it so when you attacked me in the maze."

Lady Anne shook her head. "I would not have hurt you. I was only told to warn you—"

"Told?" Kate said, her thoughts racing. "Told by whom? What is really happening here? What do you look for?"

Anne's mouth opened as if she would answer, but then the baby let out another sharp howl, and Anne swung around again, her blade waving. "Too many questions!"

"Please, Anne, let me help you," Kate said, trying to hold herself calm amid all the confusion and fear. Only by wrapping herself in ice could she discover what was happening. What part Anne played in Constable's death—and how to stop her now. "I know this cannot be your own doing. Who sent you here? For what purpose? Surely this woman and her child can pose no threat to you, or to anyone."

The baby wailed, and the mother clutched him even tighter, desperately. Anne shook her head, looking dangerously confused.

"I *must* find it, don't you see?" Anne cried, half-angry, half-pleading. The dagger steadied in her hand, still pointing menacingly at the woman. Kate wrapped her fingers around the hilt of her own blade.

"It's our last chance to be together," Anne continued. "We've longed for this so long, worked so hard for it. I *will* have it now."

"We?" Kate thought of Anne and Master Roland in the garden together, standing so close, talking so intently. She remembered seeing Anne hurrying on some secret errand as she left Nonsuch. *Of course.* How could she have thought it was some man alone? Anne did this for her lover. For Master Roland. "'Tis Master Roland, aye? You wish to marry him, yet he has debts."

Anne smiled, suddenly glowing with a terrible happiness. "We plighted our troth to each other last year, in secret. Not even Violet knows yet. We thought surely once Elizabeth became queen, he would be able to find a place for himself at court, build his family's fortunes again quickly, and we could marry."

"He has the place with Lord Arundel," Kate said, thinking quickly. "Surely he could openly declare himself now? Why all these dramatics? All this—death."

Anne frantically shook her head. "It is not his fault! He has enemies, people who plot against him. 'Tis they who keep us apart now. I only seek to help him now, to help *us*."

Kate thought of the way Constable was found, tucked into the painted moon. Anne was a tall woman, but not strong enough for such a feat. "Why did Roland hate Constable so much that he killed him? Why did you help him?"

The raw shock that flickered over Anne's face told Kate she was right. Lady Anne Godwin had not killed Master Constable. But why had Roland done it? How was Constable Roland's "enemy"?

"N-no!" Anne cried as she struggled to cover her shock. "I killed Master Constable. He took Thomas's coin and then failed to keep his solemn promise. I had to be rid of him."

"What did Roland pay Constable to do?" Kate demanded. She longed to scream with impatience.

"Lord Arundel was going to promote one of his assistants to be his private secretary, once he was married to the queen. The place should by right be Thomas's; he has worked so hard for it. But Lord Arundel had begun to think Her Majesty had no idea of marrying at all."

Kate thought of Lord Arundel's desperation to have that masquerade. "So you and Master Roland decided to—assist matters along?"

Fear and naked need lined Anne's face, usually so calm, so sardonically smiling. "We meant no harm. I swear it! I knew Master Constable was meant to conduct a séance at Lady Knollys's, and that she often counsels her cousin the queen. Thomas said he had heard Master Constable had gaming debts he, too, needed to pay. Thomas offered him a very generous sum merely to suggest that Boleyn spirits urged Queen Elizabeth to wed Lord Arundel, for the safety of her kingdom. It was a very goodly amount, more than Thomas could afford, but he was sure Lord Arundel would be very grateful once the scheme came off."

"But it did not happen that way," Kate murmured. Not that way at all. She shivered to remember Constable's howl, his empty eyes, as he collapsed to the floor.

Lady Anne's pleading expression hardened. "Master Constable deceived us. He had to pay for that."

"So you killed him and let Master Green, your friend's suitor, take the blame?"

Anne's face collapsed in fear again. She was no actor; she surely could have used many lessons from Rob Cartman's troupe in concealing her real thoughts. "Violet is better off without him. Master Longville is a finer match for her, and he would pay a handsome sum to Thomas and demand no dowry. Besides, he is so besotted with her."

Another peg slid into place as the whole twisted structure took shape in Kate's mind. The way Roland suddenly favored Longville, despite his sister's pleading. Mistress Macey sobbed in the background, but Kate could not think of her or the child yet. She had to focus, to decipher how to get them all out of there safely. "So Green takes the blame for your murder of Constable, Longville pays to marry Violet, and Lord Arundel falls down in gratitude to Roland. Only he did not. Is that why you're here now? Threatening this poor woman and her child?"

The mother, who had sunk to her knees on the hearth, sobbed over the screaming babe's head. Kate tried to signal to her, to tell her not to worry, to tell her to flee while Anne's desperate attention was turned away, but Mistress Macey was beyond seeing.

"Constable offered Thomas a book in exchange for the missing money," Anne said with a sudden, strange smile. "A book with Dr. Macey's lost alchemy. With such a thing, we would have been richer than Lord Arundel himself! But Constable lied about that, too, the dirty *cochon*."

"And he sent you to find it? He sent his betrothed, a woman, because he was too frightened to do it himself?"

Anne gave a furious cry. "I came of my own design, so we can be together at last! But this harlot vows she knows not where it, or her husband, could be." She waved the dagger in her hand again, an erratic pattern that came dangerously close to Kate's face.

Kate ducked back, raising her hands carefully to placate Anne. She felt the weight of her own dagger hidden underneath her sleeve and hoped she would not have to use it. "So what happened next? Master Roland helped you dispose of Constable in the masquerade moon?" Kate said quickly.

Her sudden question did what it was meant to do—distract Anne. She stepped back, looking puzzled.

"You would never be strong enough to do it yourself," Kate said. "*He* killed Constable himself, didn't he?"

"Nay!" Anne screamed. "He would never. It—it was me, I told you . . ."

Mistress Macey suddenly lunged forward. It all happened in an instant. Holding tight to her flailing child with one arm, she wrapped the other around Anne's legs and tried to pull her to the floor. They all were tangled in the voluminous folds of Anne's cloak, and Kate couldn't see what was really happening. She could only hear the ring of terrified screams.

She pressed herself back to the wall, trying to shake her dagger free. But she was trembling, and it fell to the floor with a clatter. She glanced up just in time to see Anne grab the baby out of Mistress Macey's arms. She knew she had to act.

She threw herself into the fray and shoved Anne

hard to the floor, grabbing up the child as her former friend fell. She half tossed the child to Mistress Macey, praying she would catch him, as Anne screamed. Kate summoned up every ounce of strength she possessed and tried to hold Anne down until Mistress Macey could flee, but Anne in her fury was stronger. She lashed out with her blade and caught Kate's leg just below the knee. Shocked and in pain, Kate lost her grip on the woman, and Anne pinned Kate to the ground.

For one instant, Kate saw Anne's horrified face hovering above her, before Anne wheeled around and ran.

Kate tried to run after her, to catch her, but a burning pain seared up her leg. She fell heavily back to the floor, struggling against the black haze that threatened to engulf her mind. She could not faint, not now!

Mistress Macey's tear-streaked face suddenly appeared above her, pale and frantic.

"We must go after her," Kate gasped. "Shout for the watchmen . . ."

"But you're hurt," the woman cried. "You saved my baby!"

"Nay, we must catch her! Go, now."

Mistress Macey left then, but only to push the window open even further and lean out to shout at someone below.

Kate feared Lady Anne was already long gone, vanishing into the anonymous crowds of London. Running back to Nonsuch to warn her murderous lover. Whom would he go after next in his desperate schemes? Whom would he have to silence?

And Kate was helpless, the pain in her leg threatening to swallow her.

Mistress Macey deposited the child on a cot by the door and ran back to help Kate up. Kate knew she could not let the pain and fear have her, not now.

"Let me help you," Mistress Macey said. With the

threat to her child gone, she seemed much calmer, more deliberate in her movements. It made Kate feel calmer, too. "I may not know how to read my husband's books, but I *have* learned something of healing from him. We must wrap your leg to stop the bleeding."

Kate looked down at her leg. The wound had torn her hose, and horribly warm, sticky red blood stained her skin. She gritted her teeth to steel herself. "Where is your husband, Mistress Macey? He has vanished from Surrey. His mother thought he would come here."

Mistress Macey shook her head, her face grim. She methodically gathered up herbs from the scattered mess on the floor, tore a sheet into strips. "We have not seen him, I fear. It was quite a plain day here until *she* appeared. Now— Oh, I do fear for him!" Her voice broke on a sob.

Kate feared for him as well. That fear was worse than the pain in her leg. "When did you last see him, Mistress Macey?" she asked, forcing herself to keep talking, to focus on the vital matter at hand and not on the burning ache.

Mistress Macey carefully applied her herbal poultice and wrapped the linen strips over it, tightening it as Kate grimaced. "It has been some weeks. I begged him not to go back there, or at least to take us with him, but he would not. He said he had to finish his work, his father's work, and he never would if we were there to distract him." She frowned but did not look up from her work. "Mayhap he thinks me too foolish."

"Then why would he marry you?"

Mistress Macey shook her head. "I know not sometimes. Perhaps because I listen to his work. It is fascinating. There," she said as she tied off the end of the bandage. It was tight, but the ache was less. The herbs were doing their numbing work. "You should stay off this leg for a time, or I fear the bleeding may start again."

But Kate felt the urgency to be on the move again. "I must be back to Nonsuch as quickly as possible. Lady Anne will be far ahead of me to warn her lover—and who knows what he will do next?"

"Will he hurt my husband, do you think?" Mistress Macey said, her own panic returning. "If Timothy can be found . . ."

"I should go now." Kate tried to push herself to her feet, but pain shot through her leg again, a fiery sword cutting into the blessed numbness of the bandage.

Mistress Macey held her arm. "Then I will go with you," she said firmly.

"Your child . . ."

"He can come, too. I can look after you both, and I know I can help you find my husband. I cannot stay here anymore."

Kate nodded, even as she feared for this woman and her child. She knew she could not do this alone, and Mistress Macey was right—she would feel better if she was doing something to find her husband. "Very well. I know someone else who can help us, too. If you will send a message to Master Hardy the lawyer's house . . ."

CHAPTER TWENTY-TWO

"So Lord Marchand was Master Longville's cousin?" Kate asked Anthony as they jolted along the road back to Nonsuch, slower than they had come. *Much* slower than she would like. As each precious moment slipped away, the odds of finding Lady Anne and Master Roland became slimmer and slimmer.

She had been forced to give in to Anthony's demand that she ride in a cart rather than on horseback, for her leg still ached like hellfire. With every painful jounce she cursed Anne Godwin, and herself, for daring to trust in friendship again. Mistress Macey and her baby slept now, curled up amid the blankets that also held Kate's leg in place, and Anthony rode his horse alongside, telling her of what he had learned in his law ledgers.

She was most glad of his tale, not only for the holes it filled in the story she herself had gathered, but for the distraction it gave her from the pain and fear.

Anthony's words were lawyerly, concise, careful, but spiced with humor. He never insulted her intelligence or assumed she could not understand something, but spoke to her as an equal. A friend. Dared she trust in that with *him*?

"Indeed so," Anthony said with a wry smile. "And it also seems Lord Marchand had even more dangerous friends than his nephew, Master Longville, does. When

Thomas Culpeper was arrested for his affair with Queen Catherine Howard, Marchand was a known drinking companion of his, and in fact they were often seen carousing together late into the night at Nonsuch. Marchand was questioned deeply about this friendship, but naught could be found of his own guilt in the matter and he was released."

"And that was when he vanished from court?" Kate thought of the horoscope of Queen Catherine Howard. Had Marchand stolen it to protect his friend Culpeper? Was that where it had come from? Perhaps he had killed Dr. Macey as a diversion. Culpeper and his friends would never want anything to make the king cease to think of Queen Catherine as his "rose without a thorn." Their positions, their very lives, at court depended on her. An ill-starred horoscope might have seemed reason enough to kill.

"Wouldn't you absent yourself, after such an event?" Anthony said with a humorless laugh. "I would be finished with the doings of kings myself after a mess like that."

"Such things are surely not likely to happen now," Kate said, though in her mind she felt a tiny, cold touch of doubt. She closed her eyes and thought of all she had learned. Roland had killed to gain the favor of his lord. The queen's enemies always surrounded her, outwardly smiling but inside always scheming. Always plotting. It had been thus in King Henry's time; it was thus now.

But Elizabeth saw things clearer than her father ever had. Surely she would not be blinded by false love, as he was with Queen Catherine.

She opened her eyes to find Anthony watching her closely. She tried to read his expression, to see past the solemn concern, but she could not see anything else. Nothing but a frown he tried to hide behind a quick smile.

"What is amiss, Anthony?" she asked, trying to smile in return. To conceal how worried she really was. "Except for the fact that we are hurrying to stop another murder in the queen's garden, of course."

He shook his head. "I do worry about you, Kate."

Did he? She didn't want to read more into those words than there really was. "I can look after myself well enough."

"You have put yourself in danger again," he said. "After last winter . . ."

"I must help the queen when I can," Kate answered. "In whatever small way possible."

"Queen Elizabeth has no more loyal subject than I, as well," Anthony said. "I have been most glad to help you in these searches, Kate. I confess it makes me feel—alive, as dusty law books cannot." The smile that always warmed Kate finally did appear, briefly but long enough for hope. "But if you were seriously hurt, I could not—that is, I think . . ."

Mistress Macey stirred awake just then, and Anthony fell silent. Kate leaned back against the pile of blankets, her confusion growing until she could barely stand it.

She wanted to scream and throw something, just like the queen; she knew that explosive feeling, when it was all just too much.

The gates at Nonsuch finally came into view. Kate's gaze frantically took in the fanciful towers of the castle, where the queen's standard fluttered, and the white sea of tents beyond glowed in the darkness. Everything seemed quiet, peaceful. No clouds of smoke hung over the ramparts; no screams split the air. It was as if nothing but joy and pleasure had ever hidden behind those walls.

But Kate knew that so often serenity hides the worst sins.

"The queen is at the hunt," the gatekeeper said as he let them in. "They'll all be in the forest hours yet."

Kate nodded. If Queen Elizabeth was hunting, surely Robert Dudley would be near her and she would be safe enough. But where was Master Roland? Where would he leap next in his murderous desperation? He seemed mad enough to do anything now.

"Has one of the queen's ladies come this way today?" Kate asked. "Lady Anne Godwin? She surely would have been ahorse, riding fast."

The man scratched his head. "Aye, there was a lady earlier. Said she had been on an urgent errand for Her Majesty."

Kate nodded grimly and gestured for the cart driver to move on. Anne had been through hours ago, more than enough time for Anne and Roland to plan their next move.

As they rolled to a stop in the courtyard, Kate saw that the house really was very quiet. *Too* quiet? There were only a few servants going about their business.

"We must find them," she said urgently. "But there are so many hidey-holes . . ."

"I will start with the kitchens," Mistress Macey said stoutly, climbing down from the cart with her sleeping babe on her shoulder and determination written on her face. She had certainly proven herself to be a woman of sense on the journey—and of resolve to find her husband and take her revenge on Lady Anne. Kate was most glad of her help.

"I will search the chambers upstairs," Kate said. Starting with her own. Hopefully Lady Anne would be careless and leave some clue there.

"How will you get up there?" Anthony said.

Kate looked up at him, setting her chin stubbornly. He could not know it, but she was a Boleyn—and Boleyn women could accomplish whatever they set their minds to. That thought steeled her resolve all over again. "I will find a walking stick."

"Bloody-minded woman," he muttered. Before she knew what he was about, he swung her down from the cart into his arms and carried her into the house, past the giggles of maidservants, none of whom had seen Lady Anne.

"Which way?" he said, and Kate guided him to her own small chamber, glad of his strength against her. She could never have moved so fast without him now, even with Boleyn resolve.

The room was empty, of course, with no sign of Lady Anne or of Violet. The beds were neatly made, the clothes chests pushed against the walls. But a dark cloak, splashed with mud, was tossed on Lady Anne's bed.

And in the middle of Kate's counterpane, pierced down with a dagger, was a hastily penned note.

I have Violet in the temple by the lake. Come fetch her alone—if you dare.

CHAPTER TWENTY-THREE

The temple was the same one Kate had studied when she sat beside the lake with Rob Cartman after they first came to Nonsuch. Was it only a fortnight ago? It seemed a century. The classical-style building was small, round, and enclosed, and marble pillars lined the outside walkway.

Today, the walkway, like the whole lake, was deserted. Everyone was at the queen's hunt. The boats were moored along the shore, and the bench where she'd sat with Rob was empty. Silence like this, with sunlight spangled between the trees and swans gliding in pale serenity along the water, was eerie.

How could such wickedness lurk there? Kate could see no sign of Violet. She leaned on her newly acquired walking stick and studied the stony silence of the temple.

"Kate," Anthony said warningly. "Let me fetch the queen's guards now. This is no matter for you, for a lady."

Kate shook her head. She thought of Violet, of her sweet smile, her good, simple heart, her love for Master Green. Violet had been Kate's friend, and she had few enough of those in the world. She couldn't abandon Violet now.

"The note said I should come alone if I wanted to help

Violet," she said. She looked up at Anthony, and he studied her with such doubt and caution on his handsome face. "You should wait here, keep watch for me."

He gave her a grim smile. "If you are determined to leap from this cliff, I will go with you. I won't let you go in there alone."

Kate nodded, secretly glad he was with her. That she was not indeed alone. She started slowly toward the waiting temple. Her leg still hurt with every step, but she was determined to see this to the end. Too many had been hurt by greedy schemes, by fear and panic. She couldn't let it go any further.

Anthony walked close behind her, a solid, warm, reassuring presence as she climbed the stone steps to the covered walkway. The door was closed and she could hear nothing beyond it. She felt the weight of the dagger at her wrist, the brass head of the stick in her other hand, and they gave her another measure of courage.

She reached out and pushed the door open.

A low sob echoed in the small, round space. The ceiling was high, domed, covered with buckram painted in a pattern of stars and moons on a dark azure background. It caught and distorted every sound. The only light came from a lamp set on a low table.

Kate quickly took in the scene before her, trying to pretend it was merely a set piece in one of Rob Cartman's plays. That the people were not real, only characters.

She wasn't entirely able to convince herself.

Violet sat on a low stool beside the curved wall, her skirts spread around her like red rose petals. Her golden curls were loose and tangled, her face buried in her hands as her shoulders shook with sobs, just as Mistress Macey's had. Kate felt a wave of burning anger that anyone should so threaten these women, should drag them down so violently into tangled plots that were none of their own doing.

And Master Roland did this to his own *sister*. He stood over Violet, his sword in his hand, shouting at her as she cried. Lady Anne was there, too, her gown torn and muddied, her hands held out as if she beseeched her lover for mercy he had gone too far to give. Behind her, huddled in a heap on the floor, was Master Macey, his hands bound behind his back and his mouth gagged. So Roland had found him after all and dragged him here in some futile attempt to find that book. Macey was not unconscious, despite a bleeding cut on his brow, and his eyes widened above the gag.

Roland spun around at the click of the heavy door, his sword raised. The fine courtier, Lord Arundel's loyal servant in his velvet clothes, was gone, and a wild madman stood in his place, with hair tangled over his face and reddened eyes. "I told you to come alone, you stupid wench."

"Did you think I would allow her to face a murderer all alone?" Anthony said, his voice low and furious, though he held himself still.

Roland gave a harsh laugh. "It matters not, I suppose."

"Please, Master Roland," Kate said softly. "I have only come to see about Violet. Let me take her back to the queen. She has nothing to do with this—she is your own sister. I am sure you cannot want to hurt her."

Roland looked down at the crying Violet, his face gray and harsh. He laughed again, and it was not a reassuring sound.

"Kate!" Violet cried. She did not look at her brother but directly at Kate, frantically. "He is the reason why Master Green is in gaol. He dragged me here and won't listen to me at all. I'm so frightened! I don't understand any of this. . . ."

"Kate is right," Lady Anne said, her own voice just slightly off the edge of panic. "You must let Violet go, Thomas. Come away with me now. We can run to France or Spain."

"France?" Master Roland growled. His face twisted in fury. "After all my work here, my sacrifices? I have been trying to build a life for us here. What use would France be?" He spun around and paced away from his crying sister, from Anne's pleas, his sword hanging loosely in his hand. He banged it against the stone wall, making Anne cower in the corner, sobbing as if her formidable will had at last broken. "We were so very close . . ."

"Keeping Violet and Master Macey here will only make matters worse in the eyes of Lord Arundel, or the queen," Kate said. She struggled to stay calm despite everyone else's panic, her thoughts racing. She had to somehow get them all out of there, safe and alive. "What has your sister to do with any of this? What can I do to persuade you to let us leave now?"

"You are the one who has Dr. Macey's notebook," Roland said, rounding on her with his sword raised. "The page boy said Constable sent you a message. Where is it?"

Kate thought of the horoscopes, the book, tucked in her trunk. At least, she hoped with all her might they were still there. "Master Constable did send me a message, but not about any notebooks. I know not of what you speak."

"Don't lie to me!" Roland shouted. The sword crashed down with a clatter, and Violet sobbed even harder. "I have had enough of courtly lies, of people who think they can take my coin and double-cross me. Violet, my own sister, refuses to marry my choice for her, as a dutiful woman should. Constable took money to persuade the queen that the spirits urged her to marry

Lord Arundel, and he did not. He vowed to pay me back with the book, so I could decipher Dr. Macey's alchemical secrets for myself."

"I have no such book," Kate repeated, pushing down her own growing desperation. "It was merely my horoscope Constable sent me. Surely such a book no longer exists at all."

"So this varlet says," Roland said, kicking out at Master Macey with his boot.

"Brother, you must stop this, I beg you!" Violet sobbed.

"Be silent!" Roland roared. "I will have no more lies. I will have my due—*now*."

He suddenly charged toward Kate, the sword raised high. She instinctively ducked away, and her injured leg gave way beneath her. She fell heavily to the hard stone floor with a cry. She twisted around in time to see Anthony counter Roland's blade thrust with one of his own, from a short sword she didn't even know he carried.

Kate shoved away the waves of pain that threatened to overwhelm her and pushed herself to her feet. Roland and Anthony fought in a blur of shining swords in the faint lamplight, and she could barely see who was who, who shed blood. She knew she had to move quickly.

She shook free her own dagger and cut Master Macey's bonds. As he disentangled himself, she spun away and grabbed Violet's arm to pull her up from the stool. Kate pushed the hilt of her dagger into Violet's hand and clutched at her stick as her last weapon.

"Macey, take Violet and run," she said, trying frantically to see what was happening in Anthony's fight. If her friend was hurt now, because of her . . .

"Stop this, now!" Lady Anne screamed. Before Kate could stop her, she raised the heavy oil lamp from the table and hefted it at the two struggling men. The glass shattered with a deafening crack, and flames shot up the painted curves of the walls.

The screams and cries became overwhelming, a wild cacophony Kate couldn't even begin to decipher.

The small space swiftly filled with clouds of dark gray smoke, thick and choking with a sulfurous scent from the paint. Flames crackled and spit, but Kate could barely see a foot ahead of her. She choked on that nauseating smell and pressed her doublet sleeve to her nose to try to breathe.

She reached out blindly and grabbed Violet's hand again. Her friend held on to her tightly as they inched their way forward.

Through the smoke, Kate heard the terrifying sounds of screams and shouts, the clang of metal.

"Kate!" she heard Anthony shout through the darkness.

"I'm here!" she cried back, immeasurably grateful to hear his voice. The pain in her leg, and the thick smoke, made her head swim, and she fought to stay upright. She held out her free hand, dropping her stick, and he grabbed onto her through the smoke. He pulled her and Violet forward, and suddenly she found herself tumbling from the hellish heat into the light and air of the summer's evening.

The three of them fell down on the grassy rise of the lake bank, next to Master Macey, who had also made it out. For one terrible moment, Kate couldn't see anything at all; her eyes stung and darkness swirled in front of her.

Then she heard Violet scream, and she whirled around to see Master Roland emerging from the flames that shot out of the temple. He was scarcely recognizable at all now, so blackened and wild was he.

The domed roof gave a creaking noise, slow at first, then louder and more horrible until it was all she could hear, all she knew. Slowly, eaten away from the inside by the fire, it caved in on itself.

"Anne!" Roland shouted, the most agonized cry Kate had ever heard. He plunged back into the inferno. The roof crashed in, taking the stone pillars down with it, and Roland and Lady Anne were both lost in the triumphant red-orange crackle.

Violet cried out and took one stumbling, running step toward the temple, before Anthony grabbed her arm and pulled her back to safety. She fell against his shoulder, sobbing and screaming, and Anthony looked toward Kate. His face was pale and bleak beneath the bleeding cuts and the streaks of soot.

Kate could only stare numbly at the remains of Lord Arundel's pretty temple, dedicated to classical love and learning. How ironic. She knew now what had happened to Master Constable, the whole sordid, ambition-centered truth. The unjustly accused Master Green would surely be freed, and Master Macey could continue his father's work. But at what price?

"Mistress Haywood!" she heard someone shout. She pushed herself around to find Robert Dudley running toward them, his sword unsheathed. His guards ran after him, but they all stumbled to a halt at the sight of the temple.

Anthony helped Kate to her feet, holding her close as she struggled to compose herself. She was glad of his steady arms holding her up, for she felt so numb she feared she would topple back to the ground.

Sir Robert looked fearsome, almost like a demon himself with his dark hair and beard in the red-gold light of the flames. He wore no doublet, only his shirt and boots over his hose, as if he had dressed in haste. "Are you injured, Mistress Haywood?" he demanded. "Is there anyone to be saved in the temple? The queen saw the flames from her window and was most alarmed.

She wanted to rush down here herself, but I persuaded her to let me come instead."

"Thank heavens for that," Kate said. She shuddered to think of the queen in the midst of this dangerous mess, her royal life in danger at every side. "Aye, there were people in there, but they won't have survived, I am sure."

Dudley gestured to his men to stay back from the flames. Instead, one of them helped Violet to her feet. She was sobbing hysterically, and the man wrapped his cloak around her to still her violent shivers. The rest of them fanned out to secure the banks of the lake and try to put out the last of the fire.

"What happened here, Mistress Haywood?" Dudley asked, gently but firmly. He still held his sword, his gaze scanning the dying flames.

Anthony's arms tightened around Kate. "You don't need to talk yet, Kate, if you don't feel strong enough. You have had a most terrible experience."

Kate drew in a shuddering breath. "Nay, I can talk now. Everyone should know what happened."

Robert Dudley focused closely on her, and she knew that ultimately they both had the same goal—to keep the queen safe. That was all that really mattered. She quickly told him all that had happened. Of how Master Roland had killed Constable, of his scheme to marry the queen to Lord Arundel and thus gain his own ambitions, of the part the horoscopes played in it all.

She glanced up at the cold, indifferent stars and had the sudden, most irrational urge to curse them. Humans were fools to think they could harness the powers of something so very far away.

Dudley rubbed his hand over his jaw, his expression weary. "Dr. Dee will be glad at least to know what happened to his pupil, and to his old teacher."

Kate thought of Master Macey's cottage, all those

herbs and bubbling cauldrons, and the strange volumes. "But what of *you*, Sir Robert? You know Dr. Dee, and his student, very well, I think."

Anger flashed across his dark, starkly carved face, but then he gave a wry laugh. "Ah, Mistress Haywood. You do see more than you ever should. 'Tis a blessing and a curse, as I well know."

Anthony's arm tightened around her again, and Kate felt a cold tiredness sweep over her. "I want the same thing as you—to keep the queen safe."

Dudley nodded. "It is no secret, really. I have been fascinated by Dr. Dee's work ever since I was a student of his as a lad. His work is very important. He seeks no less than the secrets of the heavens, to harness them to serve the forces of good here on earth. He has always served Queen Elizabeth, too, even at risk of his own life. When he wanted to set up a laboratory here to pursue Dr. Macey's unfinished work, as well as continue at his own house at Mortlake, I happily agreed to help."

"And Master Constable?"

Dudley shook his head. "I merely thought him Dr. Dee's assistant. Dee has many of those. Until . . ."

"Until?"

"Until I saw him hovering too closely around Her Majesty, and you saw him outside her rooms when he should not have been. Then, as you know, I asked you to keep watch on him. I thought perhaps he would use Dr. Dee's studies for his own ends, but not quite in this way. I didn't think him quite clever enough. But anyone can be greedy without being clever. 'Tis another lesson, I suppose, that I should be more careful in judging others."

Kate looked to the last fiery embers of the temple. It was a lesson she needed to remember, too. Forgetting it had almost cost her life. But how could she have been

suspicious of Anne, who was her own friend? Anne—
who had died for love.

Suddenly, it felt like the night sky was collapsing
down on her. Everything that had happened was too
much to bear for another instant. Her knees collapsed
under her as her mind turned heavy and foggy. She felt
Anthony catch her up in his arms, heard him call her
name.

Then there was only darkness.

CHAPTER TWENTY-FOUR

The queen's court was preparing to leave Nonsuch, in a chaotic fervor as great as that with which they had arrived. From her seat at the top of a hill, near the now-deserted banquet hall, Kate watched the servants scurrying around the line of carts like liveried ants. They heaved chests and bits of furniture into piles, Kat Ashley watching them with her wary eye and her lists that missed nothing.

Robert Dudley, followed by his own vast retinue, saw to the queen's horses. They pawed at the ground as if they, too, were most eager to be away from the ruined fairy tale of the palace.

Except for the wisps of smoke that still drifted over the trees from beyond the lake, there was no sign of the terrible events of only a few days past. The rubble of the temple had been cleared, and Master Roland and Lady Anne Godwin buried—along with their secrets. Violet Roland and Master Green were betrothed, with permission of the queen, and the eventful stay at Nonsuch ended with a banquet and a play by Rob Cartman and his troupe. Almost as if nothing had happened.

Kate watched the flurry of activity, feeling numb, removed from the whole bustling scene. In only a few days, they would all be at Windsor, but what would have changed? The queen's enemies would always be near.

Kate looked down at the bouquet of bright yellow primroses in her hand, along with a folded letter she had yet to read. When Anthony Elias had departed with Master Hardy in the train of the Duchess of Somerset, whose visit had gained no advantage for her son, Kate was closeted with William Cecil, telling him all she had learned from Master Roland. Anthony had left those tokens, and now she clung to them as if they were a last rope on a stormy sea.

Anthony's friendship meant so much to her amid all the uncertainty of court, all the secrets and ever-shifting loyalties. She missed him already.

Yet how certain *was* his friendship, truly? He had his work, and she could not see how she could fit into such a life. How she could be the mate he needed, a wife like Mistress Hardy?

There were so very many things Kate was confused about now. Her family, her place in the world, her purpose—she had no idea of any of it. Music and her little family with her father had been her life for so very long, and now she had the court, the queen, which was so very different. Would she ever learn to be a part of it? To know whom to trust?

Aye. She knew that no matter how she might long for it in her secret heart and how much she cared for Anthony, she could not make a life for them such as the comfortable, prosperous one the Hardys enjoyed. She had seen too much, learned too much, longed for too much. Love was dangerous, just as her horoscope warned. Master Constable had been fatally wrong about so many things, but he was right about that.

And also, she realized with a spark of hope, she was only beginning to learn her own strength.

Kate looked down at the letter and carefully refolded it, tucking it away in the purse tied at her belt. Anthony asked if she would write to him from Windsor, and she would. She just didn't know yet what she would say.

My dearest Kate, the letter read, in Anthony's neat, legalistic handwriting.

> *Forgive me for departing court so quickly. Master Hardy's business has called us away, and much work awaits us in London. Yet I fear so many of my thoughts will stay here at Nonsuch.*
>
> *I beg you, my dear friend, to be careful always until I can be with you to help you again. Court is most dangerous; I see it in my work now every day, and I also see that your good heart leads you into trouble. I wish you could be more cautious.*
>
> *But I confess, it is your tender heart, your courage, your great care for all your friends, that I adore so very much, that keeps drawing my thoughts back to you. Without it, you would not be my Kate, and that would be a great sadness indeed.*
>
> *Be careful, I beg you, and God willing we shall meet again very soon. My work increases, and soon I shall be at liberty to form my own career and life. Then, I hope you will allow me to speak more freely. To tell you all the hopes I have in my heart.*
>
> *Write to me, I beg you. I stand ready to help you, and will always be.*
>
> *Your Friend,*
>
> *Anthony Elias*

"Mistress Haywood!" she heard someone call. She scrambled to her feet, leaning on the elaborately carved walking stick Queen Elizabeth had sent her, and turned to see Timothy Macey hurrying up the hill. His cuts and scrapes were beginning to heal, as hers were, and he looked eager to move forward. His wife stood at the bottom of the hill, their child in her arms, and she waved and smiled up at Kate.

"Master Macey," she said with a smile. "I am glad to see you looking most recovered after such an ordeal."

"And I you, Mistress Haywood," he answered. He shuffled his booted feet, looking rather abashed. "I fear I can never thank you enough for all you have done for my family. I am sorry for ever doubting your motives when you first came to the cottage."

"Your work requires much secrecy," Kate said. Especially if men like Robert Dudley were involved. "I do understand, Master Macey. I hope you and your wife and mother will be well now, and in a place where you can carry out your studies in peace."

"Dr. Dee has found us a cottage near his own home at Mortlake, where we will have room for our work together. And a garden for the child to play in, of course. Bett is happy about that." He turned and waved to his wife, as the baby laughed back. "My mother will go with us, now that we know my father is truly at rest."

Kate shivered, thinking of those bones with their strange black stone ring and that royal emerald. At least none of them had ended up thus now. "I am truly sorry about Dr. Macey." Once she had thought perhaps the two murders were connected, Macey and Constable. Now she knew they were only connected by an ambition that burned out of control.

"Nay, now we know the truth," Master Macey said with a frown. "He should never have become involved in schemes with the likes of old King Henry and his wives. Trying to hide what he knew of that poor Queen Catherine led to his doom. I hope I have learned my own lesson from that."

And Kate hoped she, too, had learned a lesson from it all. She just wasn't sure what it could be yet. "I do have something that rightfully belongs to you." Kate took the fragile old book from its wrappings and held it out to him. "I believe Master Constable took it when he should not have, along with Catherine Howard's old horoscope. It is why I wanted to see you before I left, to make sure it was again safely in your hands. I cannot read its secrets, but I know there are those who would give so much to possess it." Who would kill for it.

Master Macey looked down at it, his face stunned. "My father's book?"

Kate nodded. "Master Roland was right about that—I did have it. I found it the night Master Constable had his séance in Lady Knollys's chamber, and I knew not what to do with it. You are its rightful owner."

He nodded slowly, turning the book slowly over in his hands. "My mother has long mourned my father, as have I, fearing his work was lost. I hope I shall never give my own wife reason to so grieve. Thank you, Mistress Haywood, for returning him to us at last."

Kate nodded, fearing she might cry at his words. She thought of her own mother, her father who had always grieved for Eleanor Haywood's loss. Of King Henry and the loves he had thrown away.

She glanced toward Mistress Macey and saw that Rob Cartman stood with her now. He studied Kate with solemn eyes, for once not masked with his usual careless charm, and she tried to ignore the strange feeling she suddenly felt deep inside.

"Kate," Rob called, hurrying up the hill toward her. "Her Majesty bade me to fetch you to her. It is almost time to depart."

Kate nodded, glad of the distraction. "Godspeed to you, Master Macey," she said. "I hope all your ghosts shall be at rest now."

"And I hope the same for you, Mistress Haywood," he said, bowing over her hand. "Though I fear it may be some time for both of us to see that come to pass."

He hurried away to his wife's side, and Kate hobbled down the hill to take Rob's offered arm. She had not spoken with him since a few words before his final performance here at Nonsuch, though she had watched his play most carefully from her place in the gallery. He looked more handsome than ever, his hair brighter in the summer sun, his features as carefully carved as the classical statues on the palace's walls. Yet there was a new wariness in his eyes, as if he had seen far too much now—and Kate feared she looked the same.

"I did hear from Lady Knollys that Lord Hunsdon has asked you to perform at Eastwick House next month," she said. She peeked up at him to see his reaction, but there was only a polite smile. "My congratulations. You have succeeded in your errand here at Nonsuch."

He looked down at her, his smile widening. "At one of my errands, perhaps. But I fear I failed to make my apologies to you, Kate. You have been a true friend to me, and I should have been more honest about my goal here at court. I should have been of more help when you were in danger."

Kate nodded, though she didn't know how she felt about his words. How she felt when he touched her hand like that. "We have both had more adventures here than we bargained for, I think," she said with a laugh. "I look forward to some quiet days at Windsor for a time, with only my lute for company."

"Not *too* quiet, I am sure," Rob said. "You would run mad in a week with no adventures at all, Kate."

"I . . ." Kate wasn't sure how to answer that. She certainly wanted no more adventures involving fires and daggers! But a quiet life, like the one she had once known at Hatfield with her father . . . did she really want that again? "I do not think so."

"Nay, I know it to be so," Rob said. "Because we are alike in that way. I saw it when I first met you at Hatfield House. We are too curious to stay quiet at our hearth. We need to see the world, hear people's tales. Find ourselves useful. People like us, Kate, we need art and adventure to feel alive. We cannot be content with an ordinary life."

Kate was startled by his words. Could he be right? She had enjoyed her life at court, all the people she met, the different countries and faraway lands she heard tales of, the music and the dancing. She had come to crave the life of it all.

But that life also came with danger and pain. With no knowledge of what lurked around every corner.

She wasn't sure how to answer him. They reached the edge of the graveled drive, where servants and courtiers alike scurried around the waiting carts, making sure all was in readiness for the complexities of the queen's journey. Kate glimpsed Elizabeth standing on the marble steps. Her gloved hand shielded her eyes from the sun as she scanned the crowd. Did she look for Kate?

"I have something I want to give you, Kate," Rob said quickly, eagerly.

Something in his tone pulled her attention back fully to him. "Something for—for me?"

He reached into the pouch tied at his belt and withdrew a tiny silk-wrapped bundle. He took her hand in his and placed the bundle carefully on her palm.

Kate stared down at it, at their hands joined together, and she felt a reluctant tiny thing like hope touch her deep inside.

"Aren't you going to open it?" he said. She glanced up to see he was smiling, but there was something shadowed in his beautiful blue eyes.

Kate swallowed hard and nodded. She carefully folded back the silk—and her breath caught when she saw what was there.

It was a lute, tiny and perfectly made in every detail. Polished enamel made up the chestnut-brown body, while hair-thin gold cords made up the strings. Tiny sparkling diamonds looked just like the inlay of her mother's lute. It was strung on a satin ribbon for a pendant.

"Oh, Rob," she whispered, enchanted by its delicate beauty. By the care that must have gone into it. Care *Rob* had for her.

"Do you like it?" he said, and Kate heard a most uncharacteristic note of doubt in his voice. "I tried to remember the design of your lute, but perhaps my memory was faulty. It can be remade . . ."

Kate laughed and sobbed at the same time, more confused than she had ever been. She had thought Rob was drawing away from her for some reason, ever since that afternoon by the lake. "It is the most perfect thing I have ever seen. But it must have taken so much time, and care. And—and coin."

"I have a friend who is a goldsmith. He began working on it in the spring. I knew I would have to wait to give it to you at the very right time."

"The right time?" Kate whispered, her head still whirling.

"When I could feel worthy to give you gifts. When I had something more to offer than a starving player's lot." He suddenly smiled, like the beautiful sun breaking through a cloudy day. "That was why I could not tell you at first why I came here, to meet with Lord Hunsdon. I only wanted to tell you when I knew for certain I would have a place."

Kate shook her head in confusion. "What are you telling me, Rob?"

He took the tiny lute from her hand and leaned forward to tie it around her neck. For an instant, he was so close to her she could feel the warmth of his skin. His lips brushed her cheek.

"Lord Hunsdon is going to be the patron for my troupe, to give us a place in his household. You have made me want this, Kate," he said with another smile. "You have made me want to be a better person. To strive to be a gentleman. Please, give me a chance to show you that I can do that. That I can make a better life. That is all I ask right now."

"Kate Haywood!" Elizabeth called out impatiently. "To me."

There was no time now to demand Rob tell her what he truly meant, to sort out her own tangled ball of feelings. He took her hand in his and raised it to his lips. The warm touch on her skin made her shiver.

He smiled up at her over her curled fingers. "I shall see you soon, Kate, I am sure," he said with a grin. *That* was more the Rob she knew, the man who hid all darker, deeper feelings behind teasing smiles and jests. "When Lord Hunsdon bids us perform before the queen, mayhap?"

"Kate!" the queen called again.

Rob turned on his heel and left in a swirl of his short satin cloak, and Kate had no choice but to go to the queen. She clutched Anthony's bouquet close to her side, walking slowly with the aid of the queen's gift of an elaborately carved stick, and felt the tingle of Rob's kiss on her other hand.

The queen's coach was waiting, but Elizabeth sent her other ladies away with a short word and a wave to Robert Dudley to stay the horses. Kate gave a careful curtsy.

Elizabeth shook her head and took Kate's hand firmly in her gloved grasp. "None of that now, Kate.

You must be most careful. You have kept my physicians too busy of late."

Kate certainly intended not to do *that* again. She had had enough of their bleeding blades and noxious potions. "Your Majesty has been most kind."

Elizabeth looked at her, her pale face strained behind her smile. "It was the very least I could do, sending you my own physicians and apothecaries, and Mistress Ashley with her infamous possets, after you risked your life to rid my court of a villain's schemes—again. I fear I have had little enough gratitude of late for those who have served me most faithfully."

Kate was bewildered by the queen's words. "Your Majesty?"

Elizabeth's dark gaze swept over the swirl of the crowd in front of them. "Come, let us walk for a moment. We will not go far. Lean on my arm, Kate."

Kate slowly took the queen's offered arm. Her heavy satin sleeve was warmed by the sun, and she smelled of roses, stronger and sweeter than the gardens around them. They left the others behind, even as they stared after the queen curiously.

"William Cecil and Mistress Ashley, who have both long been like parents to me when I had none, urge me to marry now, as you have seen," Elizabeth said. She stared off into the distance, at the trees of the woods where she had hunted, the lake where the fire had carried off the temple. "They say it is my first duty, and I neglect it at England's peril. Do you agree, Kate?"

"I think only Your Majesty can know what is best for you—and for England," Kate said carefully.

Elizabeth gave a deep sigh. She suddenly looked tired, paler, older than her twenty-six years. It had been a most merry summer progress, endless warm days of dancing and games, only to end in danger at the prettiest palace of all. "Ah, Kate. Always so careful, so kind.

I fear I have found being queen to be—not all I once dreamed of."

"How so, Your Majesty? Surely you have always been destined to be where you are now."

They came to a stop beneath the shade of a grove of trees. The wind stirred at the rich green leaves above their heads, adding to the hum of the distant crowd. Elizabeth watched it all with a distant frown on her lips, as if she saw the palace not as it was now, but as it had once been, the half-finished folly of an old king desperate to impress his young wife. To turn back the hands of time. As if Elizabeth saw only the ends of things in Nonsuch's rare beauty, and not joyous beginnings.

"When I was a very little girl, when my mother—died," Elizabeth began, "I was sent far away from court, and there it seems I was forgotten. My governess, Lady Brian, who was an excellent woman, had to write begging letters to have my outgrown clothes replaced, food for our table. I was but three, but I knew everything had changed when I was suddenly called 'lady' and not 'princess.' I learned then that no one could ever be relied upon—and everything that happened from there only proved that to me. Stepmothers came and went, my brother rejected me, my sister hated me. I had only myself."

Kate nodded slowly. She knew how that felt, the hollowness at the pit of the stomach that could only be loneliness. "But you *are* queen now."

Elizabeth's rosebud lips twisted into a semblance of a smile. "Ah, yes—I *am* queen. Once, I thought a crown, if I was ever strong enough to win it, would set me free at last. I would be beholden to no one else for my fortunes, for my very existence. I would control my destiny, and nothing, not even Dr. Dee's horoscopes or the voices of his spirits, would gainsay me. I would control the very stars. But that is not so."

"Nay, Your Majesty?" Kate said. If the queen could control nothing, what hope was there for the rest of them? The stars would always pull them hither and yon.

Elizabeth shook her head. The white plumes of her hat danced in the breeze. "I am tossed about on the waves of fortune even more than before, and nothing can steady me but my own hand. What is more, I carry so many other people's fortunes with me, which I have forgotten. Cecil says I have been careless this summer."

"Surely even a queen deserves to enjoy a warm summer's day," Kate said, thinking of all the palaces they had seen in the last weeks, all the dances. The queen riding off to so many hunts with Robert Dudley laughing at her side.

"Nay, he is right," Elizabeth said. "I am twenty-six years old, Kate, and I have not known a light moment since I was three. Now there is dancing and feasting, all for me. I am the one who is courted, sought after. I can keep company with all those I enjoy. But I forgot many of those hard lessons of my youth."

Kate glanced back at the crowd, and she saw Robert Dudley observing them, his gloved hand resting on his horse's bridle. He watched the queen with such longing it made Kate's heart ache.

"I must be ever vigilant," Elizabeth continued. "When I am not, the people I care about—people like you, my Kate—are put in harm's way, and I can do nothing to save them. I *have* been careless this summer, but no more, I vow."

Kate took a deep breath. She thought of her own carelessness, her own wild desires she could not fathom. What did *she* want in this new life, this new England of Elizabeth's? She was no longer sure at all.

"I think I, too, must look to the future, Your Majesty," she said.

Elizabeth glanced back at her sharply. "I do hope you see your future here at my court, Kate. I could not do without you. I have little enough family as it is, and you have proved your loyalty and bravery over and over. These unfortunate matters here at Nonsuch have shown me that so clearly."

Kate nodded. She *did* need her music, and she needed to serve the queen. England was never safe without Elizabeth. But was that all she wanted? "I hope so, too, Your Majesty. As you say—family is most important."

Elizabeth laughed. "For better or worse. Often for worse, I fear. That is why I need you, and my Carey cousins. Without my mother's family, I would have only the Greys, Mary of Scots, and Margaret Lennox. Vipers all. You are like my family now."

Kate thought of the queen's tangled family, and of the Rolands and the Maceys. Family was a strange thing indeed, but one could never do without them. Nothing could ever be taken for granted. "I will always be at Your Majesty's service. But I fear I must ask for a few days' leave before I travel to Windsor. There is something I must do."

"What matter is that, Kate, that is so important it will take you from us?"

Kate squared her shoulders. "I must see my father. Things between us have been unsettled for too many months. He is the only one who can tell me the truth about my mother . . ."

And if she could come to know her mother, perhaps she could come to know herself. Just as Queen Elizabeth must. The stars had spoken.

AUTHOR'S NOTE

Kate Haywood and her adventures are, of course, a work of imagination (even though she often feels like a real friend to me, now that I've been lucky enough to follow her through three books!). But one of the fun perks of writing, I've always found, is the research. The chance to jump into a time hundreds of years in the past, discover the people and places and events, and try to make it feel "real" again—I love all of that.

Ever since I did a history report on Anne Boleyn in elementary school (complete with costume and a lute made of cardboard), the Tudor era has held a special fascination for me. It was an exciting time of enormous social and political change, as well as amazing artistic achievement (especially in poetry and the theater) at a level beyond anything before or since. Bawdy, colorful, fast-paced, and populated by so many fascinating characters—what's not to love?

I also discover new things every time I happily dive into my research library. For *Murder in the Queen's Garden*, I loved exploring the worlds of the Elizabethan fascination with astrology and the occult; the intriguing figure of Dr. John Dee; and the gorgeous (and now sadly vanished) Nonsuch Palace.

The building of Nonsuch Palace, in Surrey, started on April 22, 1538, about six months after Prince Edward was born, but it took several years to complete. In fact, it was still incomplete when Henry VIII died in 1547. It was meant to compete with the glorious châteaus of France and cost more than twenty-four thousand pounds to construct (almost 104 million today). Though it was a simple layout, built around two inner courtyards, with a fortified gatehouse and several outer courtyards, it was gorgeously decorated with elaborate ornamental stucco panels depicting classical gods and goddesses, and tall octagonal towers at every corner that gave it a fairy-tale look. The gardens were said to be some of the most beautiful in England.

After Henry's death, the palace lay neglected for some time, until Queen Mary sold it to Lord Arundel, one of the richest noblemen in England, in 1556. Queen Elizabeth managed to buy it back in the 1580s, but it met a sad fate. Charles II gave it to his favorite mistress, Barbara Castlemaine, who tore it down to pay some gambling debts in 1682. It was excavated in 1959, and there is a lovely scale model of it that I used for much research. (I am not sure King Henry actually brought Catherine Howard there in 1541, but they did go on a long progress. Wouldn't he have wanted to show it off to her? Queen Elizabeth did visit in the summer of 1559, at which time Lord Arundel hoped to persuade her to marry him. It was always a vain hope, poor man. . . .)

Queen Catherine Howard was, of course, another sad story in King Henry's complicated marital history. Born in 1523, her real birthday is unknown, so I assigned her one in this story so she could have her horoscope drawn up. (She seemed like she could have been a Leo, though!) Her fate is well-known. She was young and full of fun, never prepared for the dangerous career of being Henry's wife, and was executed in 1542, convicted of treason by way of adultery (with Thomas

Culpeper, among others, who it seems was not a nice man).

Dr. John Dee (1527–1608/09) is one of the most fascinating figures of the period. He was a mathematician, astronomer, astrologer, philosopher, traveler, occultist, and possible spy, and his work has resonance even today. He attended St. John's College, Cambridge, while still a boy (from 1542 to around 1546). In 1555, he was arrested by Queen Mary's government, accused of secretly drawing up horoscopes for the queen, her husband, King Philip, and Princess Elizabeth (which would have been treason). He was questioned in the notorious Star Chamber but then released. He went abroad, until Elizabeth ascended the throne and summoned him back to England. He became one of her most trusted advisers, given such important tasks as choosing the best date for her coronation. He was a tutor and adviser to almost all the important figures of the day, including Robert Dudley, his nephew Philip Sidney, and Sir Christopher Hatton. For more information, you can check out the Web site of the John Dee Society (johndee.org).

Robert Dudley, later Earl of Leicester (1532/3–1588) was one of the favorites of Elizabeth I (and whom many consider the love of her life), a leading statesman of the time. He, like Dee, lived a complicated life. During this early part of Elizabeth's reign, when she was nearly inseparable from him (and when he was married to the ill-fated Amy Robsart), he caused a great deal of gossip, both at the English court and abroad. The Venetian ambassador wrote in April 1559, "My lord Robert Dudley is very intimate with Her Majesty," while the Spanish ambassador wrote to King Philip, "Lord Robert has come so much into favor he does whatever he likes . . . it is even said that Her Majesty visits him in his chamber day and night." He fell from favor for a time in 1578, when he secretly married Lettice Knollys, cousin to the queen and widow of the Earl of Essex.

We briefly glimpsed the beautiful, lively, flirtatious Lettice at her mother's séance in this story—but we will be seeing more of her in later books, I'm sure! Her mother, Catherine Carey, Lady Knollys (1524–1569), was one of the queen's favorite ladies-in-waiting. The daughter of Mary Boleyn and (purportedly) Sir William Carey, she was often rumored to be the natural daughter of Henry VIII. She was always acknowledged as the queen's closest cousin and married Sir Francis Knollys in 1540. They went on to have fourteen children, which didn't keep the queen from constantly summoning her to court. She served as lady-in-waiting to both Anne of Cleves and Catherine Howard and was said to have stayed with her aunt Queen Anne in the Tower before her execution (though this is probably a legend). During the reign of Queen Mary, she and her family lived in exile, only to be summoned back to royal service by Elizabeth. Catherine Carey was buried with much fanfare in Westminster Abbey.

Her brother, Henry Carey, was made the first Baron Hunsdon by Elizabeth in 1559. The queen also gifted him many estates, including Hunsdon and Eastwick in Hertfordshire, and many titles, including eventually Lord Chamberlain of the Household. He was long married to Anne Morgan but was notoriously unfaithful. (One of his mistresses was the musician Amelia Lanier, possibly Shakespeare's "Dark Lady," who was forty years his junior and gave him a son.) He was most famous for being a great patron of the theater. Shakespeare's Lord Chamberlain's Men were under his protection.

Lady Catherine Grey (1540–1568), another cousin of Queen Elizabeth, didn't fare so well as the Boleyns. As the granddaughter of Henry VIII's sister Mary Brandon, Dowager Queen of France, she had the closest claim to the throne after Elizabeth (Henry VIII having excluded his sister Margaret's Scots descendants from the throne, including Mary, Queen of Scots), but the position didn't serve her well. Elizabeth was always suspicious and mistrustful of her, and Lady Catherine was not the most clever of politicians. She secretly married Lord Hertford, and—well, we will see what happens to her later!

I hope you've enjoyed reading Kate's adventures as much as I've loved writing them! Watch for more of her tales in 2015 and 2016. In the meantime, be sure to visit my Web site, http://amandacarmack.com, for more behind-the-scenes history and excerpts. If you'd like to read more about the period, here are a few sources I found particularly helpful in writing *Murder in the Queen's Garden*:

Lacey Baldwin, *Catherine Howard* (1961)

Martin Biddle, *Nonsuch Palace: The Material Culture of a Noble Jacobin Household* (2005)

Peter J. French, *Dr. John Dee: The World of an Elizabethan Magus* (1972)

Eugenio Garin, *Astrology in the Renaissance: The Zodiac of Life* (1990)

M. Levine, *The Early Elizabethan Succession Question 1558–1568* (1966)

Derek Wilson, *The Uncrowned Kings of England: The Black History of the Dudleys and the Tudor Throne* (2005)

Frances A. Yates, *The Occult Philosophy in the Elizabethan Age* (1979)

Turn the page for a sneak peek at the next
Elizabethan Mystery from Amanda Carmack,

MURDER AT WHITEHALL

Available from Obsidian in November 2015.

"'Holly and ivy, box and bay, put in the house for Christmas Day! Fa la la la . . .'"

Kate Haywood laughed at hearing the notes of the old, familiar song, the tune always sung as the house was bedecked for Christmas. Queen Elizabeth's gentlewomen of the privy and presence chambers, along with the young maids of honor, had been assigned to festoon the great hall of Whitehall Palace and its long corridors for the night's feast, the first of the Twelve Days of Christmas.

Long tables had been set up along the privy gallery and covered with piles of holly, ivy, mistletoe, and evergreen boughs brought in from the countryside that morning, along with multicolored silk ribbons and spangles. Under the watchful eye of Kat Ashley, Queen Elizabeth's Mistress of the Robes, they were meant to turn all those random bits into glorious holiday artistry.

Kate sat at the end of the table with her friend Lady Violet Green, who was expecting her first child after the new year. They twisted together loops of ivy and red ribbon as they watched two of the queen's maids, Mary Howard and Mary Radcliffe, lay out long swags of greenery to measure them. The Marys sang as they worked, sometimes stopping to leap about with ribbons like two wild morris dancers, until Mistress Ashley sternly admonished them to sit down and cease acting like children who had eaten too many sugary suckets.

Kate laughed at their antics. Surely Christmas was the time for *everyone* to behave like children again. To dance and sing, to feast on delicacies until one was about to burst, to tell stories by the fire until the night was nearly gone. She had always loved this time of year the best of all, these twelve days when the gloomy darkness of winter was set aside for a little while, buried in music, wine, and bright silk ribbons—and then more music again. Always music for Kate, as one of the queen's principal musicians.

Kate snatched a ribbon from one of the twirling Marys and laughed. She might have been missing her father, her only family, that Christmas, but she was surrounded by such merriment that she scarcely had time to feel melancholy.

Nay, Kate thought, she could only miss her dear father very late at night, in the darkest hours when the rest of the palace finally slept, when she was working on new music for the queen's revels. Then, in the silence as she bent over her mother's lute, playing old songs her father had taught her when she was a child, could she miss him.

The queen's court at Whitehall was full to bursting for the holiday. There were groups from Sweden and Vienna, pressing the marital suits of their various princes and archdukes; as well as the Spanish under Senor de Quadra; and the French, insisting on friendship from the queen's cousin Queen Mary of Scotland, the new Queen Consort of France. To make things even more complicated, a group of Scots Protestant lords had also arrived to ask the queen's aid in their rebellion against Queen Mary's mother and regent, Marie of Guise. It was enough to make every courtier's head spin to decipher who was against whom.

Sir Robert Dudley, the queen's favorite and her Master of the Horse, had been named Lord of Misrule for the holiday, and under his direction everything was a blur of lavish merriment—and the Twelve Days had not yet even begun!

Kate reached for two bent hoops and bound them into a sphere for the base of a kissing bough. She picked out the greenest, brightest loops of holly and ivy from the table, twining them around and tying them with a length of red satin ribbon.

"Are you making a kissing bough, Kate?" Violet asked teasingly. She tied together her own twists of greenery into a large wreath for one of the great hall's fireplace mantels. She looked most plump and content in her pregnancy, her blond curls bouncing and her eyes shining. "They say if you stand beneath it and close your eyes, you will have a vision of your future husband."

Kate laughed. "I think I would be too nervous to do such a thing. What if I saw a vision of an ancient, gouty knight with twenty children? We can't all be as fortunate as you and your handsome Master Green."

Violet blushed, and laid her hand over the swell of her belly. "We are wondrously happy now, it's true, but that only makes me want to see my friends equally well matched! Have you had no suitors since I was last at court?"

"No one new at all. There is no more room at court for more ambitious young lords. And if there was, they would all be in love with the queen herself."

As Kate snipped off the end of a branch with her dagger, she thought about Queen Elizabeth in the past months, as they had moved from Windsor to Richmond to Whitehall. After the frivolity of the summer progress, the queen's pale oval face had taken on a newly solemn expression, and she spent many more hours with her privy council poring over her stacks of documents. Yet there were still days at the hunt and nights dancing, still suitors and sonnets.

And still Robert Dudley, richly arrayed and ready to pour lavish gifts at Elizabeth's feet.

"What of the delegations visiting now?" Violet said as she tied off an elaborate bow. "There are so many here. The French are so charming, so well dressed, and they say the Swedes are most generous with their gifts to anyone who will help them in their prince's suit. Or the Scots! Some of them are quite handsome indeed. Very tall, such good dancers. You could marry one of them!"

Kate laughed. Violet was right—some of the Scots lords visiting Elizabeth's court, asking for aid against their Catholic regent, *were* rather exotic and dashing. But . . . "And be carried off to some drafty old castle beside an icy loch? I don't think that would be enjoyable at all. They seem rather quarrelsome for my taste as well. If they aren't fighting duels with Frenchmen, they're glaring at the Spanish over the banquet table, or even arguing among themselves. I would prefer a more . . . harmonious household."

"Very well. No Scotsman, then," Violet said with a giggle. "What of that actor who was at court last summer? I vow he was the *most* handsome man I have ever seen, except for my own husband, and he did seem to like you very much."

"Rob Cartman?" Kate frowned as she thought of Rob. He was indeed very handsome, with his golden hair and sky blue eyes, and full of laughter and poetry. But also full of secrets. "I haven't seen him for many months." Though she *had* received letters from him, telling her of how he and his theatrical troupe were faring as they toured the country under the patronage of the queen's cousin Lord Hunsdon. She didn't want to admit how her heart beat just a little faster whenever she saw his handwriting on a missive.

Or how she wore his gift, a tiny jeweled pendant in the shape of a lute, beneath her gowns.

"Oh, well. If you don't fancy a cold Scottish castle, I daresay a traveling actor's life wouldn't be good, either. You should find someone who would keep you here at court."

"I told you, Vi—I don't care to marry yet. I suppose I am like the queen in that way. And I am much too busy right now."

Violet pursed her lips. "I know, Kate. It is just as I said—I want all my friends to be as happy as I am. And I owe you so very much. If you had not saved my life at Nonsuch last summer, I would not even be here. Nor would this little one." She laid her hand gently on the small swell of her belly, beneath the green velvet of her loose Spanish gown.

Kate swallowed hard at the terrible memory of what had happened to them at the fairy-tale Nonsuch Palace, the fire—and the murderer—that had almost ended both their lives. She reached for a branch, trying to banish the dark thought beneath the brightness of Christmas. "Anyone would have done the very same as I did, Vi."

"I do not think that's true. Few would have been as brave as you. So, if you will not let me matchmake, you must at least be godmother to my babe when he or she arrives. And, if it is a girl, she shall be Katherine."

"That I would be most honored to do," Kate said with a smile, thinking of the gift she would get her future godchild—a child-sized lute.

"Good! Now, you should put mistletoe into your

bough. It is the most important element. Otherwise the magic won't work."

Kate laughed, tucking a thick branch of glossy green mistletoe dotted with lacy white berries into the center of her circlet. Surely there *was* some kind of magic floating in the icy winter air. She felt lighter already with the holiday upon them. After she had spent months worrying over the queen's safety, it seemed the perfect time to have a bit of fun.

"'Holly and ivy, box and bay,'" she whispered, "'put in the house for Christmas Day . . .'"

Also available from
Amanda Carmack

Murder at Hatfield House
An Elizabethan Mystery

England, 1558. Dark times rule—and the country's greatest hope lies in the young Princess Elizabeth. And Kate Haywood, a talented musician in the employ of the Princess, will find herself involved in games of crowns as she sets out to solve the murder of Queen Mary's envoy...

"An evocative and intelligent read."
—*New York Times* bestselling author Tasha Alexander

Available wherever books are sold or at
penguin.com

facebook.com/TheCrimeSceneBooks

Also available from
Amanda Carmack

Murder at Westminster Abbey
An Elizabethan Mystery

1559. Elizabeth is about to be crowned queen of
England and wants her personal musician Kate
Haywood to prepare music for the festivities. New to
London, Kate must learn the ways of city life—and
once again school herself as a sleuth after her close
friend at court, Lady Mary Everly,
is murdered.

"Amanda Carmack writes beautifully."
—*Historical Novel Society*

Available wherever books are sold or at
penguin.com

facebook.com/TheCrimeSceneBooks

Penguin Group (USA) Online

What will you be reading tomorrow?

Tom Clancy, W.E.B. Griffin, Nora Roberts,
Catherine Coulter, Sylvia Day, Ken Follett,
Kathryn Stockett, John Green, Harlan Coben,
Elizabeth Gilbert, J. R. Ward, Nick Hornby,
Khaled Hosseini, Sue Monk Kidd, John Sandford,
Clive Cussler, Laurell K. Hamilton, Maya Banks,
Charlaine Harris, Christine Feehan, James McBride,
Sue Grafton, Liane Moriarty, Jojo Moyes, Jim Butcher...

You'll find them all at
penguin.com
facebook.com/PenguinGroupUSA
twitter.com/PenguinUSA

*Read excerpts and newsletters, find tour schedules
and reading group guides, and enter contests.*

Subscribe to Penguin newsletters and get an
exclusive inside look at exciting new titles and the
authors you love long before everyone else.

PENGUIN GROUP (USA)

penguin.com   s0151